Praise for Karen F... ...ce,

Prince ...

"Finally, a heroine ... ...ero who knows what a ... ...ook for us all to adore. Thank you Karen Fox for creating the most lovable hero romance has seen in a long, long time."

—Maggie Shayne, author of *Eternity*

"A fantastical journey into the faerytale realm of myth, magic, and happily-ever-after . . . Karen Fox's fantasy romance is sweet and charming, with plenty of Fae magic to burn up the pages." —*The Romance Journal*

"What a fun read! I zipped through *Prince of Charming*, turning pages as fast as I could . . . I urge readers of paranormal romance to pick up this book as quickly as they can."

—*Scribesworld.com*

"I breezed through this most enjoyable book and am eagerly waiting for more of the same from Karen Fox."

—*Romance and Friends*

"Fun and lively."   —*Old Book Barn Gazette*

"*Prince of Charming* is an amusing fantasy romance that will enchant subgenre fans . . . Enjoyable . . . humorous . . . Karen Fox writes a novel that is fun to read."

—*Bookbrowser.com*

"Highly enjoyable and well written. I could almost believe the magic existed . . . Here is an author that aims to please."   —*Huntressreviews.com*

Jove Titles by Karen Fox

PRINCE OF CHARMING
BUTTERCUP BABY

Buttercup Baby

KAREN FOX

JOVE BOOKS, NEW YORK

This is a work of fiction. Names, characters, places, and incidents are
either the product of the author's imagination or are used fictitiously,
and any resemblance to actual persons, living or dead, business
establishments, events, or locales is entirely coincidental.

MAGICAL LOVE is a registered trademark of Penguin Putnam Inc.

BUTTERCUP BABY

A Jove Book / published by arrangement with
the author

PRINTING HISTORY
Jove edition / October 2001

Visit our website at
www.penguinputnam.com

ISBN: 0-515-13169-5

A JOVE BOOK®
Jove Books are published by The Berkley Publishing Group,
a division of Penguin Putnam Inc.,
375 Hudson Street, New York, New York 10014.
JOVE and the "J" design
are trademarks belonging to Penguin Putnam Inc.

PRINTED IN THE UNITED STATES OF AMERICA

10 9 8 7 6 5 4 3 2 1

To Gail Fortune and Meredith Bernstein—
thanks for believing in me.

And to Lise Fuller,
for providing a much needed sanity check.

And, as always, to the Wyrd Sisters.

One

This is it? Ariel peeked over the edge of the crib at the sleeping infant. The boy was small and ordinary for what he represented—Oberon's grandson. Odd that the King of the Fae should have a completely mortal grandson. Odder still that he had any children at all. They did not exist among the Fae, as the Fae could not procreate among themselves, and only a few half-breeds lived outside the magical realm, the result of Fae/mortal unions, such as that of Oberon's son, Robin Goodfellow.

Ariel snorted in disgust. That Robin would trade his magic and immortality to marry a mortal only reaffirmed the Queen of the Fae, Titania's assertion that he didn't belong with the Fae. And proved once again how foolish Ariel had been in impulsively defending Robin to Titania when he had first arrived in their magical realm.

As a result, Ariel was not only banned from Titania's court for eternity, but she had been removed from her position as Queen of the Pillywiggins—the flower faeries. It wasn't fair. Ariel had served Titania faithfully for centuries. She didn't deserve to be cast away so callously.

All her life she'd felt needed . . . necessary. Though six other women made up the royal court, Titania had often called on Ariel and her pillywiggins to complete numerous tasks. After all, they made up the largest section of the Fae. Now Loralei, her second in command, led the pillywiggins and Ariel had nothing.

Since her abrupt dismissal, she had wandered aimlessly through the magical realm, bereft. With no one needing her, she felt lost, abandoned. Where was her purpose now? What was she to do for the rest of eternity?

Fortunately, Oberon had taken pity on her and given Ariel the assignment of checking on Robin's first child. She could report that the baby was healthy and had the look of his father and grandfather. The infant released a soft breath and Ariel paused. He *did* have a certain appeal, his black hair tousled and tiny fists clenched. His pudgy pink flesh begged to be touched.

Extending her finger, Ariel brushed the baby's cheek. His skin was soft, like that of a rose petal, and his sweet scent teased her senses. Like a flower, but none that she could name. And she knew them all. Interesting . . . this tiny mortal.

She rested her arms on the side of the crib and studied him as he squirmed into a new position. Part of her ached to hold him close, to place kisses on his tender skin. Why? The Fae had no use for children. Why did she feel this strange attraction?

She reached down and gathered up the baby, cuddling him to her chest. He emitted one cry, then snuggled against her, his fist clutching her long hair, almost as if he belonged there. Ariel cradled his head in her palm and nuzzled his face. So soft, so dependent. So needy.

The ever-present ache in her heart eased as she held the baby. A longing she didn't completely understand filled her.

She wanted a child.

"He should be waking up from his afternoon nap soon," a voice outside the bedroom said.

Ariel quickly placed the infant back in his bed, then turned to the dresser and shrank to her original faery size, ducking behind the lamp as the door opened. Three mortals entered the room. She recognized one of them—Robin Goodfellow's mortal wife, Kate. The other two were strangers and Ariel studied them with interest.

The man and woman shared similar facial features—high cheekbones, a sculpted nose, and full lips. The woman joined Kate in cooing over the baby while Ariel watched the man. Though he was a mortal, she found him appealing. He was tall and well built, a man obviously used to work, with a broad muscular chest even a heavy shirt could not disguise. His hair shone with the dark color of tree bark and layered back along his head, stopping just above his collar.

Ariel blinked. She wanted to touch his hair, to see if it truly felt as soft as it looked. She shook her head. What was wrong with her? First, a longing for a child, and now for a mortal man. Had despair driven her insane?

He tried to appear disinterested, his arms crossed as he leaned against the doorway, his expression bored. But his deep brown eyes followed the women's actions closely. *Not so disinterested after all.* He had a pleasant appearance, as if he smiled a lot. Perhaps he did, for the corner of his lips rose as the women exclaimed over the baby's cuteness.

"Isn't he adorable, Rand?" The other woman glanced over her shoulder at him.

He shrugged. "If you've seen one baby, you've seen them all."

The woman shook her head. "Men." She grinned at Kate. "He's perfect, Kate, and already the spitting image of his father. The ladies will have to watch out when he grows up."

Kate laughed. "I'm not looking that far ahead at the moment." She caressed the sleeping infant's back. "I guess he's not ready to wake up yet. I picked up some photos yesterday. Would you like to see them?"

"Of course." The women turned toward the doorway. "Coming, brother?"

"Go ahead," he said. He stepped aside for them to leave, then stood by the doorframe for several long moments after they left. Ariel frowned. What was he doing?

She crept out from behind the lamp to the edge of the dresser. The disinterested expression left Rand's face and was replaced by a gentleness that tugged at Ariel. She saw little of that among the Fae.

A slight whimper emerged from the crib and Rand moved to the bed. "*Now* you wake up," he murmured, laughter in his voice. He picked up the baby, supporting the child's head in one hand and body in the other with practiced ease. As the infant awakened to reveal bright green eyes, Rand smiled. "And how are you, young master Goodfellow?"

Rand suddenly grimaced. "Wet." He glanced toward the doorway, then placed the baby on a nearby raised table. "I'll let them look at their pictures." He moved swiftly, undressing, cleaning, then redressing the child, his broad hands efficient yet gentle.

Ariel sighed. A sudden ache built in her chest, a longing she had never experienced before. If a man could be so tender and caring with an infant, could he also be as considerate with a lover?

Ariel had not experienced much tenderness in the magical realm . . . and she wanted it. Would having a child fulfill that need?

Lifting the baby again, Rand held him against his shoulder and stroked the tiny head. "Time to see your momma." He smiled softly as they left the room.

Resisting the urge to follow, Ariel leaned against a white container that smelled of the infant's unique scent. The ache in her chest intensified. She wanted a baby. Not Robin and Kate's, but one of her own . . . to cuddle, to care for, to raise. Then she would be needed, then she would have a purpose to her life again.

But the only way to create a baby was to mate with a mortal. The Fae could not impregnate each other. Fae men had often mated with mortal women, which sometimes resulted in children born to those women. Yet Ariel had never heard of a Fae woman giving birth after trysts with mortal men.

She frowned, recalling a mention of babies many centuries ago. What was it? After several moments, she shook her head. No matter. If it had been important she would've remembered.

There had been no pregnant Fae because they could control whether they conceived or not with their magic. Had no other faery ever wanted to be a mother? Ariel hesitated, remembering Titania's hatred of the half-breed Fae. If Ariel did have a child, she would have to keep it far from the Queen of the Fae.

She sighed. Since she was banned from court for eternity, keeping her distance would not be a problem. The magical realm was large enough for her to make a life with her baby far from the royal court.

But first she would have to find a man to be the father. Other mortals she'd met in the past had been crude and rough. She did not want that . . . for herself or for her child. She needed someone kind and gentle, but intelligent and hardworking.

She smiled. Of course—Rand. He appeared healthy and was quite pleasant in appearance. Very pleasant indeed.

But she knew little of his character save that he was gentle with babies. Before she made her final decision, she needed to know more about him. But how?

Ariel kicked at the container in frustration, only to have it waver, then crash to the dresser, coating her with a fine white substance. She sneezed several times, swiping at her gown in a futile attempt to dislodge the stuff. *Enough of this.*

With a swish of magic, she transported herself outside the house. Ariel glanced around. No one in sight. She changed her clothes to resemble those of the women inside—heavy blue coverings on her legs called jeans and a ribbed sweater; then she assumed mortal size.

Glancing at her reflection in a car window, she grimaced. She looked mortal enough in these strange tight-fitting clothes. But could she pass as one of them?

A cold wind blew past her and she wrapped her arms around herself. Even with the afternoon sun, the chill was noticeable. The tall ash trees along the walk were dark and bare, with a few brown leaves dangling helplessly from stripped branches. The mortal season of winter was approaching—a terrible period of cold and snow. She had experienced it once and vowed never again. The eternal warmth in the magical realm was far better.

Ariel paused. Before she returned home, she needed to meet Rand and find out if he had all the qualities she wanted for her child. To do that, she needed to get inside the house . . . as a mortal. But how?

The baby. She smiled as the answer came swiftly. Rand and his sister had come to see the baby. Ariel had been sent to do the same. Only now she would approach through the front entrance.

She reached the heavy wooden door and rapped twice before it opened. Kate smiled at her, a question in her eyes. "Yes?"

"I'm Ariel. I've come to see the baby."

A slight frown creased Kate's face. "Do I know you?"

"No." Ariel hesitated. Kate knew of the Fae but Ariel was unsure how much to reveal. "I know Robin."

"Robin?" Wariness entered Kate's expression. "How do you know him?"

"I know his father better." Ariel met Kate's gaze and smiled when awareness dawned in the woman's eyes.

"Oh." Kate held open the door. "Come in." As she turned toward a large room, she glanced back at Ariel. "Oberon sent you?"

"The child *is* his grandson."

Kate smiled. "So he is."

As they entered the main room, the other woman

looked up from cooing at the infant in her arms, but Ariel focused only on Rand, standing by the fireplace. He turned to meet her gaze, and a tingle spread through her body. Ariel drew in a deep breath. Was he the one?

"Ariel, this is my friend, Stephanie Thayer, and her brother, Rand. Steph, Rand, this is a friend of Robin's, Ariel . . . LeFay." Kate gave Ariel an impish smile as she created the surname and motioned her forward.

Stephanie looked up from her position in a large chair. "Did you come to hold this fella, too?"

Remembering the baby's softness, Ariel nodded. She'd had to release him too soon before. She settled in a nearby chair and cuddled the infant close when Stephanie placed him in her arms. "Have you given him a name?" Ariel asked Kate.

"Brandon." Kate stood beside them, her expression worried until Ariel settled back, the baby cradled against her arm.

"He's very much like his father," Ariel said. She could easily picture the infant being her own with his dark curly hair and blue eyes. Her chest grew tight, her breath catching in her throat. For a brief moment, moisture threatened her eyes.

Ariel blinked. Tears? Impossible. The Fae did not cry.

But she could not deny the onslaught of emotion that washed over her. She wanted a baby. Her own baby. Perhaps then this unbearable loneliness would fade.

Glancing up, she found Rand gazing at her and she gave him her most brilliant smile. His eyes widened, then a slow smile crept across his lips—lips of such sensual fullness that Ariel instantly decided she would taste them even if he was not the one to father her child.

"Do you like children?" she asked.

He crossed the room to stand before her, so tall she had to tilt her head back to meet his gaze. "As long as they're someone else's."

Stephanie laughed. "We have so many nieces and nephews that it feels like we've always had children."

"Are you good to them?" Somehow Ariel had to determine if he met all the necessary requirements.

Rand shrugged. "Okay, I guess."

"Don't let him fool you." Stephanie grinned at Ariel. "They all adore him. He's their favorite play toy."

This sounded good so far, though she was not completely certain about "play toy." But to ask would give away her unfamiliarity with this realm. "I see."

Brandon stirred, crinkling his face as if about to erupt. Kate reached for him at once. "Time to eat."

Standing, Ariel relinquished her chair to Kate. The woman sat and nestled against the back, then raised her sweater and brought the infant to her breast. He suckled with fierce tugs, his tiny fists resting against her skin.

Warmth swept through Ariel. To have that kind of closeness . . . to give of herself . . .

"I think we ought to be going," Rand said behind Ariel.

She turned into him and stumbled, but he caught her arms in a firm but gentle hold. Mischief lit his eyes. "All right?"

"Yes." Ariel hated to look away. Men did not normally look at her with warmth and a sense of fun. "I . . . I should go, too." Though Rand appealed to her, she still was not certain that he fulfilled all her requirements for a mortal father. How could she learn more?

"Thanks for coming. Forgive me if I don't show you out." Kate smiled at them. "I'll be sure to tell Robin you stopped by."

"Don't worry, Kate." Stephanie embraced the woman and baby. "You both look great. Tell Robin I said to take good care of you."

"Oh, he's doing that." Kate beamed with happiness, an expression that lingered with Ariel as she walked to the door.

Such wide variances in emotion rarely appeared among the Fae. Especially happiness. She frowned. Had she ever been that happy? Content perhaps, satisfied with her place of honor in the court, but radiant like Kate? No.

Oddly enough, she wanted to experience that.

"Have you known Robin long?" Stephanie asked, falling in step beside Ariel.

"Over two hun—" Ariel caught herself. "Yes, a very long time."

They paused on the sidewalk beside a parked brown truck. "Where's your car?" Rand asked, searching the road. No other vehicle sat within a block.

"I . . . I walked." Ariel grinned. *With some magical help.*

"Do you live near here?"

He actually appeared interested in her answer. Ariel's pulse skipped a beat. "No, I'm visiting this area."

"Been here long?"

"Just today."

"Then you haven't seen the sights yet?" Stephanie's eyes lit up. "Well, we have to show you." She glanced at her brother. "Right, Rand?"

"I . . . ah . . . sure." Though his voice remained pleasant, Rand aimed a dark glance at Stephanie before he opened the door to the truck, but she only grinned in reply.

Ariel beamed. This was exactly what she wanted—more time with Rand.

When he motioned her forward, she climbed into the vehicle, strange tremors in her belly. She had seen these metal transports—cars and trucks—but had never ridden in one before. This would be an adventure.

Rand closed the door after Stephanie slid in beside Ariel, then went around and took a seat behind the large wheel in the front. Ariel's throat tightened as he closed his door. Though she could see out the clear glass before her, she felt trapped. A painful ache crept along her bones—a reaction to the vehicle's iron. Was learning more about Rand worth this?

"Are you all right?" His deep voice cut through her rising panic.

"I . . . I . . ." She turned to look at him, her eyes wide.

He touched her arm, concern in his eyes. "Ariel?"

His fingers blazed an imprint into her skin, shooting fire through her blood. Ariel exhaled slowly. Yes, this man could very well be worth some momentary discomfort. She forced a smile. "I've never been in a vehicle like this before."

His face lit up with satisfaction as he started the vehicle and sent it into motion. "Yep, a 1958 Ford. She's a classic."

"Don't encourage him," Stephanie added dryly.

Confused, Ariel glanced at the woman. "I don't understand."

"You'll learn more than you ever wanted to know about this truck." Mischief danced in Stephanie's eyes as she glanced at her brother. When he ignored her, she turned her attention back to Ariel. "What would you like to see?"

Ariel blinked. When she had come to this city, she hadn't planned to stay. "What is there to see?"

"Lots of things—museums, the Pro Rodeo Hall of Fame, Seven Falls, Garden of the Gods—"

"Garden of the Gods?" The name caught Ariel's attention. As a pillywiggins, she adored gardens and flowers of all kinds, though the buttercup was her reigning flower. "Is it a large garden?"

Stephanie shook her head. "It's not really a garden at all. It's a grouping of large stones in a wide variety of shapes. They look like they're growing from the earth."

Stones? Growing from the earth? Ariel's heart skipped a beat. The Stones in the magical realm were a site of great power. "I would very much like to see that."

"I'm on it." Rand wove his vehicle between others at such quick speeds that Ariel shut her eyes, her stomach rolling with the movement. "You'll be able to see it soon."

She cracked one eye open to peer in the direction he indicated. Magnificent red rocks towered in the distance above the surrounding homes and trees. Fully alert now, she leaned forward to watch as Rand took them closer. "By the Stones," she murmured. Though very different from the ones she knew, this place held magic. She could feel it.

"They're red sandstone," Rand said. "And noted for their different shapes." He pointed to a ridge of rock. "That's called Kissing Camels."

Though Ariel had only seen a camel once in her centuries of existence, she could make out the two faces nose-to-nose. "I see them." Laughter bubbled to the surface. She had never expected to find camels among the rocks.

"You have to go to Balanced Rock, Rand." Stephanie's enthusiasm shimmered in her voice as she turned to Ariel. "It's this huge rock that looks like it should fall, but doesn't."

Ariel gasped when Rand stopped the car beside that formation. "How does it stay there?"

"It's very steady." Rand slid from the truck, then came around to help the women out. As Ariel placed her palm in his, a trickle of excitement soared through her. Was it this man or the energy surrounding this area?

He didn't release her hand even after her feet touched the ground, but stared at her, his expression curious and confused. She met his gaze, surprised by the sudden tug at her insides. What was it about this mortal?

"Come on." Stephanie waved at them, already scampering up to the base of Balanced Rock.

At her call, Rand dropped Ariel's hand and stepped back, motioning for her to precede him.

A swift wave of disappointment washed over Ariel and she frowned. She was looking for a father for her child, nothing more. True, it would help to find the father attractive, but other qualities were more important. Gentleness, kindness, intelligence. Rand possessed those, but did he have the most important of all? Did he believe in the magic that flowed through her veins?

She climbed up after Stephanie to stand beside the precariously balanced rock. The magic was strong here. It filled the air and tingled beneath her feet. Ariel ran her fingers lightly over the pitted surface. These were not the

Stones of the magical realm, but they contained a power of their own.

Small sparks danced from the rock to her hand and she jerked it away. Before she could step back, Rand appeared by her side. "What happened?"

She glanced up at him. "The energy here is stronger than I thought."

"Energy?" He frowned as he looked from her to the stone.

Ask him now. Ariel paused. His answer mattered. More than she wanted it to. "Do you believe in magic?"

He raised his eyebrows, then broke out in a wide grin. "I believe there are things that can't be explained away. I guess you could call that magic."

He believed. Ariel resisted the urge to dance. Instead, she took his hand and placed it against the rock with hers over it. A tremor of energy vibrated beneath their palms. "Do you feel it?"

His jaw dropped. "I do."

The pinpricks of electrical shocks surprised Rand. *Who is this woman?* Was the vibration beneath his palm from the rock or his reaction to her? He found himself wanting to wrap his arms around this tiny creature. He'd just met her, yet something about her intrigued him. Her tumbling black curls accented her porcelain skin and vivid blue eyes, and her smooth oval face was too lovely to be true. But it was something more than her stunning beauty and soft British accent.

She had an air of innocence yet her eyes appeared to hold the wisdom of the ages. The depth in those eyes hinted at secrets—secrets he irrationally wanted to discover.

Shaking his head, Rand pulled away from the rock and Ariel. He was losing it. After growing up with ten sisters, the last thing he needed was another woman in his life. "I need to talk to Stephanie."

Before Ariel could react, he climbed down the rock to

join his sister. She met his dark look with an impish smile. "Problem?" she asked.

"Are you trying to fix me up, Steph? I'd expect that from Mom and the others, but not you." Stephanie was as avowedly single as he.

Surprise flitted across her face. "Fix you up? No. I like her, Rand. That's all." The corner of her lips lifted. "Why? You attracted?"

"She's pretty enough." He spoke grudgingly. Yeah, pretty enough to light up any room she walked into. "But I'm not interested."

"Okay." Stephanie turned to greet Ariel as the petite woman approached. "There's a path over here, Ariel, if you want to see more."

Ariel's face glowed with her smile. "I would like that." She gave Rand a curious glance, but fell into step with Steph, leaving him to follow.

He couldn't stop watching her as she viewed the towering rocks. She acted as if they were truly magical. Rand rolled his eyes. Good thing his friend Dean hadn't heard him admit to a belief in magic. Dean tended to rib him enough about his feminine-influenced upbringing.

Still Rand couldn't have stopped his response. At that moment, he probably would've agreed with anything Ariel asked him. His chest tightened with more than a hint of panic. She was definitely dangerous. The sooner they parted company, the better.

The women stopped abruptly, their conversation dying, and he came up behind them, half expecting to see a snake in their path. Instead a large buck emerged from behind the pines. Full-bodied, with a rack that would be the envy of any hunter, the deer didn't run, but stopped and stared at them.

Rand barely breathed. He'd never been this close to a wild deer before. The creature held its head erect with an air of majesty, its brown eyes giving the impression of intelligence.

Ariel approached the buck without any hesitation and,

to Rand's surprise, it didn't run, but remained in place until she stood by its head, gazing into its eyes. They appeared to be communicating by some unspoken means. Rand grimaced. Crazy thought. More likely, she was endangering herself. The buck could gore her easily, especially with that rack.

"Be careful, Ariel." Rand moved toward her and the buck jerked to attention, then fled in one smooth leap, vanishing into the trees. By the time Rand reached Ariel's side, she'd turned to face him.

"He wouldn't have hurt me."

"You don't know that." No one could speak with such confidence about a wild animal.

"Yes, I do." Again, the wisdom of someone much older than her apparent twenty-five years shimmered in her eyes. "He was merely examining the area. It will be an early winter this year and he expects it will be difficult to find food."

Rand didn't reply. What could he say to that? She honestly thought she could speak with the creature? Obviously, she deluded herself. Good—a solid reason why he shouldn't be attracted to her.

"Oh, no," Stephanie cried, glancing at her watch.

"What?" Rand frowned at her.

"I promised Tammy I'd watch the kids tonight." She grimaced. "And I'm supposed to be there in fifteen minutes."

"You're a glutton for punishment, Steph." She'd been surrounded by their older sisters' children most of her life, just as he had.

"I know." She gave him a wry smile. "But I lost a bet."

"Better you than me. Come on." He led the way back to the truck, not turning to see if Ariel followed. But he knew she did by the way the back of his neck tingled, as if he could feel her presence.

"I'll drop you off, Steph, then take Ariel home." Then he could be done with this insanity. He'd found plenty of women attractive in the past, but none had affected him like Ariel.

"Works for me," Stephanie said.

The women climbed into the truck as he started the engine. Tammy lived farther north, across the highway, so he had to hurry to make Stephanie's deadline. Fortunately the traffic wasn't too bad and he arrived only five minutes late.

"Have fun," he told his sister as he stopped in the driveway.

"Hey, you can help." Her face brightened. "The kids adore you."

"No, thanks. I'm meeting some guys at Smiley's after I drop off Ariel."

Stephanie rolled her eyes. "What's so great about hanging out at a bar? It's a macho thing, right?"

"Exactly." And Rand relished the macho things in life. After twenty-nine years of girls and dresses and tea parties, he needed them.

"I suppose Dean is going to be there, chugging beer and all."

"He's supposed to be." Rand darted a sideways glance at his sister. As much as she complained about his best friend, she always asked about him. "A doctor needs time to relax, too, you know." He grinned. "Want to come along?"

"No, thanks." She slid out of the truck. "I'd rather watch kids." She paused to smile at Ariel. "I enjoyed meeting you."

Ariel nodded. "Thank you for taking me to see the stones."

"Any time." With a cheery wave, Stephanie started up the walk.

Rand waited for her to enter the house, then pulled away. Ariel didn't move from his side despite the extra space available and he inhaled deeply, more aware of her than ever. She had a unique scent—floral, but not one he could readily identify. And he thought he'd suffered through them all with his sisters.

"Where do you live?" he asked.

"Far from here. Too far for you to drive." Amusement tinged her voice.

"Okay, then, where are you staying?"

She paused and studied him, the silence lengthening while Rand's gut knotted with apprehension. "I don't have a place here."

Well, no matter what ploy she was pulling, he wasn't taking her home with him. He didn't dare. Just the thought of her inside his house made his pulse leap. "How about I drop you at a hotel?" Any hotel. Just out of his truck, which seemed a lot smaller than it had when Stephanie was there. His sweatshirt felt tight around his neck and he tugged at the neckline. "The Holiday Inn is close."

"I would like to stay longer with you."

No way. "Sorry, I have plans tonight." He accelerated the truck and headed for the hotel.

She didn't respond, but appeared lost in thought. He didn't want to know what she was thinking. Whatever it was couldn't be good for him.

He reached the hotel in record time and pulled into a spot beside the building, his heart hammering as much from the unwanted attraction as trepidation. He went around to open the passenger door. Ariel slid to the edge of the seat but didn't climb down. At this height, her face was even with his, her expression yearning, her kissable lips only inches away.

Alarmed by that thought, Rand offered his hand to help her out, but she caught his shoulders and pressed her mouth to his. His first instinct to break away faded beneath the gentle pressure of her soft lips. He found himself responding, unwilling to stop. She tasted sweet, intoxicating.

Fire sparked through his blood, heading straight for his loins. He pulled her closer until her breasts molded against his chest and he nestled between her knees. Heat claimed his entire body as his desire grew. He wanted her, needed her—needed to touch her, to kiss her, to bury himself within her.

She ran her hands through his hair, igniting his senses. She moaned, her lips parting, and he delved inside to claim more of her sweetness. Lord help him, he couldn't get enough.

Cupping her rear in his hands, he pressed his erection between her legs. God, she was hot. He ached to remove the barriers between them.

The sudden sound of a car door slamming jerked Rand back to reality and he broke off the kiss in stunned surprise. What the hell just happened to him? He'd never lost it like that before. Never.

He lowered Ariel to her feet and released her at once so he could step back. He still craved her, his senses swimming from the feel of her mouth beneath his, her body meshed with his. "I'm sorry." His words emerged husky from his thick throat. "I don't know what—"

"I know." Her kiss-swollen lips lifted in a smile. "You are the one, Rand Thayer."

Warning alarms rang in his brain. "The one?"

"Yes." She spoke with confidence. "You are the one to father my baby."

Damn. He stared at her in disbelief. *All I did was kiss her.*

Two

"You're crazy." Rand stepped back even farther.

Ariel frowned. Why didn't Rand look happy about her proposition? From her past experience, most men were eager to lie with a woman.

"No." She'd approached this very reasonably. "You have all the qualities I desire in my baby's father." She gave him her most dazzling smile. "Shall we go to your home now?"

"No way." His eyes took on a wary expression.

Ariel hesitated. She hadn't expected this reaction, especially after his heated response to her kiss. He desired her, yet he refused to mate with her? A sharp pang stabbed her chest. Surely his reaction didn't bother her; yet, she didn't understand her strange sense of disappointment. "You don't want me?"

He clenched his fists, a brief glimmer entering his eyes that revealed he had felt something. "No, I don't." Keeping a large distance between them, Rand hurried to his truck and slid into the driver's seat. He glanced at her and for a moment Ariel thought he might change his mind, but he brought the metal beast to a roar.

She watched him drive away, her chest aching. She could not have a child without mating with a mortal man; yet, the one she wanted most for this special mission had rejected her.

"Are you all right?" A man stood beside the car he'd just parked, his gaze holding an all-too-familiar gleam.

Ariel sighed. This man would not hesitate to do as she asked. But she didn't want this man. She wanted Rand Thayer.

"I will be," she told him. Somehow she had to convince Rand to give in to his desire. She'd felt the heat of his kiss, the hard bulge in his trousers, and her body had responded at once.

But what could she do?

She could locate him easily enough with a simple spell. Then what? Explaining what she was would not change his mind, even if he believed her.

She could cast a spell to ensnare him. . . . No. That might achieve her ultimate goal, but she wanted more than that from Rand. She wanted his honest desire, the caring he'd displayed with Robin and Kate's baby.

This was not going to be easy.

She would return to the Garden of the Gods. Perhaps among the magic of the mortals' stones she would think of something.

The man from the car had entered the hotel. No one else was in sight. Ariel glanced around once more, then teleported away.

Rand's back itched as he pulled away . . . as if he could feel Ariel's gaze boring into him. Why him? Why had she picked him? He was an everyday handyman. Nobody special.

And the last thing he wanted to do—no matter how desirable the woman—was father a child. He had more than enough children in his life now—fifteen nieces and nephews by last count. He didn't intend to add to that number.

He slammed on his brakes to miss an approaching car. Damn, he'd better pay attention to his driving or he wouldn't have to worry about fathering anyone's baby.

He headed for Smiley's. A night with his friends would ease the tension lingering in his neck. It was his time—the only time he could escape the demands of his job and incessant pleas from his sisters.

Dean's new BMW sat outside the bar and Rand pulled in beside it. What would his friends have to say about this crazy lady? Rand grinned. Probably a lot.

He entered the building and waved at the bartender as he made his way to the back where his three friends sat. "A draft, please, Smiley."

Smiley waved back and Rand pulled a chair up to the table. "Sorry I'm late. It's been one of those days."

Roger nodded. "Fixing your mom's sink again?"

"Not this time." Rand's beer arrived and he took a large swallow. "Had to run Stephanie by some friends' to see their new baby—"

"She has a car," Dean interrupted. "Why are you running her around?"

"Her car is in the shop. The timing chain went out. Besides, that's not—"

"She has sisters she can call on." Dean shook his head. "You let them take advantage of you, pal."

Rand sighed. They'd had this discussion many times. Since his father had died almost ten years ago, he'd been the sole male in the family and his mother and sisters depended on him. As much as he longed for more freedom, he couldn't desert them. Dean knew that. "Look, I'm trying to tell you about this woman I met there. You want to hear it or not?"

The three men sat upright. "Woman?" Dwayne raised his eyebrows.

"A looker?" Dean asked, his interest obviously caught.

Rand paused. Oh, yeah, definitely a looker. But she was more than that, too. Besides her beauty, her petiteness and air of innocence made him want to protect her. "Not bad," he said finally.

"So, what happened?" Dwayne leaned forward. "You finally decide to relent and go out with a female who isn't related to you?"

Rand grimaced. Okay, so he didn't date much. He had enough women in his life. "You're not gonna believe this." He hesitated for a moment, enjoying his friends' responses.

Dean displayed his usual wry expression but his dark eyes gleamed. Dwayne showed more obvious interest while Roger sat back in his chair, his arms crossed, an enigmatic smile on his lips.

"She wants me to father her child," Rand said.

Dean almost fell off his chair, roaring with laughter. "Father her child? Do you *know* this woman? Does she know *you*?"

"Just met her today." Though he wasn't likely to forget her soon.

Dwayne roared with laughter before he spoke. "Why you?"

"Beats me." Rand shrugged. "I didn't hang around to find out." Though something in her eyes nagged at him. Why a baby? Why him? Maybe what she'd really needed was to talk to someone. Maybe he should've listened to her instead of panicking.

He frowned. He hadn't panicked. He'd just fled as quickly as possible. Hell, that *was* panic.

Roger snapped his fingers in Rand's face. "You have some seduction secrets we don't know about?"

Rand laughed and shook his head. "Hey, I'm just me. This woman was new in town so Stephanie and I took her to see the Garden of the Gods. That's all."

"So, what'd you tell her?" Dwayne was practically drooling. Of course, Dwayne considered sex a sport worthy of the same enthusiasm as football.

"No, of course." Rand took another hearty drink. "I'm not stupid."

"You crazy?" Dwayne rolled his eyes. "A good-looking woman asked you to have sex with her and you refused?"

"This wasn't just sex, Dwayne." Her appeal had been more heartfelt than that. "She wants a baby." Not that Dwayne would understand. To him, women were conquests, and he enjoyed sharing his exploits with his friends. Rand couldn't do that. Being raised with ten sisters had made sure of that. He respected women too much.

"There are ways to prevent that, my friend," Dwayne replied.

"But none is foolproof." Dean grinned. "I have plenty of business delivering babies as proof of that." He frowned abruptly and glanced down at the pocket on his shirt. Pulling a pen out of his pocket, he grimaced. "Damn thing is leaking. This is the second one in a week. Cheap pens."

"Just like those leaky condoms, eh, Dean?" Roger asked with a grin.

Dean tossed the pen on the table and examined the ink stain on his shirt.

"Soak that in milk and it'll come right out," Rand said without thinking.

When Dean glanced at him with raised eyebrows, the corner of his lips lifting, Rand groaned. He'd done it again. Damn. No matter how hard he tried to be macho, he messed up. It was difficult after growing up among eleven women.

Dean spoke before Rand could say anything else. "I delivered twins today and they're naming one of them after me."

"Again?" Rand smiled, thankful for the change of subject. "This town is going to be full of little Deans at this rate."

"Enough to make one wonder," Dwayne added.

Dean lifted his beer. "Can I help it if I'm a great obstetrician?"

They all laughed and Rand relaxed. This is what he enjoyed most—time with the guys. Lord knew he had little enough of it. And no one—not even a lovely woman—was going to change that.

Ariel paused outside the building and glanced at the blinking neon sign. Smiley's. One eye of the smiling face beside the words had burned out, making it appear as if the face was winking. A challenge? She'd never turned away from one and was not going to start now.

Her spell said Rand was here, yet she hesitated. Even after an hour with the calming stones in the Garden of the Gods, she hadn't arrived at a solution. Perhaps he just needed more time to know her—not common among men of her acquaintance, but possible. Therefore, she would give him more time . . . with her.

Pushing through the door, she stepped inside, then squinted as her eyes adjusted to the dim lighting. The establishment was different from taverns she had visited in prior centuries, yet much the same. Men sat around small tables, gulping their brew. Smoke and loud music filled the air. A bar lined with bottles stretched along one wall and the other end of the room held billiard tables where men flaunted their skills. She saw few women and those few were nothing like the harlots she remembered in previous eras. Good.

Ariel spotted Rand at a table in the back and smiled. Three other men sat with him. She stepped closer as she studied them. Should she approach Rand now or wait?

Too late. He'd spotted her.

Rand's expression changed from laughter to surprise, then wariness. Ariel's heart gave an extra thump. Maybe this wasn't a good idea. Maybe she should look elsewhere for a man to father her child.

No. This was the man she wanted. He was kind, gentle, caring, and believed in magic. She wanted those qualities for her baby.

Rand pushed back his chair and stood, his expression veiled, yet he made no attempt to approach her.

Ariel drew in a deep breath. She would be friendly to

him and his friends. Then Rand would realize she wasn't dangerous. He might even like her.

She approached the table and studied the other men sitting there before meeting Rand's gaze. "Hi."

"What are you doing here?" he asked, tension lingering beneath his words.

"I . . . ah . . ." She glanced around the bar. "I came to have a drink." A friendly drink . . . with him.

"Here?" He sounded even less pleased.

"I . . . liked the name." A place called Smiley's should have smiling people inside it. Only Rand wasn't smiling.

"You didn't follow me?"

"How could I follow you?" She'd always found it best to answer with another question. "You drove away."

A hint of regret crossed his face and her spirits lifted. Maybe . . .

"Join us. Please." One of the other men hurried to pull a chair forward for her. He was taller than Rand and broad shouldered enough for two men. His blond hair stood up in tiny spikes, but his expression was familiar. She had seen it often enough in the past. This man was another who would not have refused her request. "I'm Dwayne Masters," he said as he seated her.

She sat beside him then stared at Rand until he, too, took his seat. "I'm Ariel," she murmured, then recalled the mortal last name Kate had given her. "Ariel LeFay."

"A very whimsical name." Equally as attractive as Rand, the man sitting at her other side boasted a styled crop of black hair and mischief dancing in his dark eyes.

How did she respond to that? "It's *my* name."

He grinned. "I didn't mean to imply it wasn't. I'm an obstetrician and I thought I'd heard all the names in the world, but I haven't run across one like yours before." He extended his hand. "I'm Dean Carstensen."

She slowly placed her hand in his, studying him. Though he was welcoming, she sensed a protectiveness in his manner. Was he protecting Rand from her? "Are you Rand's friend?"

"We let him think so." The remaining man leaned forward to shake her hand. Slighter of build, he had longer dark blond hair and a mustache. "Roger Alvarez."

"Mostly we put up with him." Dwayne grinned. "I've worked with him on some jobs. I'm in construction."

"What does Rand do?" she asked. She'd been so eager to learn of his character, she'd never thought to inquire of his position.

"Nearly everything." Dean cocked his head toward Rand. "Carpentry, plumbing, electrical. If it can be built or repaired, Rand can do it."

"That would be a good skill to have." She dared to glance at Rand, who was watching her warily. "Do you enjoy it?"

"Most of the time," he said finally.

"So, how do you two know each other?" Tony asked.

Before Ariel could reply, Rand responded. "She's a friend of Stephanie's."

"Is Steph with you?" Dean asked, his gaze darting toward the door.

Evidently Rand wanted his friends to believe his words. As one of the Fae, she couldn't lie, but she did know the answer to this. "No, she's watching Tammy's children tonight."

"You'd think she'd get enough of that." Dean nudged Rand. "She's as gullible as you when it comes to your family."

Rand shrugged. "They're family." He said the words as if that explained everything. Perhaps they did. Ariel had never known what it was like to be in a family. The Fae had bands, such as her pillywiggins, but those were determined by each member's magical leaning, not blood.

But a child would be her family. Restless yearning tugged at her heart. Perhaps then she'd experience some of the joy she'd seen on Kate's face.

"Want a beer, Ariel?" Dwayne asked. Before she could even nod, he waved at a nearby woman server who promptly delivered a thick-glass mug of ale to their table.

Ariel sipped at it. Though slightly different in taste from the ale of centuries past, the drink was good. She took a larger drink, then wiped off the foam around her lips.

Dwayne laughed and covered her hand with his. "Now that's a woman after my own heart."

His touch was heavy, overpowering, far different from the longing Rand's touch created. She withdrew her hand from beneath his and focused on Dean. This man knew Rand and cared about him. "How long have you known Rand?"

"Most of my life. Growing up, I lived around the corner from him." Dean grinned at Rand. "He used to flee to my house when he couldn't take any more of his sisters."

"Don't you have sisters?"

"Not a one, thank God." Dean drained his mug. "But Rand has more than enough for all of us."

"How many sisters do you have, Rand?" Ariel had met Stephanie and knew about Tammy. Were there more?

As Dean frowned, she realized she'd erred. As a friend of Stephanie's, she should know this information.

Rand leaped to reply. "I don't suppose you've had a chance to meet all of them yet, have you? Counting Steph, I have ten sisters." A hint of a smile appeared around his lips. Was he finally accepting her?

Ariel hesitated. Ten was not such a large number. She'd been queen to thousands of pillywiggins. And the mortal families she recalled from centuries past had been large. Yet Dean acted as if having ten sisters was a great disaster. "And you're the only male?"

Grimacing, Rand nodded. " 'Fraid so."

Perhaps that explained it. "Then it's good you have a friend like Dean."

When Rand smiled, the tight band around Ariel's chest eased. She had said the right thing. The light in his eyes was now one of interest, not fear.

"I have to agree with that."

Recalling Stephanie's words about Dean, Ariel

frowned. "Then why does Stephanie dislike him so?"

Rand burst into laughter as a scowl crossed Dean's face. "That's because he tormented her mercilessly while we were growing up."

"It was a long time ago," Dean added. "And she was the only one younger than Rand so she tended to tag along with him."

Ariel didn't completely understand, but she nodded.

"Hell, you still tease her every chance you get," Rand said. "No wonder she avoids you."

Dean grimaced. "I should be so lucky."

Indignation filled Ariel. "I like Stephanie."

"So do I," Rand admitted. "She's the only one still single so we pretty much stick together against the others."

"Against the others?" Now she was confused. Rand had made it sound as if his family was important. Now he was fighting them?

"My mother and sisters believe it's a sin to be unmarried." Rand sighed. "And they'll do about anything to change that state for Steph and me."

Marriage—the mortal binding together of a couple for the rest of their years. How boring. No wonder Rand wanted to avoid it. "Then it's good you and Stephanie band together."

He blinked. "I . . . ah . . . yes."

After that, Rand relaxed even more, or was it the numerous ales the men consumed while they talked through the night? They grew more boisterous, each trying to outdo the other in the tales they told.

Ariel enjoyed it all, even though ale did not affect her as it did the mortals. These men were true friends, especially Rand and Dean. She had never had a true friend, someone she could trust. She had trusted Pansy when she'd defended Robin's right to be in the magical realm and Pansy had betrayed Ariel to Titania, leading to Ariel's removal as Queen of the Pillywiggins. Ariel would not make that mistake again.

"That's it, folks. Closing time." The round bartender paused by their table. "Everyone okay? Should I call any cabs?"

Dean stood as he shook his head. "I'm fine, Smiley. Thanks. Only had two. I can't afford a hangover when I'm on call tomorrow." He pulled some green bills from his pocket and dropped them on the table. "See ya later, guys."

Roger followed him. Ariel rose slowly, her gaze on Rand. Was he now willing to take her to his home?

"Don't set your hopes on Thayer," Dwayne said, placing a possessive hand on her arm. "He's sworn off women."

Men *did* that? Ariel looked at Rand in surprise.

He stood, avoiding her gaze. "I have enough of them in my life right now."

Ariel didn't respond. What could she say to that? All this had been for nothing?

Dwayne tugged at her arm. "Come on. I'll take you home." He managed to lead her to the parking lot before she realized he intended to place her in his car.

She dug in her heels and he turned to her in surprise. "What's the problem?" he asked.

"I can get home on my own." His intent was obvious. As much as she wanted a baby, she also wanted to choose the father.

"Oh, come on, doll." Dwayne drew her closer, wrapping his arms around her to pull her close to him, one hand drifting down to caress her bottom. "The night's still young."

"No." He did not attract her. In fact, his touch annoyed her. She'd encountered too many mortals like him in the past. "I'm fine on my own."

Instead, he tightened his hold, crushing her against his solid body. The solid length in his trousers spoke of lust.

Ariel sighed. What would he think when she suddenly disappeared? She tried not to use her magic around mortals, but in some circumstances, she had no other choice.

The tavern door swung open. "Let her go, Dwayne."

Ariel's pulse leaped as she twisted free and faced Rand. Had he changed his mind?

"I'm just taking her home, man," Dwayne said. He placed his heavy hand on Ariel's shoulder, but she pulled away.

"You never just take a woman home, Dwayne, not if you think you can get something out of it."

"So?" Dwayne's tone grew belligerent. "That's never bothered you before."

"It's never been Ar—a friend of Stephanie's before."

"What if she wants to come with me?"

"But I *don't* want to go with you, Dwayne," Ariel said.

He looked at her, stunned. Evidently he had not considered that. His surprised expression made her offer him a small smile. He wouldn't have forced her to go with him if she'd refused, unlike some men she'd encountered in the past. Because of that, she could forgive him.

"But thank you for offering," she added.

Dwayne grimaced. "Yeah." Without another word, he climbed into his vehicle and drove away.

Unsure what to expect, Ariel turned to Rand. His expression was unreadable as he stared at her.

Abruptly, he sighed. "Get in the truck."

She hurried to comply, her heart leaping against her ribs. This was better.

Much better.

Three

He was making a big mistake. Rand knew it, but he couldn't let Ariel leave with Dwayne. Something about this woman made him want to protect her.

Releasing a sigh, he jumped into his truck and started the engine, refusing to glance at her. He didn't need to. Every nerve tingled with awareness of her just a short distance away. "Put on your seat belt," he ordered as he drove away. That would keep her by the door, at least.

She fumbled with it for a while, but finally he heard the distinctive click of the buckle. "I'll drive you to the hotel."

"I'm not staying there."

When she didn't elaborate, he dared to look her way. The brief flashes of passing streetlights surrounded her with a glimmer that made her appear unreal, almost ethereal. She met his gaze but didn't speak.

She didn't need to. He felt her vibrancy, her passion. It filled the truck and threatened to steal any remaining ounce of sense he had left. Irrational desire sparked to life, arrowing straight for his crotch.

Damn, what was it with her? Sure, she was pretty . . .
beautiful . . . gorgeous, but he'd dealt with good-looking
women before. None of them had triggered a sudden hard-
on quite like this.

She should've stayed at the hotel. "Don't you have any
money?" he asked. Was that the problem?

After a moment's hesitation, she answered. "I have no
money."

"I see." What now? He wasn't about to take her to the
homeless shelter. She'd last about five seconds there. Yet
she needed a place to stay—at least for tonight.

He grimaced as he made his decision. After all, Steph
owed him one.

Turning toward his sister's apartment, he rehearsed reasonable explanations. Only none of them sounded reasonable. Hell, none of them *was* reasonable.

"Are we going to your home?" Ariel asked.

He tensed, his fingers strangling the steering wheel.
"No." Danger signals flashed in his brain. "I'm taking you
to Stephanie's. She'll let you sleep there tonight." *I hope.*

"I'd prefer to stay with you."

His already swollen erection tightened even more and
he almost considered it. *Get a grip, Thayer.* "That's not
going to happen."

"I see." She sounded disappointed. "You don't like
me."

"It's not that." Actually, he *did* like her. She'd held her
own with his friends tonight, laughing in the right places
while giving each of them equal attention. For a short
while, he'd been able to forget her earlier ridiculous statement.

He wasn't about to father anyone's baby. "I don't *know*
you."

"Is that so important?" Instead of coming off as flip-
pant, she acted as if she really wanted to know.

"Yeah." Dwayne might not mind a casual encounter,
but Rand did. He'd seen the effect of one on Lizzie, his
next oldest sister, when she'd sobbed a night away over

some scumbag who'd taken her virginity, then never spoke to her again.

Rand had made a brief visit to the scumbag that left them both bruised. It hadn't brought back Lizzie's virginity, but the guy probably thought twice after that before seducing someone else's sister. Thankfully, Mom had never known about it.

Ariel sighed, drawing his gaze. She looked so sad he had to resist the urge to touch her.

"This is not going as I expected," she murmured.

His curiosity caught. "And what did you expect?"

"Men in the past have been more than willing to lie with me, yet you are not." Her tone implied it was his fault.

He frowned. "You do this often?" So much for his illusions of her vulnerability.

"No. I've never done this before. I only said they were willing." Derision colored her words. "Too willing."

Rand could believe that, especially if she affected other men the same way she did him. He considered himself a sane man—hardworking, honest, and single because he preferred it that way. As a rule, he kept women out of his thoughts and out of his bed. Yet being trapped in his truck with Ariel had him thinking of hot sex, and lots of it.

He punched the accelerator. He needed to reach Stephanie's. Now.

When he spotted his sister's apartment complex, he eased a sigh of relief. Until he happened to glance at his stick-on dash clock. *Steph's going to kill me for waking her at this hour.*

But at this moment, he preferred fratricide to Ariel's attraction. Getting involved with her would be dangerous.

After parking, he went to help Ariel from the cab, but kept his distance despite his screaming hormones. Her small palm disappeared in his, her body heat sizzling up his arm. As soon as she touched the ground, he pulled away and turned toward Steph's apartment.

Before he could pound on his sister's door, Ariel

touched his arm, capturing his attention. He turned to face
her, then wished he hadn't. She was so petite, so delicious,
he was tempted to scoop her up and taste her.

"What?" He needed to keep control.

"Thank you for caring about what happens to me." She
reached up to touch his face and he couldn't have drawn
back even if he wanted to. Her gaze held his, a gleam
shining deep inside that burned through him.

As she rose up on her toes, he knew she intended to
kiss him. He could still turn away, still refuse to meet
those full lips. Yeah, if he'd been made of stone, maybe.

Her initial touch was tentative, less aggressive than before, but unnerving just the same. Rand told himself to
remain neutral, but not one single part of his body listened. He wrapped his arms around her, drawing her
closer, seeking her mouth with the thirst of a man lost in
the desert.

She moaned, tightening her arms around his neck,
bringing her body against his, her soft curves meshing
with his solid planes. She was sweet. She was hot. She
was driving him insane.

He longed to bury himself within her, to experience that
passion simmering just beneath the surface. The woman
was an aphrodisiac all by herself.

Leaving her mouth, he pressed kisses along the slender
column of her neck, lingering at her rapid pulse. She murmured his name—once, then again. The urgency of her
tone soaked slowly into his sex-starved senses.

Gasping, he released her and staggered back. God, what
was wrong with him? Where were his brains? In his pants,
no doubt.

"You need time," she whispered. "And I think I might,
as well."

His panic rising, Rand whirled around and pounded on
Stephanie's door. He was losing it. This woman held more
voltage than an exposed electrical wire . . . and one more
shock was going to kill him. "Hey, Steph, wake up."

His sister opened the door a crack and fixed him with

a glare designed to kill. "What do *you* want?"

He almost grinned. At least his sister remained true to form. "Can Ariel stay here tonight?"

Her eyes widened and she glanced past him to where Ariel stood. "Are you serious?" Steph asked.

Rand nodded. "Just for tonight."

"Why?"

"She has no money, no place to go." As his sister started to speak, he continued. "And she's not staying with me."

"You trust her?" Stephanie lowered her voice.

"Yeah. Yeah, I do." He couldn't explain it, but some inner sense told him the only danger from Ariel LeFay was to his well-ordered, womanless existence.

His sister stared at him for a moment longer, then swung the door open fully. "Fine. Come on in."

Rand backed away to let Ariel enter. "I need to go." He was panicking again, but he couldn't help it. "See you later."

He nearly ran back to his truck. Nothing like this had ever happened to him. He was a coward, unable to handle a half-pint.

And he didn't like it one little bit.

Ariel forced herself to examine Stephanie's home rather than run after Rand. She'd only intended to give him a gentle kiss, one of appreciation. Instead, he had fired to life, responding with an urgency that touched something deep inside her—a needing, a wanting that went beyond her desire for a child.

And it frightened her.

She shook her head. She was Fae. No mortal could frighten her.

"All I have is a couch. That okay?" Even as she spoke, Stephanie staggered through the room to a door. Pulling it open, she removed a coverlet and pillow.

"That will be fine."

Stephanie's apartment resembled the woman herself—

semiordered, semichaotic, and decorated in a wild array of color. The grouping of plants stacked in front of one window reminded Ariel of the elfin garden in the magical realm—wild yet irresistibly lovely.

Rand's sister dumped the items on the couch, then faced Ariel, her gaze not completely focused. "Don't murder me while I sleep, okay?"

"I would not do that." The Fae didn't kill. Besides, Ariel liked this woman.

"Good." Turning away, Stephanie shuffled toward another door. "I'm going back to sleep. I left Pierce Brosnan declaring his love for me."

The door closed, leaving Ariel alone with her tumultuous feelings. Desire still simmered within her, but beneath that lingered something more—a genuine need for Rand.

Ridiculous. He was merely a way for her to gain a child. Nothing more.

Unfortunately, they wouldn't be creating that child tonight.

Ariel eyed the couch with a frown. Normally she slept among the buttercups, her reigning flower, but this world lingered on the brink of winter. All the buttercups were gone.

The scent of violets drifted from the mismatched garden. That would do.

Shrinking to her normal size, Ariel settled among the flowers and finally drifted off to sleep.

The sound of running water awakened Ariel. Judging from the sun, the morning was half gone. How could she have slept so late? She quickly took on human size and clothing, barely having time to make the couch appear slept on before Stephanie emerged from a room.

"The bathroom's all yours," she called, then entered a different room.

Ariel approached the bathroom cautiously. Past experience led her to expect a horrid stench, but this room smelled of nothing but peaches and steam. The steam drifted from a walled area at one end, a large white tub at the bottom. The wall moved when Ariel touched it and she slid it to one side to peer inside. *Interesting.*

Playing with the knobs, she jumped back, startled when water suddenly erupted from a shiny pipe near the top. Ah, now she understood. The mortals used this to cleanse themselves, much as the Fae stood under a sparkling waterfall.

Only this water was warm . . . inviting. With a thought, Ariel removed her clothing and stepped inside. *Ahhh. Wonderful.* Perhaps there were some things of merit in this cold world.

She discovered the source of the peach scent in a bottle sitting at the edge of the white tub. Hair shampoo. Ariel read the directions, then poured some in her hand. She would try it, but before she did, she changed the fragrance to that of the buttercup. Subtle, but hers.

Once she finished her cleansing and played with the other shiny items in the bathroom, Ariel donned her mortal clothing and emerged to find Stephanie in her tiny kitchen drinking coffee from a large mug.

"Want some?" she asked, lifting her cup.

"No." That was one taste Ariel had never acquired. "But I will take some nectar if you have it."

"Nectar?" Stephanie frowned. "Juice? I have orange-pineapple." She opened the large chilling device—a refrigerator, Ariel recalled—and removed a bottle. After grabbing a glass, Stephanie poured the liquid in it, then handed the glass to Ariel.

Ariel sipped it cautiously. Different, but pleasant enough. "Thank you."

"Since I don't have to work today I can cook breakfast." Stephanie leaned against the counter and studied Ariel. "Are you a bacon-and-eggs type of person?"

"I don't eat meat." None of the Fae did.

"Works for me." Turning, Stephanie pulled a box from

a nearby cupboard and held it out. "I'm an eat-on-the-run type myself. Pop Tart?"

Ariel took one of the silver packages, then mimicked Stephanie's actions as the woman tore it open and bit into the pastry. The sweetness of it made Ariel blink, but again the taste was not unpleasant.

"What are your plans for today?" Stephanie asked between bites.

Ariel hesitated. "I would like to see Rand again."

"You interested in him?"

"Yes."

Stephanie finished her pastry and shook her head. "You might as well give up now. Rand swore off women a few years ago and I haven't seen one yet that came close to making him break that vow."

"Why did he swear off women?" Most unusual for a man.

"Too many sisters." Stephanie grinned. "He wants to enjoy being on his own for a while first."

Ariel didn't plan to take much of his time. Ten minutes might be enough. "I only want to see him again."

"Fair enough. He never did say why he dumped you on my doorstep." A mischievous gleam entered Stephanie's brown eyes. "In fact, he was more nervous than I've ever seen him." She tapped her finger against her chin. "Maybe you *should* see him again."

She poured the remainder of her coffee into a silver sink, then turned a handle to bring water pouring out. Almost immediately she stopped the flow. "Damn thing. It backs up almost every day now." Stephanie sighed. "I've asked maintenance three times to fix it and they still haven't shown up." She started from the kitchen. "Let me get the drain cleaner."

She left the room and Ariel peeked into the basin filled with brown water. She did owe Stephanie a boon for providing a place to sleep. With a swish of her fingers, Ariel sent magic rushing down into the pipes and the water drained away effortlessly. Stephanie would have no more trouble here.

Ariel stepped back just as Stephanie returned, a can in her hand. The woman stopped at the basin and looked at Ariel. "Did you do something?"

Unable to lie, Ariel nodded.

"What?"

"Magic."

Stephanie laughed. "Magic, voodoo, I don't care. It worked and that's good enough for me." She put the can away and motioned Ariel toward the main room. "Let's go."

Once outside, Stephanie led Ariel to a large boxlike vehicle. "Tammy let me borrow her car to get home last night, so don't look at the mess. It's her mommy mobile."

Another metal conveyance. Ariel sighed but climbed inside, ignoring the immediate ache and pressure on her chest that came from the metal beast.

Fortunately the trip to Rand's took only a short time. As Stephanie stopped the vehicle before a house, she groaned. "Oh, great."

"Is there a problem?"

"Yeah, Dumb Dean is here. That's his Beemer in the driveway." Stephanie pulled her car behind it, the two vehicles almost touching, then jumped out.

Ariel paused to examine the house. The dwelling was large, two stories tall, with a wood exterior that embued her with a sense of warmth and comfort. Bushes and trees nestled around it and the yard covered a vast area. The nearest neighbor could barely be seen through a thick grove of trees.

"This is Rand's home?" she asked as she joined Stephanie outside the vehicle.

"Yep. Nice, isn't it?" Admiration shone in Stephanie's gaze. "He built it himself."

Rand made this structure himself? Ariel paused to reflect again. His house fit the surrounding area, blending into the terrain as if a part of it. He was definitely a man of many talents with a care for nature that pleased her immensely.

"Come on." Stephanie squared her shoulders as if preparing for battle, then advanced to the front door. She knocked once, then pushed it open. "Hi, Rand. It's me."

"So much for a relaxing afternoon." Dean's voice drifted back to Ariel as she followed Stephanie inside.

The interior of the home was as warm and comfortable as the exterior, with light oak trim matching the oak furniture. The walls were bright and uncluttered with large windows letting in the sunlight. A woven rug in a variety of muted colors covered the hardwood floor in the entrance.

"Oh, is that your car outside?" Stephanie asked as she entered the main room. "I'm afraid I dinged it a little bit. It's so small, I didn't see it at first."

"What?" Dean pushed past Ariel in his rush to the door. When he returned, he glared at Stephanie. "Very funny, Steve."

"Don't call me Steve."

"Why not? I always have."

"And I've always hated it."

As Dean and Stephanie appeared to enjoy their bickering, Ariel ignored them and focused her attention on Rand, who watched her as if she were an approaching tornado. "Hi," she murmured. For some reason he looked even more desirable today, his hair hastily combed, a few strands falling across his forehead. He wore faded jeans and a brown shirt that accented his muscular frame.

"I didn't expect to see you today," he said to Stephanie, though his gaze lingered on Ariel.

"Of course you did. It's Broncos Sunday." Stephanie glanced at the magical box where men ran over a wide expanse of grass and her eyes lit up. "All right, it's on."

Ariel studied the box. She knew of this device—a television. It came as close to magic as anything she'd seen in the mortal world.

Stephanie settled into a chair and focused her attention

on the pictures moving on the screen. "Great, they're just coming on to the field. I haven't missed a thing."

Rand glanced at Dean and shrugged. His friend rolled his eyes, then sat in a chair beside Stephanie's. Uncertain what to do, Ariel took a seat on the long couch. Rand cast a quick look in her direction, then turned away. "Anyone need a drink?"

"Beer," Dean replied.

"Me, too," Stephanie added.

"Ariel?" He did glance at her now, his expression veiled.

Was he displeased by her presence? He liked her. Ariel was certain of that. Then why was he so wary? "That's fine," she said.

He left the room as Stephanie whooped. "Griese is quarterbacking today. Good deal."

Greasy? Ariel frowned. What did Stephanie mean? What was quarterbacking?

"And what's so great about him?" Dean leaned forward. "He's still a kid with a lot to learn."

"He's been doing great." Stephanie rounded on him, fire in her eyes. "You've just never gotten over Elway leaving."

"The man was the best." Dean spoke the words as if they were law.

Evidently, these were men. Ariel sighed. She'd heard mortals debate over athletes before.

"But he retired. Get over it." Stephanie took a silver can from Rand as he returned. "Thanks." She pulled back the tab and took a large swallow, then faced the television again. "Go, Griese."

Dean took his can. "I'll grant you his stats are better than last year's, but he has a ways to go yet."

"He's improving," Rand said as he handed Ariel her can, then sat at the far end of the couch from her. "The Broncos have a chance at the Super Bowl this year."

Ariel hesitated on asking about the Super Bowl. Obviously, it had some connection to the game on the television. She studied the screen but saw only a crowd of men wandering around a large field.

"You say that every year," Dean muttered.

Stephanie glared at Dean. "I bet they do. Griese can do it."

Dean frowned at her. "And what made you his head cheerleader?"

"He's cute."

Ariel peered at the television again. How could one even tell what the players looked like? They were extremely tiny and encased in bright clothing with a shell-like container that covered even their heads.

Dean rolled his eyes. "You don't judge a quarterback by his appearance, Steve."

"Why not?" Stephanie lifted her chin. "It holds as much weight for me as his season stats of two hundred sixty-seven out of three-ten."

When Dean raised his eyebrows in surprise, Stephanie gave him a smug look. "I never said I didn't know that stuff. It's just not as important."

"Time out, children. Game's starting." Rand threw a pillow at Stephanie, who caught it with one hand and flung it back.

Mortals. Ariel hadn't understood much of that exchange, except that these men on the television were involved in some sort of game. A violent game from all appearances. At least these gladiators appeared somewhat protected by their garments, but they still liked to hurt each other.

She winced as several large players fell on top of one man. "Why do they do that?"

Rand glanced at her in surprise. "They have to stop the man with the ball."

"Why?"

"To keep him from making a touchdown."

"What's that?"

Everyone in the room looked at her now. "Don't you know football?" Stephanie asked, her tone incredulous.

"No."

"Let me explain." Rand moved closer to her and spoke softly, explaining each of the players' positions and duties as the game progressed.

A ringing shattered their concentration and Rand grimaced as he reached over to pick up a telephone lying on a nearby table. "Hello? . . . Hi, Vicki."

His expression darkened while Stephanie shot him a grin. "I see. . . . Fine. . . . No, I'm watching the game. I'll come by tomorrow. . . . Yeah. . . . Yeah. . . . All right. Bye."

He replaced the telephone and settled back beside Ariel.

"What now?" Dean asked, his tone dry.

"Vicki's toilet is plugged. She wants me to fix it."

"And of course you told her you would."

Rand shrugged. "She's my sister."

Dean didn't reply, but shook his head with a dramatic sigh.

Stephanie giggled. "At least charge her this time, Rand."

"Yeah." He returned his attention to the television and pointed out the men to Ariel. "See how the defense is lined up. You can tell by their positions that they plan to rush the quarterback."

By the halftime break, Ariel understood the purpose of the game, but not the reason for the enthusiasm Rand, Dean, and Stephanie displayed while watching it. They acted as if they were a part of it.

"I'm going to order pizza," Stephanie said, bounding from her chair. "Supreme okay with everyone?"

"Works for me." Dean stood and stretched.

"What is that?" Supreme made Ariel picture a giant, though she had experienced pizza before while visiting Italy.

"Oh, yeah, I forgot. We'll need a vegetarian, too." Stephanie left the room and Ariel followed her into what had to be Rand's kitchen. Again, it reflected the soft wood tones of the house, the countertops and cupboards matching.

While Stephanie spoke into the telephone, Ariel ran her hand over the smooth counters. With every moment she spent in this dwelling, she liked it more . . . as well as the man who built it.

He'd warmed up to her finally. As he'd explained the game to her, Rand had moved closer until he'd sat right beside her, his scent triggering heat through her veins. He loved this game. Every word he spoke carried his enthusiasm.

Better yet, he'd forgotten once again to be afraid of her. Ariel frowned. Why did he fear her? He'd liked their kisses. His response had clearly indicated that. He would enjoy sharing his body with her, too.

Stephanie replaced the telephone into its cradle, then approached the large black refrigerator. "More beer?" she called out.

Both men replied from the other room. "I'll take one." "Me, too."

Stephanie opened the refrigerator and removed several more beers, handing two to Ariel. "Look at this man's fridge. I swear he lives on green Jell-O and salami." She held open the door for Ariel to look inside. "The trick is figuring out which is which."

Aside from several more cans of beer, some other liquids, and a clear package of meat, the sole dish inside contained a wiggly green substance. Jell-O? "What is that?"

"Good question." Stephanie pushed the door closed and turned back toward the main room. "Who knows? One of life's biggest mysteries." She grinned. "And it comes in twenty-four flavors."

The pizza arrived shortly after the game restarted and Ariel discovered she enjoyed the combination of bread, cheese, sauce, and vegetables. It tasted as delicious as it smelled.

As Rand continued to explain the game to her, she relaxed, her shoulder touching his, her pleasure rising in this odd event. To her surprise, she found herself joining in the cries of excitement when a Broncos player carried the football over the goal line. It was fun.

She grinned at Rand and he rewarded her with a smile that started a slow burn deep inside. He returned his attention to the game, but she continued to study him. He would father her child.

And he would do it tonight.

The Broncos won. Rand clicked off the set, filled with satisfaction. It had been a good game, especially sharing it with his sister and friend.

And Ariel.

He watched her carry empty cans into his kitchen, surprised by the sudden surge of warmth that spread through his veins. Though he'd been surprised to discover someone who didn't know anything about football, she'd learned quickly and asked intelligent questions. By the end, she'd been yelling as much as the rest of them.

If only he didn't have this urge to kiss her every time she came near.

As he cleaned up, he chuckled at Dean and Stephanie's bickering. If they ever stopped fighting, he'd be worried. Ever since Stephanie had insisted on tagging along with him to Dean's house at age five, she'd been a part of their lives.

During her teenage years she'd had a crush on Dean, but, at four years her senior, he'd been too old for her. Besides, he'd had more than enough girls throwing themselves at him at the time. At least Steph had gotten over that.

"I say they are going to the Super Bowl," Stephanie insisted.

"You're full of it, Steve. They're gonna choke."

She glared at Dean. "They only need to win eight more games to make the play-offs."

"Not gonna happen."

"Want to bet?" Stephanie planted herself in front of Dean, her expression indignant.

Rand shook his head and sighed, then leaned against the doorframe to watch them.

"Yeah, I'll take that bet." Dean extended his hand, a fierce light dancing in his dark eyes.

Stephanie placed her hand in Dean's. "If the Broncos go to the Super Bowl, you have to buy me a ticket for it."

His eyes widened. "Fine. And if they don't, you pay for skiing at Aspen."

"Deal."

They shook hands as they glared at each other. Rand frowned. Their grasp continued past the shake until finally Stephanie ripped her hand free and stalked toward the front door, pulling out some keys.

"I can't wait to see the Super Bowl," she called. "Bye, Rand."

"Ha." Dean followed her. "I'm looking forward to the slopes. S'long, Rand." As he pulled the door closed, Rand heard his friend's voice once more. "Hey, leave my car alone."

At last, silence.

Rand stood in the middle of the living room, breathing in the peace and quiet. He had far too few moments of this in his life. Between his job and his sisters, downtime was hard to come by.

He took the remnants of the pizza to the kitchen, then froze as he combined it onto one plate, the vegetarian slices triggering his memory.

Where the hell was Ariel?

He whirled around, searching the room. Last he'd seen her, she'd been heading for the kitchen. Had she gone out ahead to wait for Stephanie?

A trickle of alarm ran along his spine. Why couldn't he make himself believe that?

He raced through the downstairs but found no sign of

her. Peering outside, he noticed both Stephanie and Dean's cars were gone. And no Ariel.

A slight sound from upstairs caught his attention and his gut knotted. Ariel? In his bedroom?

Desire flooded his veins, arrowing toward his loins. The image of kissing her, touching her danced through his mind before he shook his head to clear it. That was the last thing he needed.

He climbed the staircase slowly. "Ariel?"

At the landing he paused to study the three bedrooms. All the doors were closed. His throat dry, he approached his room, then froze as the door swung open and Ariel stepped into view.

Naked.

Four

~

"What . . . what are you doing?" Rand asked. *Dumb, Thayer*. It was pretty obvious, wasn't it?

"I want you," Ariel murmured. Though her words were bold, she didn't approach him. Uncertainty filled her eyes.

How to handle this? His body definitely wanted to accept Ariel's invitation. In fact, the swelling at his groin had already issued the RSVP.

But he barely knew her. He didn't sleep with women for the hell of it.

"I . . . I don't think this is a good idea." He choked the words out through his tight throat, unable to look away.

She was exquisite—perfectly proportioned with skin like ivory. Her long black hair tumbled over her shoulders, covering enough of her breasts to tease him closer. Her breasts were high and firm, the areolas a dusky pink, the nipples hardened into tight nubs.

Rand clenched his fists, aching to touch her.

"But I think you want me, too." Ariel did step closer now, her gaze dropping to the bulge in his pants.

Well, hell, what man wouldn't respond to a naked

woman? Especially one who looked like her. He drew in a deep breath. "Not a good idea," he repeated. "Definitely not."

Her slim rib cage led to a narrow waist and gently sloping hips, drawing his gaze to the tight curls at the juncture of her thighs. His thriving libido insisted he bury himself between those thighs while the slim remnants of his sanity screamed at him to run. Fast.

She reached out to touch him and, afraid of losing what little control he still retained, he leaped into action. Edging past her, he rushed into his bedroom, searching for her clothing.

Dressed. He needed her dressed.

Now.

Where were her clothes? They had to be here. She sure as hell wasn't wearing them.

He tore through the room, nearly hyperventilating. Lord, wouldn't Dean laugh if he could see Rand now?

Unable to locate her jeans and sweater, he whirled around, then froze at finding Ariel directly behind him, her expression confused, her body a lush treat for the taking.

"Where are your clothes?" he demanded, his tone harsher than he'd intended.

"Gone." She held his gaze. "I don't need them now."

"Oh, yes you do." Rand rushed to his closet. At this point, it didn't matter what clothes she wore so long as she was covered, and even then he wasn't going to sleep well for a week with her image in his mind.

He tossed a shirt at her. "Put that on." She'd swim in his clothing, but he wasn't in a mood to be picky. Pants. What could he do for pants? Anything of his would fall off her.

Ariel hadn't even touched the shirt when he looked around. Instead, she looked at him, hurt in her eyes. "You don't want me?" she whispered.

With a groan, Rand snatched up the shirt. "It's not

that." He was beyond wanting and was edging into the painful must-have-now territory.

He took her arm and thrust it into his shirt. She didn't resist, but neither did she help him, as he pulled his shirt onto her. It hung to her knees and Rand hurried to fasten the buttons, freezing when he brushed the swell of her breast.

The soft skin beckoned him, the sensation diving deep within him like a drug. He wanted more.

He shuddered, at war with the passion surging within him. What was it about this woman? "What are you doing to me?" he murmured.

"Wanting you." She reached up to touch his face, caressing yet stimulating at the same time.

If possible, he grew even harder with need. "Don't send me away." She was hot sex personified. The longer he stood near her, the more his willpower faded. "Ariel." He groaned as she ran her hand over his chest. "I don't . . . I'm not . . ."

When she reached his rigid length, squeezing him, cupping him, he nearly exploded right there. This was insane . . . like some erotic dream.

A dream that was becoming all too real.

His senses whirled. He couldn't move as she unfastened his pants and pushed them over his hips. His briefs followed until he jutted free, rigid and swollen, needing, wanting . . . her.

Her eyes grew wide and a slow smile crossed her full lips. She ran her hands over him, wrenching a moan from his throat. He had to stop this, yet none of his limbs obeyed his mental command.

Ariel stepped back and in seconds removed his shirt, letting it drift to the floor. Facing him, she met his gaze, her expression hesitant, yet her longing clear. "Rand?"

To hell with it.

Past all reason, Rand pulled her into his arms and claimed the sweetness of her mouth. Pleasure, painful yet wonderful, rushed through him, escalating his mounting passion. Lord, what man in his right mind could resist this?

Ariel sighed, melting in Rand's hold, aching for more than his mouth on hers. His tongue dueled with hers—enticing, sensuous. He plundered, demanded, and she gave . . . willingly gave.

This was more than she'd expected. Any other mortal man would've had her on her back in moments.

But Rand was not like any other mortal man.

When he covered her breast with his palm, she moaned, delicious sensations rippling beneath her skin. Her desire flared, becoming more than a wanting—a craving. He caressed her, sliding his fingers over her skin as if touching rare silk.

Her breasts swelled, sensitive to his touch. He lingered over her tight nipple, brushing his thumb over it until her knees threatened to give way. She'd hoped for his gentleness but nothing in her imagination could equal this. Her body reacted as if experiencing this act for the first time, humming with total awareness of Rand.

She removed the remainder of his clothing with a thought, certain he wouldn't notice for his breathing was as ragged as hers. Releasing her breast, he crushed her against him, her body melding along his hard planes, her moist center aching for the solid length pressed along her belly.

He continued to kiss her, to delve deeper, to draw out desires she hadn't known she had until she could do nothing more than whimper in his hold and clutch at the muscles of his back. When he finally drew back, his brown eyes burned with longing.

"Are you certain?" he asked, his voice raspy.

Though his need was every bit as dangerous as hers, Ariel suspected he would leave her if she asked it of him. But she had no intentions of doing so.

"Very certain." She had never before wanted anyone—mortal or Fae—to this degree. Not once in the centuries she'd existed.

He scooped her into his arms and gently laid her on his bed, then proceeded to explore her body with his roughened hands, touching her everywhere until she writhed with desire. "I never want to stop touching you," he murmured, cupping her breasts. "It's addictive."

"It's wonderful," Ariel said between gasps. "But I want you in me."

"Soon. I have to . . ." He trailed off as he snared a small package from his dresser. After tearing it open, he covered his erection with the rubbery tube.

Ariel grimaced. She'd seen similar condoms in the past. However, if Rand thought that would stop her from getting what she wanted he was sadly mistaken.

"Rand—" She started to speak, but he bent forward to capture one taut peak in his mouth and Ariel arched as passion knifed through her. She'd never felt anything like this before, never dreamed this level of pleasure existed. No wonder other Fae shared their bodies with mortals.

She ran her hands over his chest, exploring the definition of his muscles, then gripped his shoulders as he nipped lightly at her nipple. "Rand." His name sounded strangled. She could hardly draw in a breath and her heart hammered in her chest with the ferocity of an angry dragon.

When he finally slid into her, she rose to meet him with a wildness that surprised her. He adjusted his rhythm to meet hers, answering her thrusts with equal need. It was wonderful. More so than the joy of new buttercups in the spring.

She barely retained coherency enough to make his condom disappear. She needed him unrestrained, his seed able to fill her.

The knot inside her drew tighter and she moved faster, harder. Nothing in her experience had prepared her for this ecstasy.

To her surprise, the knot unwound, sending a ripple throughout her body that brought a cry from her lips. She shuddered, clenching around Rand, as he finally erupted within her. Yet her body continued to pulse—an experience so new that she closed her eyes to revel in it.

Suddenly, abrupt sounds exploded around her—the clock beside the bed played music, a buzzing noise came from the bathroom, and from downstairs beeping and ringing competed for dominance. Atop her, Rand tensed.

"What the hell?" He swiped at the clock until it silenced, then rolled from the bed and yanked on his pants.

Ariel sat up to watch him leave and fought the urge to pull him close again. She had experienced some pleasure in the past, but nothing like this. Her body still tingled as if caught in a lightning storm, as if emitting bolts of its own.

Realization dawned as she glanced at the now silent clock. Had she done this? Had her reaction to Rand's lovemaking produced these noises?

It had succeeded in drawing him away, though much too soon for Ariel's liking. She wanted to share more with this man, but she had what she needed.

Resting her hand over her belly, she ensured that his seed took root within her. Already a child was forming. She would have her baby. Rand's baby.

She no longer had a reason to stay. Though a part of her longed to do just that.

The noises downstairs grew quiet as Rand dealt with them one by one and Ariel rose. It would be better if she left now before Rand asked for explanations he wouldn't believe. Yet she wanted to touch him again, to kiss him. He had been all she'd hoped, and so much more.

No. He was mortal. She was Fae. His life would be over in the blink of an eye while hers continued through time.

She heard him climbing the staircase. She could delay no longer.

"Good-bye," she whispered, then disappeared.

Rand took the steps two at a time, anxious to return to Ariel. The haywire appliances had been annoying, perhaps the result of a short. He'd worry about it later. Other things took priority right now—like being with Ariel.

Why he'd fought making love to her was beyond him. She had been unlike any woman in his experience. Every sensation, every touch had been heightened until he'd shared in the most amazing climax of his life.

And he wanted to do it again. Already he was ready, a feat Rand wouldn't have believed if he hadn't been the one living it. Guess it just took the right woman.

Abruptly, he noticed his condom was missing. Damn, had it come off inside her? He grinned. Guess he needed to find it for her.

He rushed along the hall, eager to touch Ariel again, to share their bodies once more.

Only she was gone.

He froze in the doorway and stared at the empty bed. "Ariel?" His bathroom door stood open and he hurried over to push it open the remainder of the way. No Ariel.

Where could she have gone?

He'd only taken a couple minutes to search the entire house. Empty. Had she fled while he silenced his crazy microwave? Why?

Because she had what she wanted from him. With a groan, Rand clenched his fists, then smashed his palm against the wall. How could he be so stupid? Did she think she was pregnant? Not likely. Though difficult to maintain coherent thought, he'd remembered to put a condom on, even if it was now missing.

"You, Rand Thayer, are a first-class fool." He'd never see her again. He felt sure of that.

"Dammit." Somehow he had to find her, talk to her.

And she wasn't going to be real happy when he finished.

Ariel reappeared across the world from where she'd left Rand. The gateway to the magical realm glimmered in the depths of the forest. It moved periodically to keep mortals from finding it, though several had still managed to do so. Of course, the last few locations had been in heavily populated areas of the mortal world.

Here, amid the quiet of nature, no mortal had ever stood.

Ariel paused before the shimmering oval. Home lay on the other side—a world far different from the mortal realm, and a place she loved. Visiting the humans on occasion could be fun, but she had no desire to stay in their world. However, once she returned, she would have to avoid Titania. The queen hated half-breeds.

That wouldn't be a problem. Ariel grimaced. She certainly wasn't allowed at court anymore and the magical realm was vast with areas the Fae avoided. She could raise her child there.

The life inside her was already taking shape, becoming a creature of its own. Her baby . . . and Rand's.

Regret stabbed through Ariel. She shouldn't have taken the time to know him as a man. Perhaps then she wouldn't feel this sadness, this longing to return to him.

"Enough." Her voice echoed between the trees and Ariel straightened her shoulders.

Time to return home.

She stepped into the gateway, expecting to reach the green fields outside the Fae forest. Instead, she bounced back as if pushed.

What . . . ? That had never happened before. Was someone entering from the other side?

She waited several moments. When no one appeared, she tried again to enter the magical realm. Again, an unseen force thrust her away.

"What's happening?" Ariel slid her arm into the gateway without difficulty. It was only when her body followed that she was propelled backward.

She dropped her hand to her belly. Was it the child growing inside her? Was the gate refusing it entry?

Pacing before the gate, Ariel tried to understand. Mortals and Fae could enter without problems. Why would this new life make a difference? Had her body changed just enough that the realm no longer recognized her as being Fae or mortal?

Her throat tightened. How could she return home?

The gateway allowed her arm to pass through. Perhaps it would once again accept Ariel after the baby was born.

But what would she do until that time?

Living among the mortals had been a game she'd played on occasion, but not something she wanted to experience for a great length of time. Yet what choice did she have?

Where could she go?

Back to Rand.

Her pulse leaped at that thought. It was his child within her. Surely he wouldn't turn her away. From his home or his bed.

If she stayed with him, she could share more wonderful lovemaking. She smiled. Yes, that would ease the misery of extended time in the mortal world.

She nodded, her decision made.

She would stay with Rand until the baby was born.

Then she would return home and take her child with her.

"There, it's fixed." Rand faced Vicki and held out his hand to reveal a small toy car. He didn't try to keep his irritation from his voice. "Try to keep your kids from dumping their cars into the toilet and you won't have this problem."

Vicki started, then frowned at him. "Get up on the wrong side of the bed?"

Rand didn't reply. He hadn't slept all night, his mind filled with visions of Ariel. One moment he'd wanted to make love to her again, the next he'd wanted to throttle her.

"Thanks for fixing it, Rand." Vicki gave him a smile. "I appreciate it."

"I'll send you my bill," he growled. Dean was right. He shouldn't let his family take advantage of him.

"Ah, okay." Vicki looked surprised, but didn't argue.

Good thing, too. This was his livelihood. If he kept giving away his work for free, where would that leave him?

"Next time have Peter fix it." He never did understand why all his sisters called him instead of their husbands.

"He's not good at this kind of stuff. You know that, Rand."

Rand gathered his tools and left with a curt farewell, squealing his tires when he pulled away. He hadn't gone far when he grimaced as guilt came calling. Vicki was family. He loved her and the kids. He had no right taking his bad mood out on her.

But he didn't know how to find the woman he did want to take it out on.

Glancing at his stick-on clock, he turned a corner sharply and headed for Stephanie's. She should be home from work by now. Maybe she'd have a clue as to where Rand could find Ariel LeFay.

When Steph answered the door, she looked as tired as Rand felt. Seeing him, she turned away, leaving the door open.

Rand followed her inside. "You look like hell."

"Thanks a lot," she snapped.

He shrugged. "I've always been honest with you." He went to her refrigerator and grabbed a soda. "Bad day?"

"Horrid." Stephanie flung herself onto her sofa. "I swear every single kid took hyper pills this morning, even Jeffrey, who's normally so quiet and shy I can't get anything out of him."

"That's just one of the perks of being a teacher." Rand settled into a nearby chair.

"Why do I do this to myself?"

"Because you love it." Steph had wanted to be a teacher as long as Rand could remember. Perhaps because she was the youngest and was constantly being schooled by her older siblings.

She looked at him, her expression weary. "Remind me why."

"I remember a speech about making a difference, helping the children." Rand had to smile. Stephanie had a passion for teaching, which was why she did so well at it.

"Yeah." She flopped her head back. "Must've been temporary insanity."

Rand didn't respond. He'd heard this enough times to know that by tomorrow she'd be full of ideas on how to handle her class.

After a moment, she turned her head to glare at him. "Why are you here? Other than to steal my soda?"

"Question." Rand hesitated. How to put this? "Do you know where I can find Ariel?"

"Ariel?" Stephanie paused, obviously in thought, then bolted upright. "Oh, Lord, I left her at your place yesterday, didn't I? Where did she go?"

"I have no idea." Would he have just asked about her if he knew?

His sister frowned. "Did you kick her out?"

"No." He could answer that honestly enough. After the greatest sex in his life, he hadn't been planning to do that. "She left."

Suddenly. Without a word. Without a trace.

"Weird. I didn't think she had anywhere to stay."

"Neither did I." Rand downed the rest of the soda.

"Is anything missing?"

"Of course not." Except for a condom. "I thought maybe she might have mentioned something while she was here."

"Not really." Stephanie thought a moment longer, then shook her head. "She didn't say much about herself, but I remember she said she wasn't from around here."

She had said she lived too far away for Rand to take her home. "But she had no money. How would she get home?"

Stephanie shrugged. "Check the bus station. Maybe she's hanging around there."

A possibility, though Rand couldn't see Ariel riding a bus. With her fragile, naïve beauty, she'd attract every scumbag along the way. The urge to protect her brought him to his feet, then he scowled.

After what she'd done to him, he still wanted to protect her? Where were his brains?

Hell, he already knew the answer to that one.

"I'll check it out," he said, turning for the door. "Take it easy."

Stephanie half-lifted her hand in farewell. "No problem. I'm not moving until morning."

After a short drive to the bus station, he searched the place, even asking the ticket clerk about her, but found no sign of Ariel. Rand paused by one wall to watch the arriving and departing passengers. What if she had been there? Maybe she'd asked someone to foot her bill. Would she sleep with him, too?

That thought brought an unpleasant taste to his mouth. He didn't want to believe that. She'd asked him for nothing and taken nothing—aside from his sperm.

And that had been the biggest theft of all.

His mood growing darker by the moment, Rand headed for home. He had to face it, his chances of finding this one woman were nil.

Why should he even bother?

It wasn't like he cared about her. He hardly knew her. Better that he chalk this up as an infamous one-night stand. Funny, he'd never thought he'd be on the receiving end of that.

He slammed his front door behind him, sending a shudder through his house that didn't really satisfy him. What he needed was to hit something . . . someone, and release this simmering rage.

Damn, he'd been a fool.

A slight movement in his living room caught his attention and he whirled around as someone stood up from one
of the chairs.

Ariel.

Five

Rand tightened his fists, uncertain which he wanted to do more, kiss her or strangle her. "Nice of you to come back," he muttered. "Did you forget something? A goodnight kiss, perhaps?"

She hesitated, and well she should. Did she think she could just show up in his house and take up where she'd left off? Rand scowled. "How the hell did you get in here?"

"I . . ." She licked her lips and his traitorous memory recalled their sweetness. "It's not important."

"It's important to me." He resisted the urge to cross over and seize her. Touching her would be bad. Very bad. "I locked the doors."

"Locks can't keep me out." She spread her hands in supplication, drawing his notice to the filmy gown she barely wore. The sheer yellow material covered, yet hinted at, her tantalizing charms.

If Rand stared, he imagined he could see glimpses of her rose-tipped breasts, or was he just imagining what he wanted to see?

The gown fell to the tops of her thighs, accenting her awesome legs. Abruptly, he noticed the dress was sleeveless and her feet were bare. "You were outside in that?" The words escaped him before he thought. The temperature was dropping as a cold front approached, normal for the Halloween season. She could freeze to death in that outfit.

"Yes. No." Ariel paced across the room, then turned back. "I need to stay here for a while."

"Excuse me?" *Not in this lifetime.*

"I can't go home. The gateway won't let me pass through."

Gateway? Rand frowned. "What the hell are you talking about? What does a computer have to do with this?"

Ariel sighed, then met his gaze. Something in those blue eyes called to him and Rand took a step forward before he realized it, then froze. She wasn't about to seduce him again.

"I'm . . . I'm carrying a baby you helped to create."

His stomach dropped to his knees. A child. The last thing he wanted was a child. He had enough nieces and nephews to supply the entire state. "Wait a minute. You can't know that already."

"Yes, I can." She drew closer, her gown clinging briefly to her curves then drifting away. "I ensured it would happen."

"If you mean your little performance last night, then you need to realize one time doesn't necessarily make a baby. Especially since I wore a condom."

"It does when you have magic."

Rand stared at her for a moment. Magic? Dear Lord, she was crazy. "Uh-huh," he said dryly.

Ariel paused, then sighed. "I know I'm not doing this right." She extended her hand. "Come, sit down and I'll explain."

"I'm not sitting down and you're not staying."

"I have nowhere else to go."

The sad note in her voice caught at him, but he steeled

his resolve. She wasn't going to play him for a fool again. "I've heard that one before."

She closed her eyes and drew in a deep breath. For several long moments she remained that way until Rand took another step toward her. What was she doing?

Her eyes flickered open as a look of determination filled her face. "You're not going to believe me."

"I don't believe much you're saying now." What was truth for this woman? Was this some kind of a game?

"I'm a faery," she said abruptly.

Rand's jaw dropped. Whatever he'd been expecting, that wasn't it. A faery? More like crazy. "Okay, whatever you say." He kept his voice calm.

"It's true."

"Just relax. It'll be all right." She definitely needed help.

A sad smile appeared. "No, you misunderstand. I'm a magical faery, one of the Fae."

A magical faery. Sure. Rand narrowed his gaze. She was definitely losing it. Maybe she'd escaped from a mental hospital. That made sense.

"I thought faeries had wings." He'd humor her for now until he could trap her long enough to make some phone calls.

"I can have them if that will satisfy you."

Her tone was earnest. She believed what she was saying. Yep, definitely a mental escapee. "Yeah, I'd like to see that." Now what would she do?

Ariel met his gaze briefly, then spread her arms. Wings suddenly appeared on her back.

Holy shit! Rand collapsed into a chair, unable to stop staring. "What kind of trick is that?" His voice came out hoarse.

"It's not a trick. It's magic." Ariel moved her shoulders and the wings moved as well. "But they're not necessary and are actually quite uncomfortable."

In a heartbeat, the wings vanished.

Almost like Ariel had vanished last night.

No, no, no. This had to be some kind of elaborate setup. He glanced around for a hidden camera. "What do you want?" he demanded.

"To stay here until my baby is born. The gateway to the magical realm refuses to admit me while I carry it inside me." Rand eyed her flat stomach. Her baby? Right. More than likely if she was pregnant it wasn't his, but he made a convenient stopping place. "So you want to stay here." He let his derision color his voice. "For how long? Nine months?" No doubt just long enough to rip him off completely.

"I'm not certain." Her answer surprised him. "I've never known another Fae to become pregnant, and time is different in my world."

"If no one's ever done this, then why did you?" He would trip her up here.

She looked away. "I lost my position as Queen of the Pillywiggins. I was lonely."

"Pillywiggins?"

"Flower faeries."

"And you're a queen?" What would she be telling him next? She was immortal?

"I was a queen, but Titania banished me from court." Ariel grimaced. "So Oberon sent me here to check on Robin and Kate's baby."

"Robin and Kate? Goodfellow?" How did they figure into this story? At least Rand recognized the names of the faery king and queen. His mythology class hadn't been a total waste after all. "And why would Oberon care about their baby?"

"Because it's his grandson."

Rand's head was starting to hurt. "And that's because . . . ?"

"Robin is his son."

"Robin is a faery?" Rand wanted to laugh. He couldn't believe he was asking this. Though he'd given Robin a hard time about his name, Robin Goodfellow was charming, energetic, and great with the kids at the school. The last thing Rand would call him was a faery.

"He was. He gave it up to marry Kate."

"You can give up being a faery?" This was a new one.

"Robin could, as he was only half-Fae. His mother was mortal." Ariel frowned. "Personally I think he was foolish to give up his magic and immortality for a mortal."

"This is insane." Rand couldn't sit any longer. He jumped to his feet and crossed to face her. "Are you going to tell me Robin and Kate's son is a faery?"

"No, he's completely mortal, but Oberon still wanted to know how he was doing." Ariel's matter-of-fact reply stunned Rand. Her expression softened. "And once I saw the baby I wanted one of my own. To care for. Then I wouldn't be so alone any longer."

Now his temples were throbbing. "So you picked the first man you saw to be the father?"

"I saw you with Brandon. I watched you with your sister and your friends. You are handsome, intelligent, kind, a good worker. I wanted these qualities for my child."

Great. Like a registered stud. "What? Did you have a checklist?"

"No." She reached out to touch his face. "From the first moment we kissed, I knew you were the one."

Her touch sent flickers of flame through his blood and he pulled back. "So you seduced me into making love to you."

"You were not unwilling."

Damn, but she was right about that. He'd wanted her. Remembering the passion they'd shared, he shifted uneasily, his body reacting to the memories. Hell, he still wanted her.

"And now you're pregnant," he said.

"Yes."

"But you can't get home because the . . . gateway won't let you in?" Jeez, this sounded like a plot for a sci-fi movie.

"Yes."

"And you want to stay with me for an indeterminate amount of time?"

"Yes."

She looked so innocent, answering each of his questions as if they were completely true. This was unbelievable.

He motioned her toward a chair. "Why don't you have a seat? I need to think about this." When she sat, he took a step toward the kitchen. "Want a drink?"

"I'm fine."

"Well, I want one." He rushed into the kitchen and snatched the phone off the receiver. Who to call? Nine-one-one? This had to qualify as some kind of emergency. No, better yet, he'd call Robin. Perhaps he could explain why Ariel thought *he* was a faery.

He'd no sooner dialed the first number when the receiver flew from his hand as if yanked. He whirled around to see Ariel standing behind him, her blue eyes flashing with anger.

"Everything I have told you is true," she said. "Why don't you believe me?"

"Look, I don't know how you did that wings thing, but it's some kind of trick." Though where she could've hidden those wings and mechanics in that skimpy outfit still baffled him. Rand extended his hands, hoping to placate her. "I think you need help, Ariel."

"You are such a stupid mortal." Ariel stomped her foot, then disappeared.

Rand blinked. Whoa. How the hell had she done that?

A sudden movement caught his attention and he nearly swallowed his tongue. It was Ariel—no more than four inches tall, hovering in front of him with tiny wings buzzing.

"Is this what you expect?" she demanded, her voice the same despite the change in her appearance.

It had to be some kind of hologram.

"You . . . I . . . this can't be." He rubbed his eyes. Maybe it was his lack of sleep playing tricks on him.

"It is. I am one of the Fae, Rand Thayer. Believe it." She zipped past him in spirals toward the ceiling while he gaped.

This couldn't be true. "I'm dreaming. I have to be dreaming."

The furnace suddenly clicked on, sending a rush of heat from the ceiling vent. Caught in the air flow, Ariel tumbled across the room until she bumped against the cold air vent near the floor.

In one swift movement, she disappeared inside.

Rand rushed over, dropping to his knees, alarm rising. "Ariel?"

Ariel cursed the blast of hot air that knocked her into this dark tunnel. She'd been doing so well, even using the stupid wings to convince him.

Very well. She would reappear beside him in the kitchen. That should do it.

She concentrated and felt the familiar tingling, but nothing happened. She was still in the duct. A sharp trickle of movement passed through her belly and she rested her hand on it. Was the baby limiting her magic?

Very well. She would fly out, then.

But the flight she'd obtained only moments before eluded her, as if her energy had been drained. A faint hint of fear crept into her mind. Was she losing her magic?

She caught a glimpse of Rand outside the grate, his face enormous as he peered inside. "Rand. Help me."

"Stay right there. I'll be back."

She grimaced. Where would she go? The cold darkness wrapped around her and she shivered. Her magic had never failed her before. Was this why no other Fae had become pregnant?

Rand reappeared and removed the grate, then stared into the darkness. "Ariel?"

"Down here. Lower your hand and I'll climb onto it." A demeaning way to get out of this situation, but necessary.

He slid his hand deep into the vent and waited. Ariel

paused. His palm was so large he could crush her . . . and he'd been very angry.

She had to trust him. She had no choice.

Stepping onto his palm, Ariel gripped one of his fingers for support. "All right."

He closed his fingers slightly around her and her breath caught in her chest, but as soon as he brought her out, he spread his hand flat. She leaped to the floor and stepped away from him. While in her true Fae size, he appeared a giant.

"I'm not dreaming, am I?" he asked, his expression dazed.

"I'm incapable of lying." He looked so confused, her heart ached. For a man who'd said he believed in magic, he certainly found it hard to accept. "I am Ariel, former Queen of the Pillywiggins."

Rand shook his head, staring at her in disbelief. Ariel wanted to shake him. Couldn't he believe his eyes?

Her neck ached from looking up at him. Better to become mortal size again.

If she could.

She summoned every last ounce of energy as she willed herself to grow. A flow of heat rushed through her veins, heading for her belly, but it worked. She now stood beside where he knelt on the floor.

But her knees trembled as if she'd run for hours. Her breath came in gasps. What was happening to her?

Rand scrambled to his feet and caught her shoulders as she swayed. "Are you all right?"

"I'm not sure." Her head whirled and she lifted a hand to it. "I . . . I don't feel well."

He lifted her as if she were still small and carried her to the couch. After placing her on it, he sat beside her. "Do you need something?"

"No. I . . . I don't know what's happening to me." She clutched his hand, trying to ward off her rising panic. "My magic isn't working."

"It looked real enough to me."

At his dry tone, she met his gaze. "Then you believe me?"

"Either that or I'm insane, too." He gave her a crooked smile. "And I don't think I'm crazy."

"Thank you." She squeezed his hand. "Then I can stay?"

He hesitated. "Here? With me?" He ran his fingers through his hair. "I'm not used to living with anyone. I value my privacy."

"You won't know I'm here."

He chuckled. "Why do I doubt that?"

"I'll do my best to stay out of your way. I don't want to interfere in your life, but I need a place to live until the baby is born."

Rand pulled away from her and a cold chill spread along her arm. "You've already interfered in my life." He stopped in the middle of the room. "If I believe you, you're carrying my child. How do I know you're really pregnant? How do I know it's even mine?"

"I can't lie," she said simply. How could she convince him she spoke the truth?

Doubt lingered in his eyes. "What do you intend to do after it's born?"

"Return home." Why should he need to ask?

"And the baby?"

"Will go with me." Once the child was a separate being, he or she should be able to pass through the gateway with her.

Rand's expression darkened. "Yet you're telling me this is my child, too. What about my rights?"

Ariel sat up despite her dizziness. "The child will be half-Fae." Like Robin had been. "It will have magic and immortality. It will not be of your world."

"So, I'm nothing but a mortal sperm donor?"

The bitterness in his voice made Ariel cringe. She didn't completely understand his words, but the meaning was clear. "Only a mortal can impregnate a Fae." Surely he realized she'd had no choice.

"Aren't I lucky?"

She remained silent. No answer would satisfy him now. She struggled to her feet to go to him, but found herself teetering. Instantly, Rand wrapped his arms around her, his gaze concerned.

"Don't faint on me."

"I've never fainted in my life." Though the lightness in her head made her wonder if there couldn't be a first time.

Rand scowled. "Come on. You can stay in a spare room."

As he led her toward the staircase, he glared at her. "But this discussion is not finished."

Perhaps not for him, but she wouldn't change her mind. Her child would not grow up among mortals. That was certain.

Rand left Ariel alone in the house while he went to work the next day and Ariel used the time to explore his home. For a man who declared he wanted no wife or children, he'd certainly designed the place with plenty of room. Aside from the three bedrooms upstairs, he had a large extra room beneath the ground that spanned the entire length of the house. Certainly that was sufficient for children to play. However, at the moment it contained nothing but a billiard table.

Her tour completed, Ariel paused in the living room. What now? Outside, the weather was foul—the wind bending the trees as it drove a mixture of sleet and rain before it. She certainly didn't want to go there. Yet she needed the solace of nature.

Rand's entire home contained one solitary plant—a philodendron—and it looked as if it hadn't been watered in a long time. Ariel used her magic to coax it back to life, relieved her power responded as it should. Perhaps she had been overly tired yesterday. Or too distressed about not being able to return home.

She straightened. Oberon. She needed to let Oberon

know she'd completed the mission he gave her. He had to be wondering about his new grandson.

A spell should do it. It could enter the magical realm while she could not. She would tell Oberon about his grandson and let him know she was staying here for a while.

Ariel stood in the middle of the room and created her report, then thrust it into a glowing ball of magic. Holding it above her head, she uttered the command to send it to Oberon.

"Travel over land and over sea. Deliver this message to Oberon from me."

The ball rose from her hand, then startled her by bouncing around the room, heedless of the damage it inflicted on Rand's furnishings. A lamp fell and broke. Items flew off a shelf.

"No. Stop." Ariel tried to capture the ball again, but it eluded her, moving faster than she could.

A picture on the wall shattered into pieces and Ariel winced. This was not good.

What was the spell to stop a message? At the moment, she couldn't recall. She'd never needed to stop one before.

The magical message continued to ricochet until it finally struck the front window, shattering the glass, and sailed through, evidently on its way to Oberon.

Ariel groaned. She should've released the message outside, but normally they passed through walls without damage. She surveyed Rand's living room. He was already angry with her. This wouldn't help at all.

Perhaps her magic could repair the broken items. If it worked correctly.

She managed to repair the two lamps before she heard the sound of a car door closing. Peeking through the front window, she swallowed the sudden lump in her throat.

Stephanie.

Ariel's first instinct was to shrink and hide, but she fought it. With her magic acting so erratically, she was afraid of being stuck somewhere in between the two sizes. No, better to face Rand's sister.

Stephanie evidently had a key to the front door, for a moment later she stepped inside and froze in the entry. "Good Lord, what happened here?" She stared at Ariel. "How did you get here? Did you do this?"

"I'm staying here." Ariel looked around her at the remaining destruction. "There was an accident."

"I'll say." Stephanie entered the room. "Rand is going to kill you." She crossed to a broken statue on the floor and picked it up. "He won this for being the most valuable player on the football team his junior year in high school. It means a lot to him."

Just what Ariel didn't need to hear. She took the statue pieces from Stephanie. "Perhaps it can be repaired." Turning her back to the other woman, she closed her eyes, willing her magic to do this one thing properly. Though the warmth inside her increased, she experienced no discomfort.

"I doubt it." Stephanie continued to walk through the room. "Looks totaled to me." She wrapped her arms around herself. "You need to get something over that broken window before we freeze to death."

Ariel slowly opened her eyes and released her pent-up breath. The statue was repaired. True, the head of the male figure was slightly crooked, but with luck Rand would never notice.

She turned to replace it on the shelf only to find Stephanie in her path. The woman focused on the statue. "What did you do?" She sounded stunned.

"I fixed it." Ariel met Stephanie's gaze and grimaced. She would have to explain herself to another mortal.

"But how?" Stephanie took the gold-colored item and examined it. "It was beyond even superglue."

Ariel hesitated before replying. "Magic."

"No, really." Stephanie looked up, then blinked. "You're serious."

Ariel nodded, dreading another lengthy explanation. To her surprise, Stephanie frowned.

"*Why* are you here?"

Ariel hadn't expected that question. "I'm staying with Rand for a while."

Stephanie shook her head. "No way. I know my brother and he'd sooner cut off his hand than ask a woman to live with him."

"Actually, I asked him."

Stephanie narrowed her gaze. "What's going on here?"

"I can answer that."

They both turned as Rand entered the room. He paused to search the room. "What the hell happened?"

"It was an accident." Ariel gave him a tentative smile, but he ignored her, his gaze focusing on his sister.

"She's not really living with you, is she?" Stephanie asked.

"I think you need to sit down, Steph," he replied.

"Why?"

"Trust me." Rand waited until Stephanie settled on the couch, then faced her. "I just got back from talking to Robin Goodfellow. I'm going to tell you three things, and you need to believe all of them no matter how incredible they sound."

"Is something wrong?"

Concern filled Stephanie's expression and Ariel drew in a deep breath. She already had an idea what Rand was about to say.

"One, Ariel is staying with me for the time being." Though Stephanie's eyes widened, Rand continued. "Two, she's pregnant with my child."

"What? That's im—"

He held up his hand and shot Ariel a wry glance before returning his attention to Stephanie. "And three . . . she's a faery."

Six

Stephanie looked at Rand as if he'd just lost all his marbles. To be honest, he wasn't sure he hadn't. "You're kidding, right?"

If only. " 'Fraid not." Rand glanced at Ariel standing nearby, apprehension on her face. "Ariel is a real, live, magical faery."

"But . . . but . . ." Stephanie looked from Rand to Ariel and back, her confusion obvious. "Faeries aren't real."

"Yes, we are." Ariel entered the conversation, her tone indignant. "Just because you don't usually see us doesn't mean we aren't here."

Steph rose to her feet. "I see you. I just don't believe it. You look like a normal woman to me."

Rand knew better. Ariel would never be normal. Though she'd worn jeans and a form-fitting sweater today, she still radiated a sexual energy that hummed through his veins. Rand couldn't stop himself from touching her arm. Instantly, the hum gave way to a boiling in his blood.

"She is magical, Steph. She's proven it." He smiled wryly. "You know me. Would I say this if it wasn't so?"

That made his sister stop and pause. "No, but—" She bit back her words. "Are you sure this isn't some kind of joke?" She glanced around the room, her eyes narrowing. "Is Dean in on this?"

Rand shook his head. He understood Stephanie's disbelief. Hell, he had trouble believing this himself. "No joke. It's the truth."

A sudden blast of icy wind circled the room and he whirled about to face the window. "What happened to my window?"

A guilty expression covered Ariel's face. Why wasn't he surprised?

"I was sending a message to Oberon and it went wild," she said. "I was fixing things when Stephanie arrived." She approached the window and stood before it, her hands raised. "Maybe Stephanie will believe this."

She stood silently for several moments. What was she doing? Rand stepped toward her then froze as a sound like a thunderclap reverberated through the room and the remaining glass in the window shattered.

Ariel stomped her foot. "By the Stones, that wasn't supposed to happen."

"This is how you fix things?" Rand asked. At this rate, his entire house would be destroyed within a week.

"It's my magic." She faced him, the blaze in her eyes reminding him of her passion. "Sometimes it works. Sometimes it doesn't."

"I guess this was a 'doesn't' time." Rand eyed the sleet falling on the glass shards on his carpeting. He might be able to get a new pane by tomorrow, but what would he do for now?

"I *will* fix it." Ariel faced the window again and Rand's stomach knotted.

"I'd rather you didn't." The entire front of the house could fall down next time.

She didn't respond and he hurried over to touch her shoulder, trying to keep her from walking on the shattered glass. An electrical shock raced into his body, bringing the hairs on his arms to attention. Was that from her?

Before he could insist she quit, the wind ceased and he glanced up to see the window filled with glass again, as if it had never been broken. Even the pieces on the carpet were gone.

His breath left his chest in a whoosh. Though he believed Ariel's story, these displays left him feeling sucker punched.

"That's better," she said.

A thump behind Rand made him turn and he spied Stephanie sitting on the floor, her eyes wide and dazed. "Merciful Mother," she whispered, the strongest exclamation in her vocabulary.

He bit back the laugh threatening to escape and extended his hand to help her up. He knew exactly what she felt. "Believe me now?" he asked.

She nodded as she climbed to her feet. "Either that or I'm as loony as both of you."

Rand grinned. "That's probably open to discussion."

As he'd hoped, she smiled and punched his shoulder. "You'd still win the prize," she retorted.

He sensed Ariel's presence as she came to stand beside him. Her unique scent reached him first, a signal to his hormones—as well as other body parts—to stand at attention.

"Are you all right, Stephanie?" Ariel asked.

"I think so." Her initial shock dissipating, Stephanie examined Ariel. "I'm sorry for not believing you." She suddenly gasped. "You really did fix my drain with magic."

Ariel nodded and Stephanie laughed. "Boy, can I use your talents at my place."

Rand sobered, a cold chill embracing him. He'd no doubt any number of people would be willing to make use of Ariel's magic. "Which is why we need to keep this to ourselves," he said.

His sister grimaced, but nodded. "Of course. Who

would I tell anyhow? Who would believe me?" She turned toward the kitchen. "I need a beer."

"Help yourself." Looking at the remaining damage in his living room, Rand called after her. "Bring me one, too."

Stephanie popped out of the kitchen, her expression incredulous. "Did you say baby?"

Ah, she'd finally remembered that part. "Yep."

"You mean you actually slept . . . ?" Stephanie faded off as she came to face him.

Rand shifted. Damn, she made him feel like a guilty child. He glanced at Ariel, who shot him a wry smile. "Hey, I'm grown up, you know."

"I know." She handed him a beer, then took a healthy swig of her own. "Mom will be overjoyed."

"Oh, Lord." Rand groaned. Stephanie was right. Their mother would look on this with the equal enthusiasm of the Second Coming. She'd been pushing Rand to get married and settle down for years. If she knew Ariel was carrying his child . . . "We have to keep Ariel and Mom from meeting."

"Why?" Ariel asked.

"I don't want anyone else in the family to know about this." They'd only jump to conclusions. "You can't let them know you're staying here."

A brief glimmer crossed Ariel's face. Hurt? Dismay? Rand grimaced. "They'll have us married so fast you won't know what happened," he added.

Ariel hesitated, then nodded. "I have no intentions of marrying."

"Good." Rand released a long breath. "That should take care of it."

Stephanie gave him a dry look. "Yeah, think again. Halloween is this weekend. You intend to leave Ariel here alone?"

Trapped. He was trapped and dying. The family Halloween gathering was tradition, up there with the major holidays. The only excuse for missing it was death. He had to go.

"I'll be fine by myself," Ariel said, bringing his attention back to her.

She might think so, but, after today, he wasn't so sure about that. The thought of Ariel and her magic loose on Halloween started a new tremor of panic. "I don't know."

"What could happen?"

He only had to look around his living room to answer that. To leave her here alone while innocent children were on the loose . . . Talk about having to chose between two evils.

"You better come with us," he said. "We can say she's a friend of yours, Steph."

His sister nodded. "That'll work."

Her willingness to help eased his tension. "I need to ask another favor, too." He'd toyed with this idea all day. With Stephanie's help, he could pull it off.

"Sure. What?"

Rand hesitated. How would Ariel take this? "I want Ariel to see Dean. She needs a check-up, but I don't want him to know the baby is mine."

"Never be able to live it down, would ya?" Stephanie's smirk was justified. He definitely didn't want to listen to Dean's comments on this situation.

"Can you take her? He already thinks she's your friend."

"Me? Take her to see Dean?" Steph hesitated. "I guess, but you owe me big time."

"You bet." In fact, Rand had the sinking feeling he'd owe his sister a lot before this was over.

"Why should I see Dean?" Ariel asked.

She'd been so quiet, Rand had taken that as compliance. He should've known better. "He's an obstetrician." At her puzzled expression, he continued. "A doctor for pregnant women. He can check you out, make sure everything is okay." And verify that she was indeed pregnant. Though after talking to Robin and having him verify much of Ariel's story, Rand was more inclined to believe just about anything.

"I'm not certain my pregnancy will be like that of a mortal's." Ariel wrapped her arms around herself. "And I am fine."

"I still want you to see him." Her hesitation shone clearly in her blue eyes. "Please. This means a lot to me." If she was carrying his child, he wanted the best care possible, and that was Dean.

"Very well." Ariel touched her tongue to her top lip and Rand suppressed an urge to cover those lips with his. "Do you intend to tell him about me as well?"

"Not unless I have to." With luck, this would be a normal pregnancy. Rand wanted to laugh. Hell, nothing had been normal since he'd met Ariel.

"So you'll get her an appointment, Steph? Soon?"

"I'll see what I can do." Steph sighed. "But I'm not responsible for anything Dean does."

No, Rand was the responsible one. For Ariel, for the child within her, for this whole entire mess.

For the fourth night in a row, he couldn't sleep. Hell, knowing Ariel slept in the room next door had him as hard as a hammer. No matter how he tried, he couldn't forget the passion they'd shared. He'd never experienced anything like it and suspected he probably never would again.

Rand grimaced. After all, how many men could say they'd made love to a faery, caressed the intoxicating skin, shared in a mind-boggling climax?

With a groan, he rolled onto his stomach but that only made him more aware of his erection. Damn Ariel. Before she'd forced her way into his life, he'd found it easy to forget the women he'd dated.

But she was different. Her every movement called to him. Her scent ensnared him. All he could think about was making love to her.

"No." He spoke the word aloud in an effort to convince himself.

He needed his sleep. He had work tomorrow—the spare room he was building for the Sandersons was only half done. Again, Ariel's fault. He often found himself thinking about her, lost in daydreams about her, and that sure as hell didn't get the job done.

Sliding from the bed, he started for the hall. He'd get a glass of milk. That usually worked.

But spotting Ariel in the doorway to her room drove all thoughts of milk from his mind. She was dressed, but barely, in a sheer gown that revealed as much as it covered. The neckline dipped low, revealing the shadow between her breasts, and her nipples were evident beneath the material. The gown fell to the tops of her thighs, hinting at the curls between her legs.

Lord save him.

"I heard you speak," she said, her gaze intense, nearly glowing in the night.

"I . . . um . . . I . . . um . . ." Damn, he couldn't even form a coherent sentence. He had thought he was rigid before, but now he ached with the force of his need.

He wanted her.

And why not? The damage was done. Shouldn't he receive some recompense?

Disengaging all thoughts but those of Ariel, he clasped her arms and covered her mouth with his. Sweet. Pure honey. A man could drink of these lips for days and still never have enough.

Within his grasp, Ariel softened, her hands going to his bare chest, her palms hot against his skin.

Rand slid his hands over her back and beneath the gown to her bare bottom, which he cupped to pull her snug against him. The heat of her femininity cradled him and he longed to bury himself deep within her. She drove him crazy.

Soft moans escaped her as he plundered her mouth,

slipped inside, and caressed her tongue. Her mouth was as lush as her body, welcoming him.

When he finally raised his head, he was gasping, his air depleted. But he paused only long enough to draw a deep breath and return to kiss her face, her throat, her shoulders. Her skin tasted sweet and was as intoxicating as a stiff shot of Jim Beam. He couldn't have enough.

Releasing her bottom, he slid her gown down her arms until it dropped to the floor, then he filled his hands with her firm breasts. They swelled even more within his palms and he brushed his thumbs over her taut peaks until she rotated her hips against him.

Desire beyond what he'd ever known flooded his senses. Now this was magic.

He slid down her body until he could draw one nipple into his mouth. Her quiet moans spurred him on to suckle first one breast, then the other, until her cries were no longer quiet.

"Rand, please." Was she begging him to continue or to stop? Dear Lord, could he stop? She wrapped her hands in his hair, but didn't pull him away.

With a final nip at her pebbled peak, he took his kisses lower. She'd be wanting more soon. She would want him as badly as he wanted her.

Finding his target, he pressed his advantage, tormenting her already swollen nub, using his lips and tongue to their full advantage. Even here she was sweet.

Ariel's cries became screams, her fingers clasping and unclasping in his hair. He held her in place, holding her rounded bottom in his palms despite her squirming. She was on fire. Hot. Burning. Fueling his answering blaze.

"Rand." As she cried his name, her body rippled with the force of her orgasm.

Now he could end his suffering.

But as he stood, he heard the familiar buzz of his alarm clock, the beeping of the microwave, the sound of the mixer running. The noise jerked him back to reality.

What the hell was he doing?

"It's you." He stepped away from Ariel, still too conscious of her breasts, the pleasure that awaited him. "You're setting these things off."

"I . . . I think so."

"Lord, I'm losing it." He turned to head downstairs, but she reached for him.

"Don't go, Rand." Her soft touch on his arm aggravated his pulsing erection and he closed his eyes to hold back the urge to take her there in the hallway.

"No. Wanting you isn't enough." This was nothing more than lust, sex for the sake of pleasure. He'd never believed in that and still didn't. Dwayne would call him a Boy Scout, but Rand needed more than that.

Ariel had tricked him once. He wouldn't be that gullible again.

No matter what some parts of him wanted.

Stephanie hesitated outside Dean's office. She hated the way her stomach knotted when she knew she was going to see him. He shouldn't bother her at all.

"What am I supposed to do here?"

Ariel's question broke into Stephanie's thoughts. "You'll get called in to see Dean and he'll give you an examination. Nothing horrible."

Indecision lingered in Ariel's eyes and Stephanie gave her a quick hug. "Trust me," she added.

No time to fiddle-fart around. Stephanie yanked open the door and led Ariel into the waiting room. Egad, she'd never seen so many pregnant women in her life.

Stephanie motioned toward an empty chair. "Have a seat. I'll let Lila know you're here."

As Ariel sat, Stephanie approached the receptionist who was busy on the phone. Lila smiled but didn't address her until she'd completed the call.

"Ariel LeFay, right?" Lila asked.

"Right. Thanks for fitting her in so quickly." Stephanie had known Lila since high school, which was the only way they could've received an appointment this soon.

"You were lucky we had a cancellation." Lila examined her appointment book. "Believe it or not, he's not too far behind. It'll be maybe twenty minutes."

"That's fine." Stephanie returned to Ariel's side. "You'll have to wait for your turn, but it shouldn't be too long."

"Is this necessary?" Ariel studied each of the other women, her hand resting against her abdomen. "I know I'm healthy."

"Hey, I believe you, but Rand needs the reassurance. You know how men are." Royal pains in the neck for the most part, though Rand was sometimes an exception.

"Not exactly." Ariel grinned. "When I think I begin to understand, I learn something new."

Stephanie laughed. "That's about right." She certainly hadn't figured out the opposite sex, which was fine with her. She was as avowedly single as Rand. She had too much to do to waste her time on men.

"Rand is upset with me, isn't he?"

Ariel's sudden question brought Stephanie's head around. "What?"

"He is polite, but reserved—not at all like when I first met him."

Okay, touchy subject. Stephanie hesitated. Where to start? "You need to know some things about my brother."

"I'd like to know many things."

"First, he has said for years that he never wanted children and now you're pregnant with his baby. I can't blame him for being upset. You tricked him." Stephanie paused. How would she feel if the tables were turned and she ended up pregnant? She was content with her classroom of six-year-olds and didn't plan for children in the near future. Still, she couldn't conceive of not loving a child— any child. She adored each and every one of her nieces and nephews and a child of her own would be . . .

A wave of wistfulness swept over her and she jerked herself free of it. Stupid idea.

"Second, he likes being on his own. He swore he'd

never get married—much to Mom's chagrin—and now you're in his life."

"I have no intention of tying myself to him." Ariel spoke so softly, Stephanie had to lean forward to hear her. "I intend to leave as soon as I can return home."

"And that's bummed him out most of all. Now that he's going to be a father, he's not one to shirk his responsibilities." Rand had explained it to her in much cruder terms than that, but the meaning was the same. "He won't let you take the baby away."

"The baby is mine." Ariel's tone hardened. "And I will keep it."

Stephanie stared at the other woman, trying to understand her reasoning. Didn't she understand a child needed two parents? "I like you, Ariel, but that's a pretty darned selfish attitude."

"I—"

"I don't want to discuss it." Stephanie turned away to pick up a magazine off the center table. "It's between you and Rand." But she certainly didn't see how it could be resolved.

Once Ariel went inside for her appointment, Stephanie replaced the periodical, unable to focus. Her insides felt jumpy as if she'd swallowed a handful of jumping beans, and the worm from a bottle of tequila as well.

It was the talk of babies. No, it was this office. Stephanie sighed. *Be honest.*

It was Dean.

She was over her infatuation with him, so this nervousness made no sense. The dumb sixteen-year-old who had adored Dean Carstensen was long gone, along with any illusions of love or romance.

Yet the memory of her sixteenth birthday continued to linger in her mind, no matter how many times she'd tried to banish it. Her cheeks warmed, recalling her boldness on that night.

Dean had come by as usual and paused outside the house as darkness fell to wish her a happy birthday.

"Sweet sixteen and never been kissed," he said with a grin that made her heart flip-flop every time she saw it.

"Why don't you change that?" she asked.

He blinked, his surprise evident. "Say what?"

"Kiss me." She couldn't believe she was being so forward, but she was tired of waiting for him to notice her, to see that she wasn't a child any longer. "Please?"

"Ah, sure. Okay." He bent down, his intention obviously to place a light kiss on her cheek, but Stephanie turned her head so their lips met.

And she melted.

The kiss was sweet and heavenly and hot, like chocolate pudding cake fresh out of the oven. She could've died on the spot and been happy.

Dean held her shoulders, his mouth moving over hers with a forcefulness that thrilled her, until the sound of a door slamming inside jarred them apart.

Stephanie stared at Dean, her heart pounding. He appeared dazed, uncertain.

Abruptly, he patted her cheek. "There you go. Have a happy birthday and stay out of trouble, kid."

Kid?

He should've slapped her. It wouldn't have hurt as much. Stephanie had whirled away to her room before he could see the tears welling. She'd never been so humiliated in her life.

Stephanie shook her head to clear the memory. Thank goodness Dean had left for the university soon after that and she hadn't had to face him again for months. By then she could feign indifference, though she had gotten even.

She grinned. Oh, yeah. She'd gotten even when she'd put superglue on his car door.

And she was over him now. Completely over him. It had been a foolish, childish thing.

"Stephanie?"

She looked toward the door where he stood, beckoning her. If only he didn't look so darned good—like some kind of modern sheik. Or didn't have a voice as smooth as Irish cream.

He ushered her into the room where Ariel waited. "I want to clarify something," he said, "since what Ariel is telling me can't possibly be true."

A flash of panic zipped along Stephanie's nerves. Ariel hadn't told him, had she?

"What . . . what did she say?" Stephanie shot Ariel a quelling look and the other woman shook her head.

"She insists she knows the day she became pregnant." Dean picked up a chart and studied it.

"Why wouldn't you believe that? I'm sure she knows when she . . ." In fact, Stephanie had no doubt Ariel could name the instant she first started a new life inside her.

Dean closed the chart and met Stephanie's gaze, his own dark and serious. "Yes, but she says it was only a week ago."

"So?"

"She has to be mistaken."

Stephanie crossed her arms. "And, of course, you would know better." Just like the male ego, and a doctor thrown in to boot.

"I think I know better about this." Dean glanced from one woman to the other. "I just examined her."

"Is something wrong?" Rand would freak out if Ariel had any problems.

"It depends on how you look at it." He paused, obviously for dramatic effect. "Ariel is not one week pregnant."

Stephanie's eyes widened. Had Ariel lied?

"She is, in fact, twelve weeks along."

Seven

"Twelve weeks?"

Ariel winced as Rand whirled around. She'd expected him to be upset at hearing this news, but she hadn't realized he'd be angry as well. "That's what Dean said."

"So you tricked me." Rand paced away from her, then back. "You were already pregnant when you seduced me, but I happened to be the first sucker who would take you in."

"That's not true." How dare he accuse her of such a thing? "I created this child when we had sex."

As Rand glanced at Stephanie, Ariel thanked the Stones his sister hadn't left. Perhaps her presence would keep Rand from killing Ariel, for he definitely looked like he wanted to at this moment. "That's a bunch of bull. You can't be three months pregnant after one week."

"Rand, on her behalf, she looked as startled as I felt when Dean told us," Stephanie said. She had remained by Ariel's side after giving Rand the doctor's verdict, which warmed a spot in Ariel's chest.

"Well, of course. She knew she was caught." Rand

curled his fists. "You'll have to leave here. Now." He stomped to the front door and yanked it open. "Faery or no faery, I'm not about to be a sucker again."

"I am carrying *your* child." Panic rose within Ariel, an unusual sensation and one she didn't like. How could she make him believe her? "I do not lie."

"Right, tell me another one."

Rand wiggled the door in emphasis, but Ariel didn't budge. She could probably find another place to stay but she liked it here. She liked Rand. If only she could explain something she barely understood herself.

"I wish I knew the answer," she said. "Perhaps I can contact Oberon and he can explain it."

Of course, that meant sending another message to the magical realm and it would be many human days before Oberon arrived. Ariel inhaled sharply. Time. Of course. That was it.

"It's the *time* difference," she added, not bothering to hide her excitement.

Rand narrowed his eyes. "Time difference?"

"I told you before that time moves differently in the magical realm. Somehow being here while I am pregnant has affected the baby's growth." That had to be it.

"If you're three months along now, then by the end of next week you'll be six months along?"

Would she? "I think so." She would have her baby even sooner than she'd expected.

Rand blinked and let the door fall closed. "You mean you'll have this kid in two more weeks?"

"I don't know that as a certainty, but I would assume so."

"Wow." Stephanie sank onto a chair. "You sure can't go back to Dean then. There's no way to explain that."

"My next appointment isn't for a month." Dean's receptionist had even written it on a card she'd given Ariel.

"And by your calculations the baby will be born before then." Rand joined them, running his fingers through his hair. "This is unreal," he muttered beneath his breath. "I thought I'd have more time."

"Time for what?" Why should the length of her pregnancy make a difference to him?

He started to answer, then shook his head, his expression grim. For a moment he had appeared disappointed. "Are you sure this child is mine?"

Ariel straightened, defiantly. Why didn't he believe her? "By the Stones of the Fae, I swear it." She could not give a more binding oath.

As Rand stared at her, her pulse quickened. Why did this matter so much? She'd never cared what humans thought of her before.

With a sigh, he looked away. "I guess time will tell."

Ariel rested her hand on her belly. The child was growing within her. She could feel it, sense it. "Indeed," she murmured.

"That's one problem solved." Stephanie leaned back and placed her feet on the coffee table. "Now, problem number two."

Ariel turned with Rand to face her. "Two?" they said together.

"Mom's Halloween bash is tomorrow." A slow grin crossed her face. "Got your costume yet?"

Rand tensed. "I am almost thirty years old. I don't have to wear a costume if I don't want to."

"Rand, Rand, Rand." Stephanie shook her head. "You know if you don't wear one, Mom will, at the very least, paint a mustache on your face." A gleam of mischief entered her eyes. "With permanent Magic Marker."

Ariel giggled, picturing the sight.

"You're evil, Steph." Rand dropped onto the couch with a groan.

"Only honest," she replied.

"What are you going as?" Rand asked.

"I found this great red cape at the flea market. I figure I'll add in a picnic basket and go as Red Riding Hood."

"I like that." Ariel perched on the arm of the couch,

then turned to Rand. "Do you have any ideas?"

"Not right now." He grimaced. "I'm not good at this."

At last, a chance to help him. "I can clothe you in whatever you wish to be."

He hesitated. "I don't know. Your magic has been pretty screwy lately. How do I know you won't turn me into a dog or something?"

"I wouldn't do that." Not on purpose anyway.

"We'll see. I might be able to throw something together." He turned his attention to his sister. "You'll pick up Ariel and take her with you, right?"

"Right."

"I can stay here," Ariel said. The thought of facing Rand's family made her chest ache.

"I'd rather you didn't." Rand gave her a half smile. "There will be too many kids on the loose, and with your magic . . ." He shook his head. "It'll be okay."

The way he said his last sentence sounded like he was trying to convince himself of that fact.

Stephanie jumped to her feet. "Well, I have tons left to do. I'll be by around four, Ariel. Be ready." She moved toward the front door. "Stay out of trouble, you two."

"A little late for that," Rand muttered.

The house seemed heavy with silence upon Stephanie's departure. Ariel dared to glance at Rand and found him studying her.

"I don't know how to handle you," he said, his tone low.

She knew plenty of ways for him to do that. "You can hold me, kiss me, share your body with me." Her voice sounded husky. He hadn't been touching her enough. She desperately wanted to make love with him again, yet he resisted all her overtures.

He jumped as if she'd slapped him. "That wasn't what I meant."

"What did you mean?" As usual, her thoughts were nothing like his.

"You're screwing up my life. I can't let you go out. I

can't keep you in alone. You're a disaster waiting to happen."

She rose to her feet, her chin held high. "I have managed to make my way in the mortal realm without difficulty for centuries."

"But you weren't pregnant then." Rand stood and came to face her. "You admitted yourself you're having problems with your magic. Can you exist without it?"

Horror raced through her. Exist without her magic? It was a part of her, as natural as breathing. She wouldn't be alive without it. "No, and I have no intention of doing so. Once the child is born, my magic will be as reliable as before."

"Well, for now, try to live without it."

She scowled and he rested his hands on her shoulders. "I know you were trying to help this morning but you blew up my coffeepot," he continued.

"How was I to know the combination of my magic and the electricity would do that?"

"You didn't know, and you don't know what using your magic will do next, so don't even try." He tightened his hold, adding emphasis.

"Magic is part of who I am, Rand. Don't ask me to give it up."

For several long moments he gazed at her, a light blossoming in his eyes. Ariel sensed his growing desire, for it fueled her own. When he pulled her closer, she swayed toward him, lifting her lips for his kiss.

Instead he dropped his hands and paced away. "You're dangerous," he said before he left the room.

"No," she whispered, aware of an ache blooming in her chest. "Just lonely."

The dance of the Fae on Midsummer Night's Eve included fewer people than the multitude filling the house of Rand and Stephanie's mother. As Ariel followed Stephanie inside, she froze, the chatter and music attacking her. Perhaps she should've insisted she stayed at Rand's house.

"It's crazy, I know." Stephanie grinned. "Come on. Let me introduce you to Mom." She wound her way through the crowded main room, greeting others as she led Ariel to an older woman busy wiping chocolate off the mouth of a little boy.

"Now stay out of the bowl, Mikey," the woman ordered. "It's for the trick-or-treaters. You'll get plenty of your own."

"But I wanna go now, Gramma," the boy whined.

"Soon." She patted him on the head. Straightening, she spotted Stephanie and a wide smile creased her face.

She had a kind face, etched with lines for laughter and tears, for wisdom and pain. Her hair was short and white in tight curls around her head. She had the same brown eyes as Rand—the kind that saw everything.

A knot tightened inside Ariel. It was too late to escape.

Stephanie hugged the woman. "Mom, I brought my friend, Ariel. Okay?"

"Of course. The more the merrier." She smiled at Ariel. "Call me Meg. Everyone does." Tilting her head, she examined them. "You call that a costume, daughter?"

"It's good enough." Stephanie swirled the cape around her, then diverted her mother's attention. "Isn't Ariel pretty? It's an old gown of mine that I hemmed in a hurry."

Ariel glanced down at the sparkly floor-length blue gown. Though loose, it fell over her figure remarkably well. The neckline above the empire waistline dipped so low, it revealed the beginning swells of her breasts. In addition, Stephanie had found a silver rhinestone tiara and thrust it on Ariel's head.

"And what are you? A princess?" Meg asked.

Ariel returned the warm smile. "A queen," she responded. Though she'd never dressed as this while Queen of the Pillywiggins. Everyone had known who she was.

A wave of melancholy washed over her. Where were

her pillywiggins now? Coaxing flowers into bloom on the other side of the world? Dancing in the grove to celebrate All Hallow's Eve?

"That's nice." Meg suddenly looked toward the front door. "Ah, there's Rand. Make yourself at home, Ariel."

Before Ariel could respond, Meg pushed her way toward the door and embraced Rand. He had dressed in a suit that heightened his handsomeness—a brown pinstripe coat with a carnation in the buttonhole, matching pants, and an old hat on his head.

"What is he?" Ariel asked Stephanie.

"A gangster." The lack of enthusiasm in her voice made Ariel glance at her friend. "Dean's with him. Doesn't he have anywhere else to go?"

Ariel hadn't even noticed Rand's friend, but Dean stood beside him and placed a kiss on Meg's cheek. He was dressed as a magician with a shiny black cape and top hat. He whipped a bouquet of flowers from his sleeve and presented them to Meg, who rewarded him with a hug.

As the men worked their way across the room, all the women stopped Dean and received a kiss, then they bestowed a hug on Rand.

"Oh, jeez, what does he think he is? God's gift to women?"

Surprised by Stephanie's sarcastic tone, Ariel frowned. "Rand?"

"No, Dean."

Before Ariel could question that remark, the men reached them. Dean paused by Stephanie and raised one eyebrow. "Red Riding Hood? Want to share your goodies with me?"

Stephanie rolled her eyes. "Not in this lifetime."

"Not even for a kiss?" He leaned forward, but she ducked away.

"I'm a little more particular about who I kiss."

"You didn't used to be." A harsh note entered Dean's voice that Ariel hadn't heard before. Usually with Stephanie, he sounded teasing.

"Well, I've grown up since then." Turning away from him, Stephanie hugged her brother. "I like the Fedora. Glad you could make it."

"Like I had a choice," he muttered. He glanced at Ariel, a question in his gaze. "How are you?"

"I'm all right." A little overwhelmed by the loud mass of people, but otherwise fine. Ariel ventured a smile. "It is chaotic though, isn't it?"

"Chaos? This?" Rand swung his arm to encompass the entire room. "For my family this is normal."

"Oh." What could she say? The Fae might have wild gatherings, but even those weren't as crowded or noisy as this party.

"How are you feeling?" Dean asked, his look more penetrating than Ariel wished.

She resisted dropping her hand to her belly. The dress fit loosely, thankfully hiding her belly. "I'm well."

"Come on, Ariel." Stephanie snagged her arm. "Let me introduce you to my sisters."

She pulled Ariel after her into the crowd, not pausing until she reached a woman of approximately thirty-five mortal years. "This is my sister, Kathleen. Kat, my friend Ariel."

Ariel extended her hand for the normal mortal greeting and found herself enveloped in a warm hug instead. "Glad you could join us." Kat grinned. "Don't mind the hullabaloo. We're not always like this."

"No," Stephanie added. "Sometimes it's worse."

Worse? Ariel stared at the women, who both laughed.

"My husband Nathan is over there." Kat pointed across the room to where a group of men stood by a table laden with food. "And three of the rugrats over there are mine." She indicated individual children out of the swarm that played by the kitchen. "Danny, Mary Lou, and Tracy."

Which ones had she meant? At least ten children clung together in a group, snatching food from the table as they talked. Their enthusiasm was obviously high for they didn't stand still for a moment.

"As you can tell, they're counting the minutes until we take them out trick-or-treating."

Ariel had heard the phrase before, but still wasn't sure of the meaning. However, she nodded, evidently the proper response, then whispered in Stephanie's ear as they continued on their way. "Trick-or-treating?"

"It's part of Halloween. Children dress up and go house to house asking for candy—a treat."

"And the trick?"

"It usually doesn't come to that, but children used to play tricks on people when they didn't get any candy."

"I see," Ariel said. Sort of like the pixies in her world. "Is that why we had to dress up as well?"

"That's due to my mom. She loves a family gathering—the more chaotic the better." Though Stephanie displayed a wry expression, her love for her mother was evident in her tone.

"It'll thin out in here soon," she added. "Most of the parents will accompany their kids when they go out."

Thank the Stones for that.

By the time the excited children departed with a group of adults, Ariel had met so many sisters she doubted she'd ever remember all the names. Megan, Susan, Vicki, Louise, Tammy, and there were the twins—Allison and Amanda.

"Is that everyone?" she asked.

Stephanie shook her head. "One sister left, but she's cool."

"Cool?"

"You'll like her."

As they approached one of the few remaining women, Ariel smiled. Yes, she would like this sister. She was holding a baby.

"Liz, this is my friend, Ariel. Ariel, my sister Lizzie." Stephanie immediately snagged the baby from Lizzie's arms and cooed. "How's Sweetums? How's my girl?"

"Her name is not Sweetums," Lizzie said dryly even as

she stood and extended her hand. "Glad you could join us, Ariel."

"It's better than Sequoia," Stephanie replied. "Who'd name their child after a tree?"

"I would," Ariel said. Why not? Trees were a vital part of nature.

"See, Steph." Lizzie grinned. "Your friend has taste."

"My friend just wants to cuddle the baby." Mischief danced in Stephanie's eyes as she glanced at Ariel. "Right?"

How had Stephanie known? Ariel had ached to hold this child from the first moment she'd spotted her. "I would like that."

Stephanie sighed and planted a kiss on the baby's face, then handed the child to Ariel. "She's older than Kate's baby," she added. "So she squirms a lot more."

The infant was heavier and held her head up on her own, her eyes wide and inquisitive. Ariel ran her hand over the tight blonde curls covering the tiny head. So soft, just like the skin.

The child's scent was similar to Kate's baby, yet unique, and Ariel inhaled it deep inside her. For a brief moment the void she'd felt ever since she had been thrown out of Titania's court was filled with a sense of contentment.

"You are a very pretty girl," she murmured.

Sequoia smiled, warming Ariel to the tips of her toes, and curled her fingers into Ariel's smooth gown.

As Ariel bent to kiss the baby's soft cheek, she sensed someone watching. Looking up, she spotted Rand on the opposite side of the room, his gaze locked on her, a peculiar expression on his face—wonder, longing, and an emotion she couldn't define.

She met his gaze and he responded with a tight smile, then looked away. Was he picturing how his child would look?

Holding this infant in her arms, she experienced a momentary pang of doubt. Rand would not be able to share in this if she took her baby to the magical realm. For the first time, she realized what that meant.

Yet she couldn't stay here among the mortals. She was magical and immortal. A visit in this world was one thing, but to spend years at a time was ridiculous. There was nothing here worth staying for.

However, Ariel found herself glancing again toward Rand, until a sudden tug on her necklace caught her attention. Sequoia had a firm grip on the chain and it took both Lizzie and Stephanie to free it from her hold.

Instantly the child burst into tears and Lizzie took her from Ariel. "Don't worry," Lizzie said. "She's just getting tired. It's bedtime soon." She searched the room, her gaze stopping at a man talking to Meg. "I think it's time Michael and I left."

Ariel's arms felt strangely empty, already missing the weight and warmth of the baby, but she smiled at Lizzie. "Thank you for letting me hold her. She's wonderful."

"I think so." Lizzie's face lit up. "Do you baby-sit at all?"

Baby-sit? Ariel frowned, but before she could speak, Stephanie touched her arm.

"Don't answer that," she said. "Or you'll be watching children for the rest of your life."

Ariel looked at Stephanie. Was that a bad thing?

"I'm shocked." Lizzie raised her eyebrows. "I thought you liked baby-sitting Sequoia, Steph."

"I do." Stephanie tickled the baby until she giggled. "I just don't want to do it every weekend. And neither does Ariel."

Ariel wouldn't mind some time with this child. It would be good experience. "I don't—"

Before Ariel could finish, Stephanie nudged her hard in the ribs and sent her a quelling look. "We gotta go, Liz," she said.

Stephanie tugged Ariel toward the food table. "Never say you're willing to baby-sit," she said, "or you'll end up doing it full-time." She grabbed a plate and began to

cover it with food. "Besides, you'll have your own to keep
you busy soon."

True, though her baby's arrival seemed a long way off.
Ariel smiled. Though two to three weeks was much better
than the mortals' nine months.

She followed Stephanie's example and took a plate, examining the variety of dishes. Some contained meat. A
shudder rippled down her spine and she concentrated on
the meatless offerings, pausing to nibble at some fruit
slices. A white fluffy dish looked interesting and she took
a tentative bite.

An odd twist wrenched her belly and she stiffened,
placing her hand over it. What was happening? The next
tremor was stronger as if she was being pushed from the
inside. Ariel dropped her plate to the table, a flutter of
panic tightening her chest.

Stephanie turned toward her, concern on her face. "Ariel?"

"Are you all right?" Rand reached Ariel's side in seconds.

"I . . . I don't know." She couldn't explain this sensation. It wasn't painful yet she'd never felt anything like
this before. "It's . . . I . . ."

She turned toward Rand, then stumbled, surprised to
find her knees weak. Rand caught her in his arms, his
strength comforting her. "I'm taking you home," he said,
his voice rough.

"Let me look at her, Rand." Dean joined them, untying
his black cape.

Ariel met Rand's gaze. Was that wise? What if Dean
found something different from the day before? "I . . . I
think maybe I ate something that disagreed with me," she
said quickly. After all, she wasn't used to these foods.

"But you—" Stephanie cut herself off as Rand glanced
at her.

"I'll make sure she gets home and lies down," he added.

Dean frowned. "Is there pain?"

Ariel shook her head. "It's . . . it's more like a rippling."

"It could just be the baby moving, though it's still pretty early for that." Dean placed his hands over her belly. "Does it hurt if I push here? Here?"

"No." Ariel didn't dare say more. The sensation was more like a pressure from within.

He straightened with a grimace. "All right then. Go home and rest. But if anything changes, and especially if you feel pain, call me at once."

"I will."

"Let's go." Rand wrapped his arm around her shoulders and led her toward the front door, pausing only when Meg came to meet them.

"Leaving already?" Her inquisitive gaze swept from Ariel to Rand. This woman was far too observant for Ariel's comfort.

"Ariel isn't feeling well. I'm taking her home." Rand leaned forward to kiss his mother's cheek.

"I'm sorry to hear that." Honest concern filled Meg's expression as she turned to Ariel. "I hope you feel better soon."

"Thank you." Ariel managed a wan smile.

"G'night, Mom." Rand headed for the door again, then stopped as he pulled it open. "You'll have to give Dean a ride home, Steph. Thanks."

He hurried Ariel outside, not waiting for a response.

"Stephanie won't like that," Ariel said.

"Why do you think I'm moving so fast?"

"You're afraid of your sister?" Ariel asked, nearly tripping over her own feet as he propelled her forward.

"Cautious," he replied. "She has evil ways of getting even."

He seated Ariel in his truck, treating her as tenderly as a fresh blossom, then rushed to take his place in the driver's seat.

They were on the road when Ariel experienced a different sensation—this time centered below her chest. She tried to draw in a deep breath, but failed.

As she tried again, a bubble rose in her throat emerging as a sharp hiccup.

Instantly, a buttercup fell from inside the roof to land on the seat.

Rand looked at it sharply. "What the—?"

Another hiccup emerged and with it another flower fell to the seat.

Rand pulled the truck to a stop by the side of the road. "What the hell is going on now?"

Eight

Why was nothing ever *normal* with Ariel? Rand watched as she hiccuped again and another flower dropped on the seat. He sighed. He should know better by now.

"Are you making these flowers appear?" Why did he even bother to ask? He already knew the answer.

"I think so. They're buttercups—my flower." Ariel's voice was so soft he could barely hear her. "I'm sorry."

He glanced at her. Were these hiccups the reason she'd looked so pale at his mother's? The tightness remained in his chest as she huddled on the seat, small and wan, her knees pulled to her chest.

"Can I do anything?" The words escaped him without thinking. How could he make her smile again?

"Just take me home." She met his gaze, her eyes luminous in the darkness. "Please."

He drove as quickly as he dared, fighting the urge to speed. Too many little goblins roamed the streets tonight for that.

By the time he reached his house, the seat held a pile of yellow flowers, their aroma subtle, reminding him of

Ariel. Ignoring them for now, he rushed to help Ariel from the truck. She leaned against him, appearing even more fragile, her eyes wide in her pale face.

Once inside, she sank onto the couch. "I'm afraid," she whispered. "What's happening to me?"

Ariel had been many things since he'd met her—enticing, infuriating, loving—but he'd never seen her vulnerable like this. Rand sat down and drew her into his arms. "You'll be fine." If he had anything to do with it.

Her head nestled against his shoulder as if designed to fit there and her soft curves were warm against his chest. Rand tightened his hold on her. Her well-being mattered.

And why not? She was carrying *his* child.

But more than that, *she* mattered. He kissed her hair lightly. Despite his defenses, she was managing to make him care about her.

"Do you think I'm dying?" she murmured, a tremble in her voice.

"Of course not." He wouldn't allow it. Besides, he'd been through too many pregnancies with his sisters. "You're just pregnant. When Vicki was carrying Jordan, she was sick and miserable for months."

"Months?"

Rand winced. Okay, maybe that hadn't been the best thing to say. "Well, for you that should only be a day or so. But Liz breezed through her pregnancy. She said she threw up once, got it over with, and was never sick again."

"She regurgitated her food?" Ariel shuddered. "A Fae would never do that." Abruptly she hiccuped and a flower dropped from nowhere to land on the couch.

"No, you hiccup instead." Rand smiled and nuzzled her hair, enjoying its silky softness.

"I'm trying not to." She relaxed against him and Rand held her close, surprised at how right she felt within his arms.

As if she belonged there.

Forever.

He tensed. *Lose that idea right now.*

"I'm sorry I made you leave your mother's early," Ariel said, thankfully jerking his thoughts from dangerous territory.

"I didn't mind, believe me." He'd been ready to leave ten minutes after he'd arrived.

She started to speak, then paused as another hiccup emerged and a flower dropped beside them. "You have a large family."

"You're telling me." He grimaced. Ten sisters. What had he ever done to deserve that?

"But they were so welcoming, so . . . so caring."

He caught her note of wistfulness. The last thing he needed was for Ariel to spend more time with his family. It had been dangerous enough allowing her at his mother's tonight. "They're pretty overwhelming."

He'd never known a time in his life when he hadn't been surrounded by women and children, though he wouldn't mind giving it a try. Until Ariel had disrupted his life, he'd been close to achieving that goal.

"I liked them. For mortals," she added quickly.

"Don't worry. You won't have to see them again." If his mother ever discovered Ariel was staying with him, he'd never know a moment's peace. And if Mom learned Ariel was pregnant . . .

Rand shuddered. He didn't want to go there.

"Do you dislike your sisters so much?"

He stiffened. What kind of question was that? "I love them," he said emphatically. "I just want to live my life without women or children cluttering it up."

When Ariel didn't respond, he fought back his rising niggle of guilt. "All I want is to be left alone, to have peace and quiet. Is that asking so much?"

"No." Ariel slid out of his embrace, her expression solemn, leaving his arms strangely empty. "I'm tired." She rose to her feet. "Good night."

He reached for her, unwilling to let her leave. "Are you all right? Do you need help?"

"I can manage." She crossed the room, then paused at

the staircase. "You needn't worry about me. I'll be out of your life as soon as possible."

Turning away, she hiccuped and a flower dropped into Rand's lap. He stared at its delicate beauty.

"Damn."

"You owe me a ride."

Stephanie jerked around as Dean spoke behind her. She'd hoped to avoid this. After a long Halloween night, all she wanted was to get home and sleep. As much as she loved her family, she always ended up exhausted after one of these gatherings.

"Get someone else to take you," she retorted. Dean's company was always dangerous.

"No, you're stuck." He grinned, so confident of himself she wanted to smack him. "I rode with Rand. Since he took off with your friend, you're the logical choice. It's not like my place is out of your way."

She grimaced. He had her there. She'd have to drive right past his neighborhood to get home from here. "Fine." She snagged her purse off the nearby kitchen counter. "Let's go, then."

Without waiting to see if Dean followed, Stephanie crossed the room to her mother. "Good night, Mom." They shared a quick hug.

"Be careful, Steph," Kathleen called. "It was getting nasty out there while we were trick-or-treating."

"Drive carefully," Mom added.

To Stephanie's amazement, Dean joined them, dropping a casual arm around her shoulders. "Don't worry, Meg. I'll make sure she drives smart."

Mom bestowed a smile on him that she reserved for gods and movie stars and Stephanie gritted her teeth. Why did he have to be so blasted charming?

Dean pressed a quick kiss to her mother's cheek, then steered Stephanie toward the door. She jerked away from him, detesting herself for enjoying the warmth of his hold.

They exchanged numerous good nights with the re-

maining family before they made it outside, with Dean
gathering more of them than Stephanie. She scowled as
she slid into the driver's seat of her small Miata. Evidently
her family liked Dean better than her.

"Keep that up and your face will freeze that way," Dean
said as he climbed into the passenger seat. He filled the
space, his head brushing the roof and the rest of him way
too close for comfort.

"Is that a medical observation?" She fired up the engine
and took off in a hurry, anxious to be rid of him. Why
did she have to be so aware of him? She certainly was
long over her childhood crush.

"Jealous?" He grinned, irritating her more. "It's not my
fault everyone in your family loves me." His smile faded
and he brushed one finger over her cheek. "Except you."

She managed not to jerk at his touch. "That's 'cause I
know what you really are."

"Oh?" For once his tone sounded sincere rather than
mocking. "And what am I?"

"You're a . . ." Stephanie struggled to find the right
word. What could sum up the way he'd treated her? "A
scoundrel."

"A scoundrel?" His grin reappeared. "I rather like that."

"You would." The car slid slightly as she rounded a
corner and Stephanie focused her attention on the road.
"Kathleen was right. It's a mess out here."

The earlier sleet had changed to snow, the heavy wet
flakes creating slick slush on the pavement. A perfect end
to her night.

"So, what's up with Rand?"

Stephanie jerked at Dean's surprising question. How
was she supposed to answer that? "What do you mean?"

"I mean the way he nearly had a cow when Ariel became ill. He took over like he had a right to."

"That's just Rand," Stephanie said quickly. "After all,
he's probably been through this as many times as you
have."

Dean was always too observant, except when it came

to her. He still thought of her as one of the guys and she'd ceased being that a long time ago.

"I thought Ariel was *your* friend." Dean glanced at her in the darkened car and she felt his gaze like a physical touch—warm and lingering.

"She is."

"Then why did Rand rush over so quickly? Is something going on there?"

"Of course not." Stephanie forced a laugh. Blast Rand for putting her in this position. "You know Rand's sworn off women."

"That's what I'd always thought." Dean paused. "Does he know she's pregnant?"

"Yes." Stephanie bristled. Of course, it *was* Rand's baby, but if he wanted Dean to know that, he could tell him.

She wrapped her fingers around the steering wheel. "You know, Rand's life is really none of your business."

Dean chuckled. "Good point, Steve."

That name never failed to make her blood boil. Didn't he realize she was a woman? "Don't—"

"Call me Steve." He finished the statement for her. "But how else can I get that gleam in your eye?"

His words startled her and Stephanie turned to look at him. "What?"

"Watch out!"

She pivoted back to see two children dash across the street. She hit her brakes only to have the car skid on the slush. As she wrestled the steering wheel to regain control, she realized Dean had thrown his arm in front of her in a protective gesture.

The vehicle slid to a stop against the curb and she threw it into park, her heart racing as much from Dean's touch as the close call. His arm and hand remained across her torso, a hair's breadth beneath her breasts.

"You okay?" he asked, his voice slightly rough.

"Yeah." It was the only word she could push through

her constricted throat. Though "okay" at the moment was a relative term.

"I'm sorry. I didn't mean to distract you."

Heck, just having Dean in her car distracted her. "Yes, you did. You like to cause trouble." And the fact that he hadn't removed his arm distracted her even further.

She met his gaze, illuminated by the nearby streetlight, surprised to find an odd gleam in his eyes. One very un-Dean-like.

"Poor Little Red Riding Hood, stuck with the wolf," he murmured.

He had to be referring to her costume. Did he see himself as the wolf? That fit.

She was afraid to move, to breathe, too aware of his palm over her ribs. "Well, you know what happened to the wolf," she said quietly.

"He gobbled up Little Red Riding Hood." Dean slowly drew his arm over her ribs, barely brushing the underside of her breasts.

Her pulse accelerated as her breasts tingled with desire, her nipples tightening. "Not this Red Riding Hood." She struggled for coherency. "This one would beat the crap out of the wolf."

He lingered, his fingers splayed across her ribs, then removed his arm. "Yes, I imagine she would."

But he didn't look away, his gaze holding Stephanie captive. Was this how the wolf worked? By hypnotizing his victim?

She blinked and forced herself to look away. Gripping the steering wheel, she started the car again. She needed to get Dean out of here.

To her relief he didn't speak again until she arrived at his sprawling house. "Good night," she murmured, her gaze straight ahead.

When Dean didn't reply, she glanced at him to find him watching her.

"Good night, Steve." He beamed his devastating smile,

the one that always brought butterflies to her stomach, and held up his hand before she could retort.

In one smooth movement he produced a large candy bar from his sleeve and handed it to her. "Thanks for the ride."

He closed the door quietly, then climbed the steps to his front door as Stephanie stared at the candy bar. Snickers. Her favorite.

But he was treating her like a child.

Again.

Ariel groaned as she stretched beneath the heavy comforter on the bed. Judging from the sunlight slipping between the blinds, she had slept late again.

Why was she sleeping so much? As a Fae, she could go days without rest. But now she relished every moment she didn't have to move.

As she stared at the ceiling, she vaguely recalled Rand peeking in several hours earlier to inquire about her condition before he ran some errands. Evidently he'd accepted her sleepy mumble as confirmation of good health.

She searched within for affirmation of that fact. The baby was still there—alive and healthy. Better yet, she no longer experienced the odd pressure in her belly. Maybe her discomfort *had* been something she'd eaten.

Ariel ran her hands down to her stomach, then froze. By the Stones. She had grown.

Jumping from the bed, she tugged off her gown and examined her figure in the large mirror over the dresser. Her abdomen jutted out, providing ample evidence of the new life growing inside her.

She was deformed, off-kilter, her swollen belly destroying the sleek lines she'd maintained for centuries. Even her breasts were larger, the peaks darker in color.

Ariel immediately sought to clothe herself to hide the hideous sight, but only succeeded in creating one leg of a pair of trousers.

"Stones." Wishing the malformed clothing away, she

searched the dresser drawers for something to wear. She found several sweaters and pulled out a blue-gray one. Tugging it on, she found the material soft against her skin. This was definitely Rand's sweater, for it fell to her knees and the sleeves hung down well past her wrists.

As she rolled up the sleeves, she examined her profile again. Better, but her belly still protruded.

No wonder it had ached and felt so tight yesterday. The baby had been growing. Rapidly.

Soon she would have a new life to cradle in her arms— a chance to feel needed again. A baby would cure her loneliness, her sense of not belonging anywhere.

With that thought foremost in her mind, she padded downstairs. Quiet filled the house.

Until the shrill ring of the telephone shattered the silence.

Ariel didn't answer the ring. No one would be calling her and Rand had made it clear he didn't want others to know she was there. But she did listen when his answering machine clicked on.

"Hi, Rand. It's Lizzie. What happened with Ariel last night? Is she all right? And what's going on with you two? Call me."

Ariel smiled. Lizzie was worried about her. Had any of the Fae ever cared for one another like that?

A warm feeling centered in her chest and ebbed out to fill her veins. Someone actually cared about her.

True, Oberon had expressed concern when she'd wandered the magical realm, alone and lost, after losing her position as queen. But this was different.

Yet she couldn't explain it. Was it because Lizzie was mortal? Or Rand's sister? Ariel had met her only briefly and found the woman as open and warm as most of Rand's family.

Why did he want to be away from them so much when they were a precious gift? One he obviously didn't appreciate. Which was another reason why she couldn't leave her child among the mortals.

This was her baby. Once it was born, Ariel would no longer be useless, unneeded. Its presence would fill this terrible emptiness inside her. It had to.

To pass the day, she tried watching the television, but she found the mortal antics tiresome. Did it truly matter if a person could guess the price of something?

She needed to do something . . . something for Rand. If he wanted to be away from his family, it was no wonder he found her irritating and useless. Perhaps if she could do something right for a change.

She had repaired his house after her incident with the message to Oberon. What more could she do?

Eat.

Ariel grinned. Her hunger pangs could not be ignored. She headed for the kitchen to peruse the refrigerator and to nibble at the fruit Rand had recently purchased. Aside from the recent addition of produce, it remained mostly empty. Even his bowl of green Jell-O contained nothing more than a spoonful.

She took out the bowl, an idea forming. She could replenish this for him. Rand enjoyed his gelatin and ate it almost every day. If she could create more, then perhaps he would like her.

Ariel hesitated. Why should that matter? He was mortal—nothing to her.

Yet he had been kind.

Setting the bowl on the counter, she poked at the wiggly substance and shuddered. How could anyone eat this?

No matter. Rand enjoyed it.

She had no idea how it was made, but surely her magic was capable of replicating this easily enough. With a wave of her hands, she set her magic to work.

Wonderful. The gelatin was growing to fill the bowl, just as she'd planned.

Wait.

Within a matter of moments, the goo overfilled the bowl and continued onto the countertop. Ariel frowned. That shouldn't be happening.

She sent a counterbrush of magic to halt the spell, but the green, gooey gook kept increasing. "Oh, no." She scooped up an armful and hurried to dump it in the sink, but by the time she returned the counter was covered again.

There had to be a way to stop this. Why did her magic constantly fail her when she needed it the most?

In a few minutes, her attempts to shove the mass into the sink were useless. The gelatin now covered the entire countertop, including the sink, and was dripping onto the floor, wiggling as it went. Was it alive?

Certainly not, but the way the substance bounced and oozed over the floor gave her a moment of doubt. She had to stop this before Rand's house filled with this stuff. He might like green Jell-O, but this was a bit much.

She tried a simple spell, but the growth only appeared to increase rather than stop. Her heart raced as she attempted to gather the gelatin into a single pile, but it refused to be contained.

What could she do? Already the floor was covered and increasing in depth. If she wasn't careful, she'd be buried in this stuff.

She found a garbage bag and tried to fill it, to no avail. The Jell-O refused to stop. It now reached her knees, undulating as if alive.

"Stop, please stop." She slipped to the floor, ending up waist deep in the green goo. This couldn't be allowed to continue. She was Fae. Her magic was more powerful than this mortal substance.

Ariel closed her eyes, trying to ignore the swelling gelatin, and drew deep on the magic within her. It had always been a part of her, as subtle as breathing. Commanding it had never been difficult.

She would not allow it to be now.

The magic swelled through her veins, hot and prickly, alive with power. Yes, this would do it.

With a cry of satisfaction she released her magic, then slowly opened her eyes. What would she see?

The gelatin had stopped. Thank the Stones.

"What the hell is going on here?"

She turned abruptly and spotted Rand in the kitchen doorway. Swiping at the gelatin coating her, she gave him a tentative smile. "Hi."

Rand shook his head. Flubber had taken over his kitchen. Dear Lord, couldn't he leave Ariel alone for even a few hours? "What happened this time?"

"I was trying to make you more Jell-O." Ariel stared up at him, her eyes almost pleading. If not for the green gook all over her, she'd be an appealing sight.

"Uh-huh." Rand didn't enter the room. Instead he surveyed the pile of gelatin almost two feet deep on the floor and several inches thick on the counter. He'd be hours cleaning it up. "Don't bother doing anything for me. I can't take any more of your help."

"I didn't mean for this to happen." Ariel's voice trembled. "My magic is out of control."

"Maybe you'd better stop using it." He sounded harsh, but, damn, she was going to ruin everything he owned with her haywire attempts to help him.

She stared at him as if he'd suggested cutting off her head. "But it's a part of me."

"Well, your parts don't appear to be working very well." He started toward her, then extended his hand when she attempted to stand. "Be careful. Don't fall." He scooped up a handful of gelatin and threw it toward the buried sink. "What a mess."

"I . . . I . . ."

At Ariel's sniffle, he frowned. Was she crying? He hated it when women cried. His sisters knew he was a sap when that happened. Blast his temper. "Are you crying?"

"No. Fae don't cry." She sounded indignant, but he caught sight of the large drops trickling down her cheeks.

"Oh, hell." He waded into the room and pulled her up into his arms, then froze, staring at her belly. "Dear Lord, you're pregnant."

"I told you I was. Even Dean said I was." Ariel swiped at her tears and he reached out to catch one on his finger.

To his shock, it crystallized into a solid white stone that shone in the light. Rand frowned and examined it more closely. An opal? "You're crying opals?" After everything else she'd done he shouldn't be surprised, but crying *opals*?

"Fae don't cry," she repeated with a quivering lower lip.

Rand had to smile. "I hate to disillusion you, Ariel, but you *are* crying." He touched that full lip, then caught more tears with his hand. As they left her skin, they instantly changed into gemstones. "And quite a cry at that."

"But I . . . I . . ." She touched her face, leaving green smears, then stared at the moisture on her hand. "It must be the baby."

Oh, yeah, he'd believe that. His sisters had been walking hormones during their pregnancies. If possible, he'd avoided them, never knowing when to expect tears or anger.

But he couldn't avoid Ariel. To be honest, he didn't want to avoid her. Even with her belly swollen, eyes red-rimmed, and green gelatin covering her clothing, she was enticing. "I'm sorry I yelled." He kept removing her tears until they finally stopped, creating a pile of gems atop the Jell-O. He surveyed the mess. She'd meant well. His chest tightened. She'd been doing this for him, to please him. And he'd yelled at her.

Rand ran his hand over her hair. "It was nice of you to want to make me Jell-O."

Her damp gaze met his. "Perhaps I should learn how to cook the mortal way."

"I'll teach you." It had to be safer than letting her magic loose again.

"Thank—" She stopped abruptly, her eyes widening as she dropped one hand to her tummy.

"What is it?" Renewed panic jumpstarted his pulse. She'd seemed fine when he'd left this morning or he wouldn't have gone. Was she still having problems?

A soft smile crossed her lips. Her face glowed. "The baby moved. Like a butterfly testing its wings."

She took his hand and placed it on her stomach. "Wait. Wait. There. Did you feel it?"

He had felt a tiny tremor beneath his palm. A sense of awe filled him. His baby was alive. *His* baby.

No matter what Ariel said, he intended to be a part of this child's life. He might not especially want women or children, but he wasn't about to neglect a life he'd helped to create. Even if it was Fae.

He brushed his fingers against Ariel's cheek. "It's awesome." From her expression, she experienced the same wonderment he did. "Thanks for letting me share." At this moment, he could almost fool himself into believing they were a real couple, a normal man and woman expecting their first child.

Ariel's eyes darkened, the color resembling the ocean depths, as she placed her hand over his. "Thank you, Rand," she whispered, her voice thick with emotion.

Emotion that burrowed into his chest and lingered, heavy and warm. Without thinking, Rand sought her lips.

She sighed and melted against him, her mouth hot and welcoming. This kiss was different, less hot but no less passionate. Only this passion was built on sharing, or caring.

Was this woman claiming more than his home, his child, his life?

"Now this has got to be a good story."

Rand jerked his head up at the familiar voice and pivoted toward the doorway. Oh, hell.

Dean.

Nine

~

"Haven't you heard of knocking?" Rand demanded. So much for keeping Ariel a secret, but he'd known all along he'd have to tell his best friend at some point. Who else could deliver the baby?

"I did. The door just swung open." Amusement danced in Dean's eyes. "Maybe you were too busy to hear me."

Rand glanced at Ariel to find trepidation in her expression. "Don't worry," he murmured, running his hand over her back. He'd trust Dean with his life. To be honest, it was the ribbing he'd hoped to avoid.

Dean grinned. "I thought there was something going on with you two."

"There's more to this than you think." Rand sighed. Where to start?

"You're telling me." Dean surveyed the room. "Starting with why you'd fill your kitchen with . . . What is this anyway?"

"Jell-O." This was as good an opening as any. "Ariel's magic went haywire."

Dean lifted his eyebrows. "Her what?"

"Magic. Ariel is a faery."

"Uh-huh. A faery." As Rand expected, Dean didn't believe him. "A pregnant faery. That's a new one."

"Trust me. She's a magical faery." Rand gave Ariel a reassuring smile, then stepped away from her, revealing her swollen belly.

Dean gaped. For a moment, he was speechless—an achievement in itself. "Now, wait a minute," he said finally. "I just saw you a couple days ago. You can't . . . this is impossible."

"Not really." Ariel spoke for the first time. "Time moves faster in your world than in mine." She stepped toward Dean, then stopped and frowned at the gelatin around her. "I can make this disappear."

"No, we'll clean it up the old-fashioned way," Rand said quickly. With his luck, she'd make his entire house disappear.

She placed one hand on his chest, her palm warm even through his sweatshirt. "It'll make Dean believe."

Dean waved his arm to indicate the room. "You're going to make this mess vanish?" He snapped his fingers. "Just like that?"

Ariel lifted her chin. "Yes."

He shook his head with a wry smile. "Do that and I'll believe you're a magical faery. Hell, you do that and I'll believe anything." Crossing his arms, he leaned against the doorjamb.

Rand knew that expression. Dean had worn it the time Rand had insisted he could get a date with the most sought-after girl in high school. True, Rand *had* been shot down, but Ariel was a different story. She *was* magical. He couldn't deny that.

And no amount of talking would convince Dean as well as a simple display of her magic. If it worked. Rand released a long breath, then nodded. "Go for it, Ariel." He crossed his fingers.

Ariel beamed at him, sending a flutter into Rand's gut. This woman affected him too easily in too many ways.

Ways that made him uncomfortable—physically and emotionally.

She closed her eyes but kept her hand on his chest. A sudden shock ripped through him and he gasped. Pulsing energy surrounded him, so strong he imagined he could see it. Was this what magical power felt like? It was exciting, tantalizing.

"Hot damn."

At Dean's exclamation, Rand glanced around. The gelatin was gone—every trace of it. And, amazingly, his kitchen was intact.

"Uh-oh."

Ariel's quiet murmur sent an arrow of panic through Rand. "What?" He looked over the room again. What had he missed?

"The bowl is gone, too."

She looked so worried he bit back his initial reaction to laugh. If that was the worst of it, he didn't mind.

"That's all right." He sent a triumphant grin toward his stunned friend. "I think you convinced Dean."

Dean entered the kitchen slowly, searching the walls and counters. "Okay, so where's the hidden camera?"

Rand did laugh now. He knew exactly how his friend felt. "There isn't one."

Pausing beside them, Dean ran his fingers through his hair. "I assume there's an equally unbelievable story that goes along with this."

"Very unbelievable." Rand clapped Dean's shoulder. "Let's grab a beer and go into the living room. You'll want to be sitting when I tell you this."

Two beers later, Dean sat in a chair, shaking his head. "Even the *National Enquirer* wouldn't believe this one."

"I hope not." Rand cast a glance at Ariel, who had said little during his explanation. If the world learned about her, she'd never know a moment's peace.

"And you're positive it's your baby?"

Rand hesitated only for a second. His mind now confirmed what his gut had told him all along. Ariel wouldn't lie to him. "I'm sure."

"Okay then." Dean stood to pace the room as if he could no longer sit still. "And you think it will arrive in a couple weeks?"

Ariel nodded. "You said I was at twelve weeks when I knew it had only been one." She indicated her belly. "And there's this."

"Hard to argue with that." Dean stopped and faced them. "All right, I'll deliver the kid." He fixed his gaze on Ariel. "It's not going to have wings or anything, is it?"

Ariel's laugh reminded Rand of tiny silver bells. "My child will look as normal as I do."

"Our child," Rand added. He didn't intend for her to forget that. She might have used him as a sperm donor, but he wasn't about to remain in that capacity. If he was going to be a father, he would be a presence in his child's life.

"The baby will be half-Fae," she said, her smile fading. "It will have magic."

"It'll also be half-human," he retorted.

Ariel rose to her feet, her eyes blazing. "You have no idea how to handle a magical being."

Rand stood to face her. "I've handled you, haven't I?"

To his horror, tears welled in her eyes. "Not very well." She brushed past him to hurry up the stairs and Rand sighed. How could he stop her from taking their baby away?

Dean rested his hand on Rand's shoulder. "Looks like it's going to be an interesting couple of weeks."

Rand focused on the single opal lying at the foot of the stairs. He only had two weeks to convince Ariel that he deserved to be a part of this child's life.

"You're telling me."

Ariel stared out the window of her bedroom, her arms wrapped around herself. Why did she feel such an emotional upheaval? She'd cried. The Fae never cried, yet she couldn't deny the moisture that dripped from her eyes.

Was this, too, a part of carrying a child? No wonder the other Fae didn't get pregnant. To lose control, to feel so unsure . . . These were not things she'd experienced before. They were too . . . mortal.

The bright sun had melted away the snow of the previous evening, leaving the dull browns of autumn. This was his world, not hers. How could Rand expect her to raise her child here? It was dirty, unsafe, disbelieving— no place for a member of the Fae.

For a being of magic.

Ariel rested her forehead against the cool pane. Yet her magic was fading more each day—another side effect of the baby growing inside her. If not for the energy she'd drawn from Rand, she wouldn't have been able to clean the kitchen.

Without her magic, she was helpless, incomplete . . . mortal. A chill ran down her spine. She couldn't endure that.

She sighed. How could she make Rand understand what her world was like? Surely if he knew he would cease his demands to keep the baby here.

He was a good man. Ariel sighed. More than that, he attracted her, affected her unlike any other man—Fae or mortal—she'd ever met.

His earlier kiss only made her want more. His touch sent tingles through her blood, reminiscent of standing in a lightning storm. The more she knew about him, the more she wanted to know.

Knowing Rand and his family shattered all the beliefs she'd held for centuries. She'd always thought mortals to be self-serving, uncaring; yet these people were different. They honestly cared, and that frightened her.

Their caring held power—as strong as any magic. She had to be on guard not to let it weave a spell over her.

She watched Dean drive away. Soon after, a soft rap sounded at her door and she turned from the window. "Yes?"

Rand opened the door, but didn't step inside. His gaze immediately sought hers as if he needed to know her feelings. Did he care? The baby meant something to him. She knew that, but was there anything more?

"It's a nice evening." He motioned toward the window. "Not nearly as cold as last night. Want to go for a walk?"

To be out among nature. Yes, she needed that. She stepped forward, then froze, glancing down at her only piece of clothing. "I have nothing to wear." With her magic so erratic, she didn't dare try to create something.

"That *is* a problem." Though the way Rand's gaze traveled over her indicated approval, adding a sudden skip to her pulse. "I'll have to get Stephanie to take you shopping."

He crossed to the closet. "Let me see what I can find." Rummaging through the few items inside, he pulled out a pair of soft blue trousers with a grin. "I thought Steph had left something here. Try these on. They'll probably be a little big, but not nearly as oversized as my stuff." He headed for the door. "Be right back."

The material was soft like a rabbit's fur as Ariel pulled on the trousers. True, the legs were too long, but the elastic waist barely encompassed her swollen middle. Rand returned with some socks and boots, which he placed on the floor.

"The boots are small on me, though I'm sure they're still way too large for you, but they're better than nothing."

"That's true." Ariel caught an undercurrent of excitement in Rand's voice as if this upcoming walk held some importance. Did it?

Finally dressed, she teetered across the room, her feet slipping within the oversized boots. Rand caught her arm with a grin. "Think you can manage?"

His smile reached deep inside her, touched a place she hadn't known existed. "I think so."

After stopping to grab jackets for each of them, Rand led her outside. While the night air held a chill, it was

much warmer than the previous evening when snow had
fallen. Ariel searched the heavens now to find thousands
of stars sharing their light.

How many other nights through the centuries had she
walked beneath the stars like this, sharing in their beauty,
bathing in their power? Thousands, yet never before had
she experienced the tight yearning she felt within her tonight.

"Warm enough?" Rand asked as they fell into step on
the sidewalk.

"Yes." She drew in a deep breath, the cool air invig-
orating, stimulating her senses. True, the world was still
barren and brown, but she found things she'd missed from
her bedroom window. A racoon scurried past, a morsel in
its mouth, then vanished into the shrubbery until she could
no longer see it in the darkness. A blue spruce vibrated
with energy, renewed by the recent snow. It evidently
liked when the white flakes fell.

Strange, Ariel had always believed nothing could like
the cold semideath of the mortal winter.

"You have an odd look on your face," Rand said, drawing her attention. "What is it?"

Ariel gave a wry smile. "I'm surprised to learn the
spruce likes winter."

He raised his eyebrows. "It talks to you?"

"Not in words." She laughed. "But I can sense its pleasure, its energy level."

"Are you attuned to all nature?"

"It's a part of my world." She struggled for words to
explain it. "In the magical realm, the plants, the animals,
the Fae, we are all created from the same material. It is
made up of the world and the magic, of a unity in living."
She shook her head. "I'm not saying it right."

"Actually, I'm envious. Is there no death in your
world?"

"No." All who lived there were immortal, transcending
the limits of time. Perhaps that was why winter never

visited the realm. "We have no illness, no reason for death."

"So everything is sweetness and light?"

Ariel hesitated. "I wouldn't say that." Not with Titania as queen. "But it is different from here. For the most part, we live in peace. We work, we play, we dance." Her voice dropped as a wave of homesickness washed over her. If she were home now, she too would be frolicking on the soft grass in the meadows among the vibrant flowers beneath a rainbow-streaked sky.

"Sounds interesting." Rand walked several steps in silence before he continued. "I wish I could see it."

"You can." Excitement flared to life in Ariel. If he could see her world, then he'd understand why she couldn't leave it. "Mortals are not welcomed, but neither are they forbidden. You just have to know where the portal is."

"I see." He paused to face her. "Could you take me there?"

"After the baby is born." With her magic so unreliable, she doubted she could transport herself to the far distant forest, let alone Rand with her. She searched his gaze. Would he consider it?

He nodded. "I'll think about it."

Her spirits fell at his noncommittal answer and she dropped her head. Was he afraid?

Rand caught her chin in his hand and lifted her face upright again. "And are all the Fae as lovely as you?"

Again Ariel found no clear answer. She had never considered herself particularly beautiful—just Fae. "They are all very much like me. We are . . . what we are."

"Then maybe I'd better not risk it." A smile teased the corner of his lips as he ran his fingers through her hair, pulling it away from her face. He rested his palm and thumb against her cheek. "I'm not sure my hormones could take it."

She frowned. His hormones?

"Do you realize how radiant you are right now?" Rand

brushed his thumb over her cheekbone and the tension within her twisted tighter. "I remember my mother mentioning how my sisters glowed during their pregnancies, but I never paid much attention. With you, it's true."

"I'm glowing?" She needed a mirror. "That only happens when I've been dancing with fireflies."

"Not literally. It's an inner radiance." His thumb moved to her lips, his touch sparking tiny shocks deep in her core. "I guess it has to do with creating a new life."

Ariel smiled. A new life. Yes, that was more important than her swollenness and emotional turmoil. It meant a new beginning for a lost, forgotten faery.

"Ariel, I . . . you . . ." Rand leaned forward and Ariel's heart leaped in her chest. Even the anticipation of his kisses thrilled her.

Before his lips could do more than place the barest of touches on hers, he drew back with a grimace. "You are a most unusual woman. Life with you around is never boring."

Something in his tone chilled her inner fire. He sounded as if that was a bad thing. "And you prefer boring?" she whispered.

"I'd like to try it sometime." He wrapped his arm around her shoulders and set them into motion again. "I really would."

Ariel walked, her mind whirling. If Rand wanted boring, she would do her best to find it for him.

All she needed to do was figure out how.

"Now that's pregnant." Stephanie arrived the next afternoon in her small metal vehicle just as Rand had told Ariel she would. She eyed Ariel's bulging belly with a wry grin. "No wonder you need new clothes." Rand had asked his sister to take Ariel shopping for proper clothing—a situation that Ariel had never faced. "Ready to go?"

"I'm not certain." Ariel grabbed a jacket from the closet, her pulse hammering. "Is this painful?"

"Only to bank accounts and men." Stephanie grinned and held open the front door. "Trust me. You'll love it."

Inside a huge building filled with people and stores, Stephanie led Ariel around one large shop to a section beneath a sign reading "Maternity." Pulling a bright blue sweater off a rack, Stephanie held it up. "This would look great on you, Ariel. What size are you?"

"Size?" Ariel looked at the numbers on the clothing. They meant nothing to her. "I don't know."

"Then we'll start low and go from there. Jeez, what does someone as tiny as you wear? A two?" Stephanie proceeded to gather an armful of items as she led Ariel through the section.

"Great. Let's have you try on these."

This shop even had small rooms for trying the clothing before purchase. What an innovative idea. A small swell of eagerness rose in Ariel as she dressed in the first outfit of blue jeans and long-sleeved shirt decorated with a smiling baby. The jeans had a special panel sewn into the front that nestled her protruding belly. Amazing. Perhaps mortals did have some good ideas.

She emerged to show the outfit to Stephanie, aware of a certain nervousness yet unsure of why. "Is this appropriate?" Ariel asked.

Stephanie grinned. "It's awesome. Even in maternity clothes, you look good. Unfair." She tapped her chin. "Looks like that's the right size, too. Try on the others while I pull some more."

Ariel tried on one outfit after another, adding steadily to a pile of those to keep. Stephanie had an amazing eye, pulling together combinations Ariel wouldn't have considered, yet she had to admit they made her look good.

After a considerable time, Ariel called a halt. "My stomach is growling and I have far too many clothes already. I should only be with child for two more weeks."

"Oops, I forgot that. Okay, let's pick out what you really like and pay for it, then we can grab something to eat. The food court here has a lot of variety."

"Pay? As in exchange coins?" Ariel had forgotten that foolish mortal custom. "I have nothing."

Stephanie dismissed her worries with a wave of her hand. "Not a problem. Rand is covering this."

Ariel hesitated. She was beholden to Rand for enough already. "I may be able to produce some currency—"

"No." Stephanie cut Ariel off and pulled her toward the counter. "We'll do this his way. It's good for him. Builds character. Trust me."

When the woman behind the counter announced the final total, Ariel felt the blood drain from her cheeks. She would have to reward Rand handsomely once her magic resumed its full strength—jewels, perhaps. Or gold? He appeared more the type of man to appreciate gold.

"Come on." As usual, Stephanie took the lead, weaving through the store's displays until she emerged in the open hallways of the massive structure. "Let's hit the restroom. You can change into one of your outfits there."

"I can wait until later." Though Ariel couldn't deny the tiny thrill that idea created.

Stephanie paused and examined Ariel with a twist of her lips. "No, you can't. Trust me. My sweats and Rand's sweater leave a lot to be desired. It'll only take a moment."

Ariel didn't need to be further convinced. She changed into a matching trouser-and-sweater combination that fit far better than her borrowed apparel, and gladly exchanged Rand's oversized boots for a pair of shoes Stephanie called Nikes. Ariel had never experienced footwear so comfortable before.

As she rejoined Stephanie, she resisted the urge to jump or run in reaction to the energy churning within her. "Better?"

Stephanie nodded. "Much better. You look human again." She took off at her normal hectic pace. "Let's go eat."

Human? Ariel's excitement faded as she glanced down at her clothing. Yes, she did look human. Mortal. More so than any time in her past visits when she'd assumed their mode of dress to blend in.

Wasn't that what she wanted? To blend in?

"Are you coming?" Stephanie called.

Ariel nodded and scrambled to catch up with the other woman, pushing her thoughts away. Of course, she wanted to appear as one of them. It was safer.

And boring.

She grinned suddenly. Perhaps this was what Rand wanted.

Noise echoed off the high glass ceiling at the food court amidst a jumble of smells, some repulsive, others enticing. Ariel stared at the variety of shops. They reminded her of a day at the market in London centuries ago—an event she hadn't particularly enjoyed.

"Is this edible?" she asked, seeing nothing but animal proteins offered. Her stomach grew even more queasy.

"Oh—oh, yeah." Stephanie grimaced. "Sorry, I keep forgetting you're a vegetarian." She headed for a small shop, cleaner than many of the others. "Let's go here. They have salads as well."

After purchasing their food, they found a small table on the open floor and slid into the seats. Ariel shifted, uneasy. The other tables were within reaching distance, the people far too close.

She met the gaze of a young man at the next table and he gave her a brilliant smile. For once she couldn't determine the meaning behind the smile. It created no sensation for her, yet she couldn't dismiss it as the type of leer she had experienced from others.

"That man smiled at me," she told Stephanie.

Stephanie turned and returned the man's grin, a twinkle in her eye. "Now, he's worth looking at," she murmured. "He's just flirting."

"I don't like it." She couldn't explain her sudden uneasiness.

"Don't worry. I won't tell Rand." Stephanie bit into her sandwich.

"That isn't my concern." Or was it? Would Rand be offended if Ariel smiled at another man? To be truthful, since meeting Rand, she'd barely noticed any other man.

She picked at her salad. Was that why she constantly wanted to be with Rand? To please him? She sighed. Yet everything she did displeased him.

"Problem?"

Ariel met Stephanie's gaze. Rand's sister would surely know what her brother wanted. "Why does Rand want his life to be boring?"

"Boring?" Stephanie blinked. "What do you mean?"

"What would he consider a boring life?" If Ariel could emulate it, she might be able to grant Rand's wish.

"Where do you get these questions?" Stephanie asked, but she didn't wait for Ariel to reply before continuing. "Well, for me, boring would be spending the entire day cleaning, cooking, and doing laundry, though I imagine others would consider it heaven."

"I'm afraid I don't know how to cook." Ariel had never needed that talent, but with her magic so erratic, she didn't dare try it for such basic necessities.

"Why do you . . . ?" Stephanie grinned. "You want to be boring for Rand? Believe me, he only thinks he wants a dull life."

"He has said it's his most fervent desire."

"Yeah, until he actually gets it." Stephanie cocked her head. "So you want to be the perfect homemaker for Rand, eh?" Mischief danced in her eyes. "I think we can handle that. Let's finish our food and hit the bookstore."

"Thank you. You're very kind." Ariel barely tasted her salad, her thoughts whirling around how her transformation would affect Rand.

"Think nothing of it." Stephanie reached across the tiny table to touch Ariel's hand with genuine affection. "You're like another sister already."

Sister? To Ariel's surprise, tears filled her eyes. Why did she have no control over this weeping? Yet Stephanie's innocent gesture meant more than she could imagine. The Fae did not share so openly or so completely.

Only now Ariel discovered she liked these new emotions surging through her. "I never had a sister," she whispered.

"I didn't mean to make you cry." Stephanie smiled dryly. "I just like you. Learn to accept it." She jerked back abruptly, then leaned forward to touch where a teardrop had fallen to the table and transformed into an opal. "What the heck is this?"

"An opal, I believe." More spattered onto the table before Ariel could swipe away her tears.

"Merciful Mother, don't do that here." Stephanie made a frantic attempt to sweep the gleaming gems into her hand. "Let's go before somebody notices."

Stephanie's obvious alarm sent shivers through Ariel. She rose to her feet, scanning the nearby tables. The young man closest to them was engrossed in his magazine. Close by, a young couple fussed over their young son. A man and woman on the other side had eyes only for each other. No one had noticed.

She hoped.

Ten

~

Ariel waved good-bye to Rand as he left for work, then hurried to her bedroom to retrieve the two books she'd purchased with Stephanie the day before—*The Betty Crocker Cookbook* and *At Home with Martha Stewart*. With these and the list Stephanie had given her, she would give Rand the boring life he desired.

She paused at the bottom of the staircase, suddenly struck by a thought. Why did she care about making Rand happy? He was only a mortal.

No, he was more than that. Admittedly, she found him attractive, more so each day she spent with him. She still wanted him, longed for his touch, ached for his kiss. Was that what she was hoping to obtain by doing this?

Ariel entered the kitchen and set the books on the counter. To be honest, yes, she wanted his loving, but he'd also been kind, despite her intrusion into her life. He'd shown her the warmth she'd never known existed.

More importantly, he'd given her the life growing inside her. The least she could do was repay him by making his life boring.

Besides, how difficult could it be to perform these simple mortal chores? After all, she was Fae.

The cleaning came first and she used Stephanie's list of instructions. Ariel examined every can under the kitchen sink until she found the ones she needed, then proceeded to dust and polish with a frenzy until even the battered coffee table shone.

Using the vacuum cleaner required a little more thought, but she managed to turn it on and run it over the carpeting of the main rooms. *This is easy.*

A sudden jerk at the cleaner caught Ariel's attention and she grimaced as she tugged the machine away from the curtain cord it was trying to eat. "Let go."

The vacuum's pull surprised her by its strength and she yanked it back with a hard jerk. The cord flew out. *Better.*

She continued cleaning until she realized the vacuum was no longer removing the particles from the carpeting. *What now?*

Turning off the machine, she searched for an obvious answer, but found nothing. Very well. She was nearly done vacuuming as it was.

She stood in the middle of the living room, her hands on her hips. It was as clean as *humanly* possible. Should she use her magic to finish the particles the vacuum had missed?

An intense sense of loss swept over her. No, she didn't dare. Her power no longer obeyed her.

Ariel rested one hand over her swelling belly. Soon. Soon, the child would be with her and her magic would return. For now, she could play at this mortal life.

After a quick lunch, she prepared a vegetarian lasagna, carefully following each step outlined in the cookbook. Rand would be pleased with this. Even unbaked, her dish looked magnificent.

She turned on the oven and slid the baking dish inside. One hour until she had a masterpiece.

Ariel danced her way to the laundry room beside the kitchen and sorted the clothes as Stephanie had directed.

How mundane. *She* was bored. Rand should appreciate this.

After loading the clothing into the washing machine, she poured the soap into the measuring cup but lacked enough to meet the line at the top. No problem. The soap by the kitchen sink looked the same. She used that to make up the difference, then set the machine into action.

Done.

Now what? The clothes were washing, the meal was baking, and the house was clean.

And she was tired. Another side effect of her pregnancy, no doubt. She'd never experienced such a lack of energy before.

Ariel collapsed onto the couch and turned on the television. There had to be something more than the silly shows she'd glimpsed before.

Clicking through the channels, she stopped upon encountering a man and woman discussing the woman's pregnancy. Now this was interesting. It appeared this man wanted nothing to do with this child, which the woman insisted was his.

So different from Rand. Despite his reluctance to have children, he insisted on being a part of Ariel's baby's life.

Which was impossible.

His lifespan was too limited, his knowledge of magic even more so. How could he hope to handle a magical being such as her child?

Yet Ariel couldn't shake a nagging sensation in her mind as she watched the drama unfold on the television. These characters were real with real problems, their emotions palpable. As the show ended, she frowned.

Where was the rest? It couldn't stop there. She had to know about Elizabeth's baby and Michael's plans and the romance building between Tyler and Mandy.

Instead, another drama, similar in tone to the first, appeared with new characters and new problems. She'd never realized the vast extent of mortal lives before.

Within moments, she found herself engrossed in this latest adventure and the one that followed it.

Only the intense smell of something burning jerked her out of the tragic plight of Sal and Ronda, torn apart by Sal's ex-girlfriend. Ariel jumped to her feet. *The lasagna.*

She raced into the kitchen only to slip in the soapsuds covering the floor. *The laundry.*

Sliding into the laundry room, she found the washing machine silent and still, a river of soapsuds trickling down the side. What went wrong? This wasn't supposed to happen.

She scooped up an armful of suds to deposit in the sink, then whirled around as smoke drifted out of the oven. *Oh, no.*

A cloud of smoke greeted her as she opened the oven door. She grabbed at the dish, then snatched her hand back at the stinging sensation. *Hot.*

The dish shattered on the floor, depositing blackened pasta among the suds.

It wasn't supposed to be like this.

Ariel realized she was crying when the first opal fell to the floor to gleam up at her from amid the mess. With a sob, she ran from the room to the living room and threw herself on the couch.

As her tears continued to fall, hiccups began, creating a garden of buttercups around the couch.

She was a failure—not only as Queen of the Pillywiggins, but she couldn't even be a good mortal.

She couldn't be a good *anything*.

Rand smelled the smoke as soon as he stepped out of his truck and he ran for the front door. Lord, what now? Had she set his house on fire?

Black smoke poured through the door as he opened it and his heart filled his throat. "Ariel." She had to be all right.

A cursory glance in the kitchen revealed the open oven and a sodden mess on the floor, but no Ariel. And thankfully no fire. The burned remains provided the answer to the smoke.

"Ariel?"

She spoke even as he spotted her on the couch. "I'm here."

She sat up, surrounded by a pile of shimmering opals and fresh buttercups, her eyes red and swollen. The tightness in Rand's chest eased. She was okay.

As she sniffled, he went to her side, pushing flowers away to create a space. Or maybe not okay.

"What happened?" he asked, wrapping his arms around her to pull her close. The feel of her, the smell of her enticed him, triggering a flow of heat through his veins.

"I . . . I . . ." She hiccuped and another flower landed on the couch. "I wanted to make life boring for you."

Rand raised his eyebrows. This was boring?

"But I can't even do simple mortal things."

The pain behind her wail tugged at his heart. This obviously meant a lot to her. "You're just inexperienced," he murmured, tightening his embrace. The mess suddenly made sense. She'd been trying to become Suzy Homemaker.

For him.

A fist of emotion pounded his chest and he drew in a sharp breath. He knew how she felt about mortals. To undertake this effort showed an unselfishness he hadn't expected.

"And it was going so well." She drew away and looked up at him, her cheeks streaked with tears. "I cleaned and made a beautiful lasagna. I started the clothes washing. Why didn't it work?"

He ran his thumb over her cheeks to remove the damp residue, dropping opals to her lap. "Well, for starters, I'd guess you forgot to take out the lasagna in time."

She dropped her long eyelashes and a charming pink blush colored her cheeks. "I . . . I was watching the television."

Glancing at the television, he caught the end of a soap opera. "Hooked, were you?"

"It was fascinating," she murmured.

He bit back the laugh that wanted to emerge. His little faery showed more mortal tendencies than she knew. "So you forgot the lasagna and it burned." Rand ran his hand over her tangled hair. "What did you do when you started the laundry?"

Her head came up. "I followed the directions."

"But . . . ?" It was never as simple as that where Ariel was concerned.

"I didn't have enough of the blue soap so I used some soap from the kitchen."

Rand shook his head as he smiled. "That's the problem. They're not the same kind of soap."

"But they look the same."

He had to admit that. Blue soap was blue soap in her world. "Well, now you know they're not."

Her lower lip quivered. "I'm sorry."

Unable to resist, he drew a kiss from her lips. "Don't worry about it." She was unharmed and that mattered most. "We'll clean up the mess and I'll take you out to dinner."

"Out?"

"To a restaurant." He knew a couple with good vegetarian selections.

"I thought you didn't want to be seen with me." Her gaze met his and he caught a brief glimpse of her uncertainty.

"I'd be proud to be seen with you." Lord, he'd screwed up trying to keep his family in the dark about her presence in his life. And, to be honest, he suffered from a touch of jealousy.

She would draw more than a few appreciative male looks, even pregnant. He smiled. Especially pregnant.

She was beautiful, exciting, and never, ever boring— no matter how hard she tried. She was Ariel.

"I don't . . . bother you?" she asked.

Hell, yes, she bothered him. Every moment spent near her sent his hormones into overdrive. "You . . ." How to explain it? "Ah, hell." He found her mouth, reveling in the soft warmth, the sweet taste that was uniquely Ariel. One kiss was never enough. He darted inside her mouth, dancing, dueling, devouring. He held her firmly, her full breasts pressed against his chest, her rounded belly molded against him.

Lord, what she did to him had to be illegal. One touch, one taste and he wanted more, wanted to bury himself inside her and never leave.

He pulled her onto his lap, her curved bottom pressed against his hardened erection. He heard a moan, but wasn't certain if it came from him or Ariel.

Or both.

She wrapped her arms around his neck, giving as fiercely as she accepted. This woman . . . this faery, affected him unlike anyone he'd ever met.

He ran one hand along the delicate line of her back, then up her side to cup her breast. Fuller now, the heavier weight only enticed him more. He brushed his thumb over the peak, which responded by forming a hard nub.

The urge to touch her flesh, to feel her writhing beneath him surged through him. This time he wanted to share in her powerful climax that triggered all his electrical equipment . . . not to mention what she did to his own personal equipment.

Before he could slide his hand beneath her sweater, something punched his abdomen—once, then again.

The baby.

Rand drew back, his breathing ragged, and glanced down to where Ariel's belly pressed against him. Again, a hard foot punched him.

Dear Lord, where was his mind?

"Don't stop." Ariel tightened her arms around his neck as he tried to replace her on the couch.

"I have to." This was the woman who'd stolen his seed and now threatened to keep his child from him. He had to remember that. "You don't need me to create a baby anymore."

"But I want you."

Her earnest words created a tight knot in his gut. Wanting wasn't enough. Couldn't be enough.

He managed to unlink her hands and set her back onto the couch. "Let's get the kitchen cleaned up." He rose to his feet before she could touch him again and shatter his already tenuous control.

She didn't answer until he reached the kitchen doorway. "Very well." Her voice was quiet with a slight tremble that brought Rand to a halt, his back toward her.

He closed his eyes, resisting the small voice that demanded he go to her and share in this passion. This woman had used him . . . more than once.

But lately he had a difficult time remembering that.

Under Rand's direction, Ariel discovered cleaning the kitchen wasn't as difficult as she'd expected. And the floor shone once she finished with the mopping.

But she didn't want a shiny floor. She wanted Rand.

Her body still hummed with the banked fires he'd brought to life, her breasts aching for his caress, her lips desperate for his kiss.

But he still hadn't forgiven her. No matter how pleasant he acted, she couldn't forget that. He saw her methods of obtaining the child she wanted in a different light. What choice had she had? She'd needed a mortal male to impregnate her and he certainly hadn't minded. Then.

Just her luck to find the one human man with a sense of responsibility.

Rand avoided touching her as they prepared to go out, even when he helped her on with a coat.

Ariel hesitated as he crossed the foyer to the front door. Should they even go? She could not endure an entire evening with him in his present mood. Couldn't he smile at her even once?

She reached out to touch his shoulder as he pulled open the door. "Rand, I—"

To her shock, he grabbed her arm and swung her behind the open door.

"Wha—?"

"Vicki, what are you doing here?" The strangled sound of his voice made Ariel grin. One of his sisters.

"You forgot, didn't you? I knew you would. And I left a message on the answering machine, too."

Peeking through the crack, Ariel spotted Vicki standing on the doorstep. She was one of the older sisters. Silly, they were all older, other than Stephanie.

Ariel recalled her introductions from the other night, trying to place Vicki in the family tree. Fifth child with three young children, and from the other voices Ariel heard, Vicki had brought them with her.

"Forgot what?" Rand didn't bother to open the door fully.

"You agreed to watch the kids for me tonight so Peter and I could celebrate our anniversary. Remember?"

Rand's groan told Ariel he had forgotten. "I have plans."

"So do we." A note of desperation entered Vicki's voice. "Peter's made reservations at the Briarhurst. Come on, Rand. It's too late to find another sitter."

He hesitated. "Fine, bring them in." He left the door open, hiding Ariel's presence as he led his sister and her children into the living room.

Ariel resisted the urge to pop out from behind the door. Rand had made it clear from the beginning he didn't want his family to know about her. This, at least, she could do for him.

"Wonderful. You're the greatest." Vicki deposited a kiss on his cheek. "We won't be very late. Just dinner. We've already fed the kids. They should all be ready for bed by eight, though Joshua has been fussy lately. He's cutting a tooth."

In a flurry of hugs, Vicki left as abruptly as she had appeared and Rand shut the door after her with a sigh. He glanced at Ariel and gave her an apologetic smile.

"Sorry. I'd forgotten about this. I'll order in some take-out."

His smile made the difference. He could've said anything and Ariel wouldn't have minded. "It's all right." Now she could spend some time with the children.

She approached the trio of young mortals, then froze. What did one *do* with children?

Before she could even guess, the two older kids threw themselves at Rand, one wrapping around each leg. He roared with mock ferocity and stomped across the floor until he reached the middle of the living room. There he plucked them off, one at a time.

"Come on, Uncle Rand. Wrestle with us." The oldest child, the boy Jordan, didn't wait for an answer, but launched himself at the far larger man.

Rand dropped to his hands and knees and was soon covered by Jordan and his sister Felicity. The youngest child, a boy toddler, stood watching, his thumb in his mouth.

"Watch over Josh," Rand called as he rolled over the floor with the older children. "I'll handle these two."

"All right." Ariel approached the little boy, her heart hammering in her chest. Though adorable with a head full of blond curls, he stared at her as if she were some kind of troll. "I won't hurt you," she murmured.

She bent down to face him, then wrinkled her nose at the foul odor. "He stinks."

"Probably needs his diaper changed. Vic left his diaper bag by the couch." Rand was quickly buried under laughing children again and Ariel snared the bag.

Was this a diaper? She pulled out a strange-looking folded pad. The diapers she remembered were cloth, but this covering was made of a paper and plastic combination. Still, nothing else in the bag resembled what she believed a diaper to be. This had to be it.

"Let's try this, Joshua." She laid the little boy on his

back on the carpeting and removed his small trousers. The item he currently wore around his bottom resembled the one she'd found. That was good.

It had no pins, but she located the pieces of tape holding it closed. Remarkable. And far easier than cloth diapers used in the past. These mortals constantly amazed her.

Unfortunately, cleaning the mess remained the same. "What do I clean him with?" she called. The noise level had risen as the children romped with their uncle.

"Should be wipes in the bag," Rand gasped between wrestling matches.

She found a container with damp white cloths. They worked despite Joshua's constant squirming. Ariel placed one hand on his chest to hold him in place as she worked.

Abruptly, a stream of urine shot into the air, hitting her face. She shot backward. "Stones!"

What a horrid creature. She couldn't clean her face fast enough, then glared at the child who watched her with big hazel eyes. Ha. Pretending to be innocent.

"Did he get you?" Rand appeared by her side, a wiggling child under each arm. "Sorry, forgot to warn you. Keep something over his . . . er . . . bottom half when you change him. He's notorious for that." Rand deposited the older siblings and reached down to tickle the toddler's belly. "Aren't you, Josh? Got me once, too."

Easing down beside Ariel, he completed the change with remarkable efficiency, then lifted the boy into his arms.

"Ra," Josh said, his pleasure evident.

"They all love you," Ariel said as she struggled to her feet.

"Only because I'm their favorite play toy," he replied. As if confirming that fact, Jordan and Felicity latched on to his legs again.

Rand rolled his eyes and handed Joshua to Ariel. "One more round and they'll be ready to sleep."

He launched into another bout of wrestling while Ariel

stared at the boy in her arms. He returned her stare, then burst into tears with a wail so loud it hurt her ears.

"Mama," he screamed. "Mama."

"Shh." She rocked him as she'd seen women do but he continued to cry. What was she doing wrong?

Doubts rose within her. She couldn't handle simple mortal chores. Now she couldn't handle this single child.

Her throat closed. What if . . . what if she couldn't be a good mother to *her* child? Fear closed its tight fist around her chest.

What if she failed at that, too?

Eleven

~

As Josh continued to scream, Rand shook himself loose from his niece and nephew and started toward him. Catching sight of the panic on Ariel's face, he paused.

Mixed with the panic were doubts as clear as if she'd spoken. The day's events had already conspired to make her feel inadequate, and Josh certainly wasn't helping. If Rand stepped in now, she'd realize she needed his help to raise their child.

But she'd also feel even more inadequate.

"He's probably just hungry." Rand forced himself to walk past Ariel and into the kitchen. "Why don't we all have some milk and cookies?"

"Yea!" said the kids. The older two raced after him and Ariel followed slowly.

In the kitchen, he made quick work of producing a package of Oreos and several glasses of milk—one with a special lid for Josh. "You'll have to hold him on your lap while he eats," he told Ariel. He gave her an encouraging smile. "We'll have dessert before dinner tonight."

She sat on a chair, her movements stiff, and tried to

fold the raging Josh into a sitting position. Rand busied himself with Jordan and Felicity, despite the urge to intervene. Ariel needed to win this battle herself.

As the older kids dove into the cookies, Ariel took one and offered it to Joshua. He seized it, his screams dying as he shoved it into his mouth, though his chest continued to heave with after-sobs.

Ariel visibly relaxed as she stared at him. "He *was* just hungry," she said.

"I know these rugrats. They're always hungry." Rand sat beside her and offered a reassuring smile. "He'll be fine."

Her gaze met his. "I didn't know . . . I felt . . ."

"Vic said he's cutting teeth so he probably doesn't feel real good, plus you're a stranger. He was frightened." Rand ran one finger over her soft cheek. "He'll get over it."

"You're good with children." She spoke softly but he heard the envy in her voice.

Pleasure floated through him. She'd noticed. "I've been around them most of my life." And for once he was glad of that fact.

"Do you think I can be good with them?" Her eyes were wide and her bottom lip quivered as she stared at him.

The hesitation behind her question made him want to hold her close. "Of course you can." He grabbed two cookies, instead of her. "Dealing with children is a learning experience. No one is born knowing how to do it."

"Then I need to spend more time with children."

Rand rolled his eyes. That was never a problem around his sisters. "It can be arranged." But doing so would reveal that Ariel was living with him and, knowing his family, they'd all make assumptions—assumptions that weren't necessarily true.

Though Ariel *was* staying with him, and attracted him more than any woman in his life. She *was* carrying his child. But the future was a black hole. If she had her way, she would disappear out of his life, taking his child with her.

Try explaining that to my family.

He couldn't let that happen. Somehow he had to persuade her to share this baby with him.

But how?

She cleaned up Joshua without any instruction, a step in the right direction in her children education, then joined them all in the living room.

"Tell us a story, Uncle Rand," Felicity said, crawling onto his lap.

Rand wrapped one arm around her and the other around Jordan while Ariel situated Joshua on her lap. "*Hmm,* a story." He could always go with "The Three Little Pigs" again. They loved it when he did the voices.

"I know a story," Ariel said suddenly, capturing their attention. "About faeries."

"Faeries?" Felicity's face lit up. "Oh, yes."

Rand nodded at Ariel to continue. What kind of story would she tell?

"Did you know there are faeries called pillywiggins?" she began.

Jordan laughed. "Pillywiggins? What kind of name is that?"

"That is what they are. They're flower faeries. They take care of the flowers all around the world."

"All flowers?" Felicity asked.

"All flowers." Ariel gave the children a warm smile that sent flames through Rand's blood. "They go wherever they are needed to make the flowers grow."

Jordan's eyes grew large. "Do they even come here? Can I see them?"

"Oh yes, they come here in the spring to coax the flowers to life, but you have to be very, very clever to see one. They don't like to be seen by mortals, and they hide whenever one is near."

Interesting. Rand enjoyed Ariel's musical voice as much as the information she imparted.

"What's a mortal?"

"A human." Ariel smiled as she tickled Jordan's stomach. "Like you."

"Oh." He looked momentarily disappointed. "What do I have to do to see a faery?"

"Be very, very quiet when the flowers first peek out of the ground and watch carefully. The pillywiggins play with the bees and butterflies so if you see them nearby, you can be sure a faery is close as well."

Rand chuckled. He could see Jordan now waiting for hours by his mother's flower bed.

"Can I capture one?" Jordan asked.

"Oh, no." Ariel's expression grew solemn. "You don't want to do that."

"Why not? I'd take care of it."

Jordan's earnestness made Rand grin. Sure, just like the puppy he'd promised to care for. Besides, Rand had learned there was a lot more to taking care of a faery than one would expect.

"The Fae have to be free to come and go with the wind. If you penned one up, she would die." Ariel's voice grew sad.

Rand stiffened. Was that how she felt? Was keeping Ariel in his home killing her? Aside from Halloween night, she appeared perfectly healthy.

"But I'm going to tell you about Esmeralda, a pillywiggins who cares for the lilacs. She's also a musical faery who sings instead of talks."

Jordan stared, his interest obviously caught, and Felicity snuggled closer to Rand, her thumb finding its way to her mouth as Ariel continued with her story. The adventures of the singing faery amused Rand as well. Ariel had a way with words that kept the children enthralled.

". . . and Esmeralda sang to Queen Titania that she would never, ever neglect her lilacs to play with the robins again." By the time Ariel finished the story, Felicity was half asleep and Jordan was stifling yawns.

"Time for bed." Rand rose with Felicity in his arms and

extended a hand for Jordan. "Come on, big fella. You can sleep in my bed."

Tucking the children into his large bed took only minutes. He smiled as they snuggled beneath the covers. They wouldn't be playing in bed tonight. The horseplay and story had done them in. Thank God.

He paused in the doorway. They liked Ariel and her stories, which meant Vicki would hear about Ariel as well. He grimaced. He'd tell his sister Ariel was a friend who happened to stop by. That would set his mother matchmaking as usual, but he'd avoid a direct confrontation.

Maybe.

Returning downstairs, he found Ariel changing Joshua's diaper again, her movements more certain, and she had a fresh diaper draped over him, warding off any potential showers. She learned quickly.

Lifting Josh into her arms again, she roamed the living room, humming a tune Rand couldn't place. The notes wove around him, creating an image of dancing faeries and magic in the air. Unwilling to move, Rand watched from the doorway as Ariel crooned Joshua to sleep, the toddler resting his head against her shoulder.

His gut twisted. One day it would be their child she sang to sleep. And he wanted to be there to see that . . . to see the baby . . . to see her.

Rand's throat went dry. Somehow, this faery was weaving her way into his life, into his thoughts.

Into his heart.

He crossed to her and wrapped his arms around her and his nephew, rocking gently. Ariel met his gaze with a soft smile that acted as a sucker punch. She mattered, damn it. She mattered as more than just the mother of his child.

Reacting rather than thinking, Rand touched his lips to hers, drinking of her sweetness, of the passion she constantly ignited within him. She was everything he didn't want in a woman, yet he desired her beyond reason.

Insanity.

Or some kind of spell.

Releasing her mouth, he rested his head atop hers, not needing words. What could he say? The feelings inside him were too raw, too uncertain to define.

They remained that way, entwined, rocking gently in the middle of the living room for minutes . . . or was it longer?

The sharp rap at his front door startled him from his sensual cocoon and Rand tensed.

The door opened. "We're back, Rand," Vicki called.

Ariel's eyes grew wide and she thrust Josh into his arms before vanishing into the kitchen, a brief second ahead of Vicki and Peter's arrival in the room.

"Were they good?" his sister asked.

"Great." He handed her the sleeping toddler, then led Peter upstairs. Rand carried Jordan while Peter took his daughter in his arms.

As Vicki fastened the children into their car seats, Rand watched, still warm inside despite the night's chill.

"Thanks again." Vicki placed a quick kiss on his cheek.

"Anytime." He caught himself. He must be under some kind of spell if he'd said that.

She looked startled, not that he blamed her. Usually he fought to avoid baby-sitting. "Are you serious?"

The image of Ariel cradling Josh filled Rand's mind and he smiled. "Yeah."

"Ah . . . thanks." Vicki's expression remained stunned as she slid into the front seat. " 'Night."

Rand saw them off, then returned to the house in search of Ariel. He wanted . . . he wasn't sure what he wanted.

He found her sound asleep in her bed, the comforter tucked beneath her chin. No wonder. She'd had a long day.

He reached down to smooth her hair, then drew his hand back, rolling it into a fist. No, if he touched her now, he'd only want more.

Something was happening, something he couldn't control, something he didn't want to examine.

And it scared the hell out of him.

• • •

Ariel laughed as Stephanie tossed more flour onto the countertop. "Do we really need that much?"

Stephanie shrugged. "I do." She plopped the dough they'd made onto the flour. "Now we knead it."

"Need it?" Of course, they needed it if they were to make bread.

"Knead—k-n-e-a-d—it," she repeated. "Like this." Stephanie folded the dough toward her, then pushed it away with the heel of her hand. "We do this until it's smooth."

"All right." Ariel took Stephanie's place, copying the woman's motions. The feel of the dough beneath her palms enticed her, especially as it grew more stretchy and smooth. This part of cooking she liked. It produced a sense of satisfaction like that she experienced when her buttercups first opened their budding petals.

She especially appreciated Stephanie spending her evenings showing her how to cook without magic. After three nights of lessons, Ariel could prepare a meal without burning it, and had even produced a dinner Rand had raved about.

Tonight Stephanie had made a meatloaf, a horrid-looking substance with meat that she'd actually shaped with her *hands*. Ariel could not—*would* not—touch that thing.

But Ariel had made the salad and now worked on the bread, though it would not be ready for several hours yet. Rand would have to be satisfied with it for his breakfast.

Stephanie leaned against the counter, watching her. "I swear you're getting bigger every time I see you."

"So is the baby." At least Ariel understood what it meant now when she suffered the extreme pressure in her belly. Usually within hours she found her belly even larger.

"Have you and Rand talked about names?"

Names? Ariel blinked. She had not thought to discuss it with Rand at all. The baby was Fae and would reveal its own name in time. "The name will come."

"Rand will want a say in it." Stephanie's gaze held Ariel's. "He *is* the father, you know."

"I know." A fact he constantly mentioned. Were all human fathers so involved with their offspring?

As if mentioning him conjured his appearance, Rand poked his head into the kitchen. "It smells good in here."

Ariel jumped. She hadn't heard the front door. "You're home already?"

"Yep, I'm done with the Sanderson job."

He entered the room, his gaze meeting hers with such intensity that Ariel's heart skipped a beat.

"A day early even," he added. "I thought I wouldn't finish up this project until Friday."

"That's good." The thought that one man could build a room still amazed her. Using magic was understandable, but to imagine him creating such a structure with his hands called for magic of a different nature.

"Now I can be here when the baby decides to come calling."

His words sent a small stab of alarm through her. Though she was adapting to the miserable changes of her body, she hadn't thought ahead to actually giving birth. She wasn't looking forward to it. Mortals usually screamed in childbirth. Would she?

Rand caught her shoulders. "Hey, it'll be all right." His gaze dropped to her mouth and for a brief moment Ariel thought he might kiss her. She ached for him to do so. Since the night they'd watched the children, he'd been polite but distant, when all she wanted was more of his touch.

Instead he released her and turned toward his sister. "Thanks for helping out, Steph. I really appreciate it."

"It's been fun," Stephanie replied. "Ariel and I are having a good time playing house."

He surveyed the kitchen, raising one eyebrow. "I hope so. Ariel doesn't make *this* big a mess even when her magic goes haywire."

Ariel stiffened but Stephanie advanced on her brother

and poked her finger against his chest. "It's hard work to make bread, brother dear, and hard work makes a mess."

Besides, the gelatin mess *had* been worse than this. Ariel scanned the countertops. Though they had managed to get flour almost everywhere.

Rand held up his hands and backed away, laughing. "Just so long as I don't have to clean it up, go for it."

The doorbell rang and he looked around. "That'll be Dean. He's joining us for dinner tonight."

Ariel sensed Stephanie's tension though outwardly the woman's expression didn't change. "Why him?" Stephanie asked.

"He's giving Ariel a checkup."

Not again. Ariel hated the intrusiveness of the exams. The baby was healthy. She would know at once if that changed. "I don't need that."

"Yes, you do. He's just going to listen to the heartbeat and check your vitals." Rand's tone left no room for argument and Ariel sighed as he left the room.

"What a pain," Ariel muttered, using the slang she'd picked up from Stephanie.

"You're telling me." Stephanie produced a wry smile. "Just what we need—men to ruin an otherwise perfect evening."

Ariel laughed. This woman had become special to her— a friend. The first friend she could recall in all her centuries of existence. And she liked the feelings it produced of sharing, of warmth, of kinship. "I guess we will survive."

"What choice do we have?" Stephanie opened a cupboard and pulled out four plates. "I'll set the table."

Rand and Dean entered the room as soon as Stephanie left. "How are you doing, Ariel?" Dean asked, his gaze going immediately to her swollen belly.

"Fine." Which was true for the most part. He didn't need to know about the ache in her back or her perpetual fatigue. Stephanie had already assured her those things were normal.

"Good." He eyed the kitchen. "So what bomb exploded here?"

Ariel lifted her chin, indignant. She and Stephanie had worked hard. "Stephanie and I are making bread."

"Figures." Dean shook his head. "Just like Steve to make a mess and leave it."

"We're not done yet." Stephanie spoke from the doorway, her tone cool.

A gleam entered Dean's eyes as he looked at her. "So you'll clean it up later?" He grinned. "I've been hearing that one since you were six years old."

"I'm not six anymore," Stephanie said.

Dean ran his finger through the flour on the countertop. "Could've fooled me."

"Go to hell."

The animosity in Stephanie's voice surprised Ariel. Though Steph often argued with Dean, Ariel had never heard her quite so angry before.

Dean looked up, startled, and Rand stepped between him and his sister. "Why don't you take Ariel into the other room? I'll help Steph get the meal on the table."

Ariel glanced back at Stephanie as she followed Dean. Fire blazed in her friend's eyes. Why? Usually the bickering between Stephanie and Dean was more playful in nature.

Why had Dean's teasing statement affected Stephanie so strongly? Obviously, Ariel had missed something.

" 'Since you were six years old.' " Stephanie muttered the phrase to herself as she stormed into the mall two hours later. She'd promised to pick up a cream for Ariel, to help with the stretch marks produced by the baby's rapid growth.

Blast Dean Carstensen. She was sick and tired of him treating her like a child. When would he finally see her as a woman? Did she have to strip naked in front of him?

Stephanie winced. Heck, even that wouldn't help. He

saw half-dressed women all the time. He'd probably only laugh at her.

Why did it matter anyway?

She lifted her chin. It didn't. He was nobody. Nothing. If he persisted in seeing her as a child, it was his loss and not her problem.

So why didn't she believe that?

She was twenty-five, a college graduate, working full-time as a teacher. She had a life, friends, activities. Okay, no boyfriend, but then no one had held her interest for any length of time. Why bother? From her experience—granted, it was limited—men were a waste of time.

Especially Dr. Dean Carstensen.

Intent on her inner fury, she collided with a man who caught her shoulders to steady her as she stumbled backward. "I'm sorry," she murmured. It was all Dean's fault, distracting her when he wasn't even present.

"No problem." The man produced a smile that lifted her spirits—a smile that said he liked what he saw.

She stared at him. "Do I know you?" Even before she finished speaking, she realized where she'd seen him. He'd been the man flirting with her and Ariel last weekend at the food court.

"I don't think so. I'd definitely remember meeting you." He released her shoulders and extended his hand. "Bob Harris."

She placed her palm in his. "Stephanie Thayer." He was definitely a looker with those bright blue eyes, blond hair, and a smile designed for Colgate commercials.

He continued to hold her hand and a secret thrill ran through Stephanie's veins. "Can I offer you a cup of coffee?" he asked.

"Well, I . . ." Though tempted, she'd just met the guy.

Turning her hand over, he examined her bare fingers. "No ring. Are you involved with someone?"

Not likely. "No." Dean flickered briefly through her mind and Stephanie straightened her shoulders. The heck

with him. Here was a man who saw her as a woman.
"Sure, I'd like some coffee."

"Great." Bob's megawatt smile warmed her. "How
about we duck into Ruby Tuesdays? They're open for
another couple of hours yet." Even as he spoke, he placed
his hand on her elbow and guided her in that direction.

"I want to know all about how a knockout like you is
running around unattached," he added. "And how I can
change that."

Stephanie smiled, basking in his obvious interest.

Take that, Dean Carstensen.

Twelve

~

Ariel danced under the rainbow sky, her figure trim, her worries gone, her magic at full strength. How wonderful to be home where the air was sweet and clear, the grass lush and green, the flowers full and colorful. Other pillywiggins swirled in the circle with her—Lily, Lilac, Ambrosia, Pansy, and Gladiola. Their laughter filled the clearing.

She'd missed this—almost forgotten how to be Fae. With her magic and buttercups, what more did she need?

Yet something nagged at her. Something . . . someone was missing.

Ariel searched among the trees and flowers, growing more frantic when she couldn't find what she sought. What was it?

"Ariel?"

At her name, she turned and spied Rand standing in the portal, a single buttercup in his hand. Behind him, she could see the gray dismal winter of the mortal world, a stark contrast to the colorful beauty of the magical realm.

She stepped toward him, then hesitated. She was happy here. Why should she leave?

"Ariel?" He said nothing more, but something gleamed in his brown eyes, an emotion that tugged at Ariel, drew her closer.

She wanted him. Needed him.

For Rand, she could spend some time in the harsh human world.

She ran toward him and he caught her in his arms, whirling her around until her head spun. When he stopped, she discovered they were in his bed and his hands and lips were touching her with his own special magic.

No matter where he placed his hands, her skin warmed, her blood boiled. When his lips found hers, she melted with pleasure. Nothing in the magical realm could equal this.

"I want you," he murmured, his voice husky. "I want what's mine."

"Yes." She'd grant him anything. No one had ever made her feel like this—cared for, desired, special.

Abruptly Rand disappeared. When Ariel turned to find him, she spotted him in the distance, walking away.

With her baby in his arms.

"No." Ariel sat upright in the bed, her chest tight with panic. For a brief moment she struggled to orient herself. Oh, yes, Rand's house in the mortal realm.

She shuddered. She'd never had such a vivid dream in her entire existence. What did it mean?

The exquisite ecstasy she'd experienced with Rand, though a dream, still lingered, her skin warm, her breasts aching. But the alarm of losing her baby overshadowed it. She'd never give up her child, nor would she live among the mortals for an extended period.

While dreaming, she'd felt the full force of her magic, the joy of being Fae. How could she deny what she was?

Yet she had gone to him without reservation, given herself to him, only to have him betray her by stealing her child. Her heart still pounded with the pain of that realization.

Was her dream a warning? Were Rand's intoxicating kisses nothing more than a means to win her affection and befuddle her mind?

If so, they were working, for she craved more each day and longed to be near him. Stones, she'd even tried to create a boring life for him.

What was she doing?

Ariel rolled over in the soft bed and buried her face in her pillow. This mortal was becoming important to her.

Unthinkable.

But true.

She couldn't allow it. Only another week remained until her baby would be born. She could endure this life among the mortals for that long, but no more kisses, no more caresses from Rand to send her pulse racing.

She was Fae. He was mortal.

That difference had blurred lately as she'd experienced more of the mortal life, but no more. Her magic might be faulty, but it was still a part of her and a part of her unborn child. They didn't belong here.

She had to remember that and remain firm in resisting him.

Unbidden, Rand's expression as he'd beckoned her toward him appeared in Ariel's mind and a tingle of longing spread through her veins.

She *would* remain firm.

She wrapped her arms around her swollen belly and whispered, "I hope."

"Almost time for the game." Rand turned on the television. Where was everyone? Ariel was still in her room, but usually Dean arrived early, with Steph not far behind.

The outcome of today's game could mean play-offs for the Broncos. Surely they wouldn't miss it.

As if on cue, Dean knocked once and entered. "Sorry I'm late."

"About time."

"Hey, I stopped for beer. It's my turn." Dean disappeared into the kitchen, then emerged with a beer in each hand as Ariel descended the staircase. "Hi, Ariel. How are you feeling?"

Rand heard the note in his friend's voice that indicated his question was more than casual conversation.

"I'm well." She gave him a tight smile, then headed for one of the easy chairs.

Rand frowned. She'd been different lately—polite but distant—yet he couldn't think of a reason for her change.

Damn, he hated to admit it, but he missed her enthusiasm, her impulsiveness, even her good deeds gone wrong. *Man, you are losing it.*

He studied her lovely features—a face he knew nearly as well as his own, yet he never tired of looking at it. Usually her brilliant blue eyes sparkled and good humor lingered in her flawless expression.

But not today.

She appeared subdued—present physically while her mind drifted elsewhere. Was she homesick?

Rand's throat tightened. Was she planning how she'd take their child there?

"You look like you need a beer." Dean handed Rand a bottle before sliding into a chair.

"Thanks." Rand twisted off the cap and took a big swallow. Unfortunately, no amount of beer could ease the uncertainty inside him.

A sharp rap on the door caught his attention. "Come in, Steph," he called.

She entered, followed by a man Rand had never seen before. What the hell? Rand started, then exchanged puzzled glances with Dean, who shook his head, evidently as confused as Rand.

The man stood slightly shorter than Rand with sandy hair layered to his collar and a neatly trimmed goatee. He wore designer jeans and a shirt on a lean figure. Though the man displayed a warm smile, his appearance suggested someone who thought well of himself.

Worse yet, he held Stephanie's hand firmly in his.

"Hi, guys." Stephanie breezed into the room. "This is Bob Harris. Bob, my brother Rand and his friend Dean."

Bob extended his hand. "Hi. Hope I'm not intruding. Stephanie invited me to watch the game."

Rand kept the handshake short. "You a Broncos fan?"

"Love them." Bob faced Dean, who didn't bother to take the proffered hand. Something dark flashed in Bob's eyes before he shoved his palm into his pocket.

"And this is Ariel." Stephanie bent to hug Ariel, then stepped back to study her. "You look odd. Are you okay?"

"I'm fine."

As Ariel answered, Bob gave her a broad smile. "Pleased to meet you." He wrapped his arm around Stephanie's shoulders. "Steph says you're good friends. I guess it stands to reason a beautiful woman like Stephanie would have beautiful friends."

Stephanie's cheeks flushed, and she sat on the couch with Bob so close to her that Rand wondered if he'd need a chisel to break them apart. Seeing his sister with a stranger bothered him. Especially one who could barely keep his hands off her.

Or maybe it was the way he looked at Ariel.

"Come on. The game's starting." Stephanie waved Rand over and he dropped onto the far end of the couch, staring at the television though his mind was anywhere but on the game.

What was going on? Steph hadn't dated anyone seriously in years. In fact, she'd claimed she wanted to remain single like Rand.

Why the sudden change? Did Ariel's pregnancy make Steph feel like she was missing out on something? Or did Steph just want to shake up Rand's life even more? If Stephanie settled down, then his mother's attempts to marry him off would be even worse.

Rand watched Ariel as she focused her attention on the television. The last thing he needed was another woman in his life. This one claimed all his energy and then some.

A rush of desire knotted his gut and centered in his

groin as he recalled the "then some." For all the problems
Ariel had caused him, Rand couldn't honestly say he re-
gretted her presence in his home. In fact, he'd even grown
to like it.

After lessons from Stephanie, Ariel's cooking had dra-
matically improved, though he still had to eat such mon-
strosities as spinach quiche due to Ariel's vegetarianism.
What was wrong with a thick rare steak?

"Go, Terrell." Steph bounced on the couch, drawing
Rand's attention back to the game in time to see the receiver weave his way through the defense to a touchdown.

"All right," he exclaimed.

"Touchdown." At the enthusiasm in Ariel's voice, Rand
glanced at her again to find a healthy glow in her cheeks
and the familiar sparkle in her eyes as she leaned toward
the television.

A beautiful woman who loved football. What was not
to love?

He tensed. *Like*. What was not to *like*?

Love was serious. It implied commitment, a radical
change from his bachelor life, and a devastation of his
emotions. No, he wasn't about to fall in love, no matter
how lovely, how enticing, how exciting, how much fun a
woman was.

"They're going to win this one," Bob declared.

"It's still early." Dean fixed his gaze on the stranger.
"A lot can happen."

Bob shrugged. "There's always another game."

"Not really." Rand had to respond to that. Hadn't this
guy said he knew the Broncos? "If you'd been following
the season, you'd know this game will have a major impact on whether the Broncos go to the play-offs or not."

"Oh. Well." Bob produced a tight smile, then focused
his attention on Stephanie, whispering something in her
ear that made her giggle.

Judging from the expression on Dean's face, he didn't
care for this intruder any more than Rand did. And Rand
couldn't find a good reason why he didn't like the guy.

After all, he had bonded pretty well with all his sisters' husbands.

Maybe he was paranoid. After all, Steph was his baby sister. That might be the difference.

Bob leaned forward with Steph to cheer a play, his hand brushing Stephanie's breast, and Rand frowned. Then again, maybe the guy really was a sleaze.

At halftime, Stephanie escaped into the kitchen while the men devoured their pizza. Maybe bringing Bob here hadn't been such a good idea, but she'd wanted Dean to know that there were men who found her attractive and grown up.

Except that Bob's attention suffocated her. Since they'd met at the mall, he'd been around constantly, which—she had to admit—did her ego a lot of good. He was a good-looking man and obviously thought highly of her.

So why didn't she feel anything more than a heady rush of pleasure? He'd kissed her for the first time last night and no chimes rang. Not like Dean's long-ago birthday kiss.

Steph scowled. That was over. Done. Dean had made it clear then and since that he saw her as nothing more than a child.

Though he didn't appear very pleased today. He'd watched the first half of the game without his usual enthusiasm and hadn't baited her once about Griese. Her pulse leaped. Was he jealous?

"There you are." She whirled around as Dean joined her in the kitchen. "I want to talk to you."

Her breath caught in her throat. Maybe he was jealous. Maybe he'd finally admit he found her attractive. Then she could reject him as cruelly as he'd done to her so long ago.

Catching sight of the fiery gleam in his dark eyes, she moistened her dry lips. Or maybe she wouldn't.

"What's the matter?" she asked. "Upset 'cause Griese is doing such a good job?"

"This isn't about football." Dean stopped in front of her, so close she only had to extend her hand to touch him. "It's about you and that Bob character."

A flare of excitement rushed through her veins. "Oh, really?" She forced herself to appear calm and disinterested.

"Are you out of your mind?" Derision colored Dean's words. "What the hell are you thinking bringing him here?"

His attack was so different from what she'd expected that it took Stephanie a moment to respond. "I . . . ah . . . why shouldn't I? We're dating, you know." If she counted two outings as dating.

"That's not the issue here." Anger blazed in his eyes. "You're putting Ariel at risk by bringing a stranger here."

"Ariel?" He was thinking about Ariel?

"She's due to give birth by the end of this week and doesn't need anyone else learning her identity."

"I wasn't going to tell him." Steph curled her fists. He should at least give her credit for some brains.

"What if she gets the hiccups and flowers appear? How are you going to explain that?"

Steph hesitated. She honestly hadn't thought of that. "I . . . I'd think of something."

"Maybe you should've waited a week to flaunt your boyfriend."

"I'm not flaunting him," she protested with a twinge of guilt.

"Like hell you're not." Dean placed one arm on either side of her, trapping her against the counter. "Let me warn you, Steph. Don't trust this guy. He's got more lines than a ream of notebook paper."

"You ought to know. It's a page from your book." How dare he lecture her? He wasn't even her brother.

"I *do* know." Dean leaned closer until his face was just a breath away. His gaze held hers prisoner. "I don't want to see Ariel hurt." He paused, the silence so thick Steph just knew he could hear her pounding heart. "I don't want you hurt."

"You're a fine one to talk about that," she whispered, unable to speak any louder through her dry throat.

Dean blinked. "What do you mean?"

Surely he knew how he'd devastated her so long ago. Or maybe he just wanted to hear her admit it. Stephanie struggled for a proper reply, difficult to do with Dean's lips so close to her own. "You—"

"So here's where you went." Bob entered the room, his loud voice so jovial Steph wanted to hide.

Dean drew away from her slowly and darted a glance at Bob before returning his gaze to her. "Think about what I said."

He left the kitchen and Steph could finally draw a deep breath, though her thoughts continued to whirl.

"What was that about?" A note of tension entered Bob's voice.

"Nothing." Steph forced a smile. "Just an old football disagreement." Though she would have preferred to put her foot in Dean's balls at the moment, she touched Bob's arm. "How about we take off? This isn't nearly as much fun as I thought it would be." And she definitely didn't want to endanger Ariel. The Fae woman was her friend.

"Actually I'm enjoying it." Bob wrapped his arm tightly around her shoulders. "Let's at least finish the game, then I'll take you to dinner."

Unable to think of another excuse, Stephanie shrugged. "If that's what you want."

"Yeah, let's do that." Bob released her long enough to grab a beer from the refrigerator. "I like your brother. Good guy."

While Steph agreed, she doubted Bob knew much about Rand. They'd barely spoken. "I think so."

"Is Ariel his wife?"

Stephanie hesitated. "Not actually."

"Just living together, eh?" Bob winked. "More power to 'em. Though it looks like she's about to pop."

"It's their business." Explaining Ariel needed a lot more time than she wanted to spend and a lot more trust than she felt willing to give.

"So it is." Bob led her back into the living room as the game resumed.

Steph darted a quick glance at Dean as she settled beside Bob on the couch, but Dean kept his attention on the television, the set line of his mouth revealing his disapproval.

Why didn't he just boil her in oil and get it over with?

At least Ariel appeared more vivacious than when Steph had arrived. Good. *Just don't hiccup.*

Only now Rand looked depressed, his gaze lingering on Ariel. Stephanie sighed. Rand was falling for Ariel. She'd bet money on it. Only problem was Ariel intended to return home once the baby was born. Not a great start for a relationship.

As Bob erupted at a referee call, Stephanie studied him. He was handsome, attentive, considerate. What more could she want?

She stole a look at Dean.

What more, indeed?

Ariel released an audible sigh as everyone finally left. Though the game had been exciting, the tension in the room had been palpable. "What's going on with Stephanie?" she asked.

Rand shook his head. "I wish I knew. Today is the first I've heard of this guy."

"You don't like him." Even without her magic, Ariel had sensed the antagonistic vibes from Rand.

"I really don't know him."

"Doesn't matter. You don't like him."

"Well, he kept glancing at you all afternoon."

Ariel grimaced. "Probably because he's never seen anyone so pregnant before." If she swelled much more, she could double as a milkweed pod.

"Maybe." Rand came to face her. "Or maybe he found you as beautiful as I do."

Ariel's throat tightened, her blood warming. Before she could lean into him, she forced herself to move to the front window, away from danger. "Look, it's snowing."

And this time several inches coated the ground. Already the grass and sidewalk were covered with white, and large flakes continued to pour from the sky. Instead of the dirty slush of Halloween night, this was beautiful, coating the world in a pristine shell. The setting sun highlighted the crystal particles, creating a brilliance equal to any spell.

"I never knew it could look like that," she murmured.

She knew without turning around when Rand came to stand behind her by the tingle that raced down her spine and into her belly.

"Haven't you ever seen snow before?"

"I usually don't visit the mortal realm during winter. It's too cold, too depressing."

Rand rested his hands on her shoulders and gently massaged them, each touch of his fingers relaxing her tense muscles while stirring the embers of fire deep within. She should move away. She really should.

But she didn't.

"Then you've missed a lot. Winter has a unique beauty all its own, especially in Colorado."

Just as her bones melted and she found herself leaning back toward him, Rand dropped his hands and moved away. She stumbled backward, then turned to look at him in surprise. "What are you doing?"

"Getting our coats. You have to be outside to truly appreciate this snow."

Despite the cold awaiting her, Ariel felt a tingle of anticipation. The storm at Halloween had been more slush than snow. What would this be like?

Stepping out of the house with Rand by her side, Ariel lifted her face to the twilight sky. Flakes landed softly on her face and quickly melted—cold, wet, yet unique, mysterious.

She lumbered along the sidewalk, her arms out-stretched, hearing the excited chatter of distant birds, sensing the eagerness of the evergreens. The mortal world held more magic than she'd ever realized.

"It's wonderful." She gave Rand a warm smile. Without his urging, she might not have experienced this.

His eyes twinkled. "Told you so." He scooped up a handful of snow and compressed it into a ball. "Ever had a snowball fight?"

Ariel eyed the snowball warily. "No. What is that?"

"This." Before she could react, he tossed the ball at her, and it smashed against her coat.

She stared at him in stunned surprise. "You hit me."

"That's the point." He reached down for more snow. "You throw them at me, too."

Another violent game. Yet Ariel eagerly joined in, packing a handful of snow into a ball and throwing it at Rand. He dodged it and she frowned.

"That's not fair."

"Nothing says I have to stand still." He threw his snow-ball at her, but this time Ariel evaded the missile and quickly grabbed another handful of snow.

Her next attempt exploded against Rand's chest. He glanced down at it in amazement, then grinned. "You catch on fast."

They continued to hurl the snow at each other until Ariel could barely move, her laughter making her chest ache. She sank onto the ground, holding her sides.

"Now you're going to learn about snow angels," he said.

"Snow angels?" Snowflakes drifted onto her face as she stared at him.

"Yep, like this." Rand lay flat in the snow and swished his arms and legs back and forth several times.

Ariel watched him. What did this have to do with snow angels?

When Rand jumped to his feet, she suddenly understood. The outline he'd left in the snow resembled a full-winged angel. She grinned and proceeded to follow his example. Only standing up again wasn't so easy.

Rand chuckled as he extended his hand. "Let me help." He tugged her to her feet, then held her close to his side as she turned to view her imprint. "Not bad," he murmured.

"*That* is a snow *faery*," Ariel said. She pulled away to sit on the snow again, anxious to try another design. This was fun.

Rand dove at her and she gasped as he pressed her back into the deepening snow on his yard. He leaned over her, propped on one elbow. "You've now been initiated to snow."

His eyes held a glimmer of passion and his gaze dropped to her lips. Ariel's throat tightened, unable to look away. She wanted his kiss. It was only one. What could it hurt?

But as his mouth touched hers, desire raged through her veins. Her breasts swelled, her insides heated with want. Coherent thought fled as she wrapped her arms around his neck to hold him close, unwilling to let him go.

One kiss became another, then another, as he worked a spell of his own with his lips, his tongue, his hands. Ariel half expected the snow to melt around them with the fire growing inside her.

He nipped at her lower lip, then drew back, studying her. Surely the blazing passion in his eyes equaled her own. "I like how you end snowball fights," she said, her breath coming in gasps.

"This gives winning a whole new meaning." His smile bathed her in warmth as he smoothed her hair back from her face.

Winning? As in winning her affections?

Ariel froze, her earlier passion dissolving. How could she be so foolish, so easily led astray? By a mortal, no less?

She lifted her hand to push him away, but found her

fingers entwined in his soft hair as he stole another kiss, lingering, teasing, weakening her resolve.

"Rand." She offered a faint protest.

Suddenly she heard a splat and Rand jerked away from her, rising to his feet in one smooth movement to face his attacker. "What are you doing?" he demanded.

Ariel tried to join him, but her bulk made it difficult. Rand extended his hand to pull her up beside him.

"Got ya, Uncle Rand." A boy of about nine stood by the front walk to Rand's house, his smile white in the falling darkness.

"He was kissing her, Derrick. You shouldn't hit him while he's doing that." An older girl joined him.

"Hey, kids." Rand sounded strange.

Glancing past the children, Ariel saw the reason why.

His sister, Louise.

Thirteen

He was in deep shit now. Rand produced a smile as he moved forward to greet his sister, very aware of Ariel beside him. A very pregnant, very tousled Ariel, whom he'd been caught kissing.

As the saying went, the jig was up.

"Hey, Lou," he said.

"Hi, Rand." Her gaze darted past him to Ariel. "Is that Ariel?"

"Hi," Ariel said, her voice soft. She glanced at Rand and he caught a glimpse of the understanding in her expression. Well, it could be worse. It could be his mother.

"Randall Thayer, do you make a habit of kissing young women on your front lawn?"

Rand jerked as he spotted the owner of that voice approaching from the driveway. Okay, it *was* worse. "Hi, Mom." He knew his smile was weak, but it was the best he could manage.

Mom came to stand beside his sister, a foil-wrapped package in her hands. "Well, are you going to invite us inside? I'm sure you and Ariel need to dry off. You're covered with snow."

"Sure. Sure. Come on in." Rand started for the front door, then paused, catching sight of the panic on Ariel's face. Hell, the damage was done now. He took her hand in his and led the way into the house.

Once inside he took everyone's coats and made a production out of hanging them up. Anything to delay the inevitable.

"I'll . . . I'll make some coffee." Ariel vanished into the kitchen at the first opportunity. Not that he blamed her. He wanted to disappear, too.

"I'll help you." Mom went after her before Rand could utter a protest.

Oh, God. He was really dead meat now.

Louise gave him a teasing grin, then sent her two kids downstairs to the family room. Probably for the best. This wasn't going to be fun.

"What are you doing here?" Rand asked. Of all nights, why did they have to pop in tonight?

"Mom and I made some bread this afternoon and we thought we'd bring you some. You've been so busy lately, we've hardly seen you." A glimmer of mischief danced in Lou's eyes. "Now I understand why."

"It's not what you think," he said quickly.

"Oh?" Louise raised one eyebrow. "You're cavorting on the front lawn kissing a young woman who is obviously very pregnant. What *do* I think?"

Oh, hell. He was truly doomed. "Okay, it's what you think." And he couldn't begin to explain.

"Why didn't you tell us you and Ariel were . . . involved?" Lou approached the subject much more delicately than their mom would. "Now I understand why you took off with her on Halloween. This also explains Jordan's incredible tale about the fat lady with the stories."

"It's a long story in itself." And one she'd never believe.

"I'd like to hear it." She grinned. "And I know Mom will *demand* to hear it."

Think fast, Thayer. "I . . . I've known Ariel for a

while." Better not to give a time period. "She's . . . she's pretty special." None of that was a lie.

"What about the baby?"

He tried to evade the question. "What about it?"

"Is it yours?"

He swallowed the thick lump forming in his throat. "Well . . ."

"Yes, Rand, tell us." His mother entered the room, Ariel by her side. "Is it yours?"

"I . . . ah . . ." No matter what he said this wasn't going to go well.

Before he could form a reply, Mom turned on Ariel. "Is Rand the father?"

Oh, no. Ariel couldn't lie.

She hesitated, her discomfort obvious, then nodded.

"I see." Mom focused on him again, her expression sentencing him to at least a dozen Hail Marys, and a couple of full rosaries to boot. "And when were you planning to tell us about this?"

"It's complicated, Mom." Not a good answer, but the best he had.

"I'm sure it is."

He waved his hand toward the couch. "Why don't you have a seat and I'll explain as best I can."

"I prefer to stand." Mom crossed her arms, her expression set.

Yep, he was a goner.

In any case, *he* needed to sit. Rand hurried to nab Ariel's arm and pulled her with him to the couch. "Don't say a word," he whispered. Whatever he came up with had to be believable and if Ariel started telling the truth, he didn't have a chance of that.

"I'm waiting," Mom said.

Lounging in a chair, Louise just smiled, obviously enjoying every moment of his discomfort. And he'd built a walk-in closet for her, too.

"As I told Lou, I've known Ariel for a while, and we . . . ah . . . we have a certain chemistry." Damn, he wasn't going to tell his mother he'd slept with her. Surely that was obvious. "Anyhow, she ended up pregnant."

"When is the wedding?" Mom's expression softened slightly as she gazed at Ariel. "A simple ceremony will have to do at this point."

Rand swallowed hard. "There . . . ah . . . there isn't going to be a wedding."

A tightness entered his mother's face that he hadn't seen since he was thirteen and had threatened to run away. "Excuse me?"

"We're not getting married." He blurted out the words, then waited for the explosion.

"You intend to bring a child into this world and not take responsibility for it?"

Mom's icy words sent rocks plummeting to his gut. "No, I want to be there for the baby. I just—"

Ariel cut him off. "It's my fault. I refused to marry him."

Rand gaped at her. Was that a lie? Or a truth that had never been voiced? He hadn't asked her to marry him. He'd thought about it, but then he already knew her answer.

"And why is that?" Mom turned the deadly glare on Ariel. "Is he not a good man?"

"He's a wonderful man." Ariel gave Rand a quick glance, then bit her lip before continuing. "However, my . . . lifestyle is very different from his. We . . . have no future together. He has been kind enough to offer me shelter during my pregnancy, but we will go our separate ways once the baby is born."

His mother dropped into a nearby chair, speechless for the first time in Rand's life. No doubt she felt much like he did—kicked in the gut.

"We're still working out the details," he added quickly, frowning at Ariel. She wasn't going to write him out of his child's life that easily.

"No marriage?" Mom sounded stunned. "Where . . . where will you go?"

"Home."

"And where is that?"

Rand jumped in before Ariel could answer. "It's far from here, I'm afraid."

"And the baby?" A note of desperation entered Mom's voice.

"Will go with me." Ariel glanced at Rand, her expression less certain than her words.

"No." Mom rose to her feet, her cheeks growing red. "That is unacceptable. I have fifteen grandchildren and have been there for all of them. I refuse to allow this one to go so far away."

Rand stood as well and crossed to give Mom a hug. "Mom, I told you. We're still working out the details. Things could change."

Wisely, Ariel remained silent.

"They had *better* change." The determination that had seen his mother through the many years since his father's death entered her eyes. "They *will* change."

"Anything is possible," he murmured. Boy, was that true.

"Come, Lou. I think we've overstayed our welcome." Mom marched toward the closet and Rand closed his eyes briefly, shaking his head.

"I'm making coffee," Ariel said, rising unsteadily to her feet.

"No, thank you." Mom stood waiting and Rand hurried to retrieve her coat and help her into it.

"But Mommy, we just got here," Derrick said, as he appeared to answer Louise's summons.

"We'll come back another day," Louise told him. She paused by Rand on her way out, her expression filled with disappointment. "Count on it."

He closed the door after them, then leaned against it. That hadn't been so bad. He was still in one piece.

Ha. Who was he kidding? The condemnation on his mother's face hurt worse than any beating.

And she wasn't done with this. He knew her better than

that. She was going to regroup and plan her attack.

Rand crossed the room to face Ariel. "Marry me." The words erupted from him without thought, yet he meant them. He had to do something to keep Ariel here. "Stay with me and let us raise this child together."

A brief flash of something appeared in her eyes as she stared at him, obviously surprised, then it vanished as her expression hardened. "You know that's impossible."

"Why is it? Robin married Kate, didn't he?"

"Robin also gave up his immortality to do so." Ariel raised her chin. "I couldn't do that even if I wanted to."

"I'm not asking you to give it up. Damn it, Ariel, you have eternity. All I'm asking for is a few years to watch my child grow up . . . to be a part of his or her life." He wanted this, wanted it so badly he ached with it.

Ariel hesitated and he pressed his advantage.

"We get along okay." That had to be an understatement. "I know you're not repulsed by me." Not with her enthusiastic responses to his kisses. "Why not try it and see what happens?"

She shivered, then turned away from him, pacing to the far side of the room. "I can't. I'm Fae. This child will be Fae. You would trap us in this mortal realm and demand we hide who we are . . . refrain from our magic. It's asking too much."

Her words held a certain amount of truth. It was difficult enough now to hide her true identity, and her use of magic had only been tempered by its diminishing power. How could he ask her to give that up? Yet how could he allow her to fill his kitchen with green Jell-O? Or worse?

If the truth about Ariel became known, his life would become a nightmare. The peace he'd long sought would cease to exist.

But he couldn't let her go. Couldn't let their child out of his life.

"We could work out something," he said, hearing the panic in his voice and hating it. He needed to take control, to do something. But what? He couldn't force her to stay.

"I can't." She sounded near to tears. "I'm sorry, but I can't."

She fled toward her bedroom and Rand let her go. What more could he say?

He was going to lose his child.

And Ariel.

And damned if he knew which one bothered him more.

She felt guilty. Ariel couldn't believe it. She sighed as she worked in the kitchen. The Fae rarely suffered most of the human emotions, and never guilt, yet she couldn't deny that the twisting, churning feelings within her had to be guilt.

Rand's point that she would have forever while his lifespan was limited still lingered. His desire to be a father to this child could not be denied either.

He would be a good father. Ariel smiled sadly. He would be an *excellent* father.

And Meg's reaction had startled her. Ariel hadn't expected Rand's mother to become so involved with this child. After all, it was Ariel's baby.

And Rand's.

She grimaced. And apparently Rand's family's.

Ariel surveyed the dining room table. She had set it for two and prepared a casserole, half with meat, just for Rand. Strange, the things guilt made a person do.

She peeked into the living room. "Dinner's ready."

For a moment, she thought Rand might refuse to eat. He'd barely spoken to her all day and she missed his warmth, his smile, the look in his eyes.

But he finally nodded and rose from the couch where he'd been reading the newspaper.

Once he was seated and served, Ariel waited, her chest tight, for his reaction to her casserole. She had experimented with a recipe to make it acceptable for both of them, something she wouldn't have dreamed of doing even a week ago.

Rand took a bite and his eyes widened. "There's meat in this."

"In half." Would he be pleased?

"I thought you refused to even touch meat."

"I managed." Ariel stifled a shudder as she recalled handling the raw substance that had once been a living creature. As long as she didn't think about its source, she had been okay. "Do you like it?"

"It's pretty good." He resumed eating and she released her pent-up breath.

Though Rand hadn't complained about her cooking, Ariel had noticed he enjoyed his meat when they ordered in. To modify the recipe had been a small thing.

Ariel picked at her serving, needing to speak but uncertain how to begin. "I've been thinking about what you said," she said softly.

Rand quit eating and interest flared in his eyes. "And?"

"You could come to the magical realm with me after the baby is born." She couldn't believe she was saying this, yet having Rand with her held a certain appeal. "Because time is different there, you'll live much longer."

"You're asking me to live with you?" He sounded stunned.

Ariel hesitated, then nodded. "Then you'll be there for the baby."

"I thought humans weren't welcome in your land."

True enough, but they had stumbled in sporadically throughout the centuries and weren't always sent away. "I am not exactly welcome myself." A truth that pained her. "But the realm is immense. We can find a place to live. My magic will return once the baby is born so we will want for nothing."

In fact, the more she thought about it, the more she liked this idea. Rand knew so much more about children than she did and the thought of making love to him often sent a warm flush through her.

He, however, didn't appear as pleased. "I'd have to give up my house, my work, my family?"

"You could visit from time to time." Ariel frowned. "Though that might not be wise as they will have aged while you will remain much the same."

"I can't leave my family." The decisive tone in Rand's voice sent Ariel's hopes plummeting. "They need me."

While no one needed her. Not the Fae. Not the mortals. Only the life inside her would need her.

"And I cannot live here without my magic."

"Why not? You're doing it now." Rand's gaze held hers. "Has it been so bad?"

At first, yes, but now . . . She was becoming adept at living as a mortal, though it still terrified her . . . and pleased her. Their existence was much more complex than she had suspected, and, in many ways, more rewarding.

But to live without her magic . . . ? Ariel shivered. No, she couldn't do that.

"It's been tolerable," she said. "But nothing I want to do for a lengthy period of time."

"Then we're at a stalemate." The resignation in his voice echoed her feelings.

Was there no solution to this problem?

"We could share the baby," he said slowly. "I'll keep it for a while in my world, then you have it for a while in yours."

To be without her baby for any time was unacceptable. Besides, Rand would lose out considerably. "You forget, six months in my world would be years in yours."

"Damn." Rand pushed his plate away and stood. "There has to be a way."

He refused to live in her world. She refused to live in his. Ariel saw no other answer.

She rose, then froze, her senses tingling. "Someone is outside."

Rand headed for the front door and she shook her head. "No, watching us." She struggled to understand the warning sensation. "There." She pointed toward a window just in time to see a movement outside it.

"I'll get him." Rand ran for the door.

"He'll be gone. I can find out who it is." A simple
seeking spell would provide the information she needed.
*"Magic seek, magic search, magic find. Bring the answer
I seek to my mind."*

The spell worked. She felt the power surge from her
into the outer world.

Rand froze in the entryway. "Is that a good thing to
do?"

"It's a very simple spell. There's nothing to it. What
can go wrong?" She waited, expecting a face or a name.

Instead, she heard barking outside the house. Ariel
looked at Rand in surprise and he opened the door a crack,
then closed it again, shaking his head.

Laughter filled his voice. "Ariel, you've managed to
call every dog in the neighborhood."

"What?" She joined him and peeked outside. Indeed,
the front yard contained several barking dogs with more
running to join them. "That's not supposed to happen."

Rand wrapped his arms around her even as he laughed.
"With you around, nothing happens as expected."

"But . . . but . . ." She had sent out a simple spell, an
elementary spell, one so basic it required practically no
magic at all. How could it go so wrong? Had her magic
truly deteriorated *that* much?

"It's okay." Rand placed a gentle kiss on the top of her
head. "Whoever was out there is definitely gone by now."

"But who was it?" The thought of someone spying on
them sent a chill along her spine.

"Good question." Rand tightened his hold even as he
frowned. "I don't like it. What was this person expecting
to see?" He leaned back to meet her gaze. "Magic?"

Ariel's heart skipped a beat. "But who could know?
I've hardly gone anywhere." Except to the mall. She
blanched. "I cried at the mall."

"Oh, Lord." Rand released her and hurried to bolt the
door and close all the drapes. "If someone saw you . . ."

"But no one did. They were all doing other things."
Reading papers, taking care of children, eating meals. If

someone had seen her tears, surely she would have noticed their reaction.

"I hope you're right." Rand stood in the middle of the room, alert, tense. "Otherwise we could be in for a world of trouble."

Ariel's stomach churned. Always before, when confronted with mortal knowledge of who she was, she'd relied on her magic or could return to the magical realm. Now she had neither of those options.

For the first time in her existence, she was defenseless.

After dressing the next morning, Ariel eyed her belly dubiously. It had swelled even larger—something she hadn't thought possible. The baby nestled beneath her ribs, making it difficult to draw a deep breath, and she could barely stand erect.

How could mortal women do this over and over again?

As if in response, the baby moved within her and Ariel smiled. That was why. Creating a new life came from a magic more powerful than anything among the Fae.

She descended the stairs to the smell of toast. Rand smiled at her over his shoulder as she entered the kitchen.

"Two eggs over easy, right?" he asked, even as he cracked the eggs into a pan.

Within minutes, he produced a plate containing the eggs and toast. Ariel accepted it eagerly, her stomach rumbling. "Thank you." She settled at the small table in the kitchen to eat.

Rand pulled out the opposite chair. "Will you be all right if I run over to Tammy's for a while?"

"Of course." Seeing the worry in his eyes, she smiled. "I'll keep the door locked."

"Good. I wouldn't go if Tam hadn't said it was important. Her garbage disposal managed to clog up again and she tried to fix it on her own." Rand sighed. "I showed Malcolm how to clean it out last time she did this, but I guess he's at work. Anyhow, she broke the pipe and made an even bigger mess."

"She's lucky to have you." In just the short time she'd been here, Ariel realized how much his sisters depended on Rand. At least one called every day, not always with work for their brother, but checking on him.

"Yeah, lucky." Rand stood with a dry smile. "Not every family has a built-in fix-it man." He paused by the kitchen doorway. "I shouldn't be long. An hour at the most."

"I'll be here." Where else was she going to go?

After he left, Ariel cleaned up the kitchen. Though Rand complained about assisting his sisters, he had still chosen them over her. They needed him, so he stayed.

They were family.

She'd never completely understood all that word meant until meeting Rand's sisters and mother. The love and understanding that wove them together was beyond anything in the magical realm.

Love.

Ariel paused. That emotion held no place in her world, yet the more she knew of it, the more she respected it, admired it. Watching the soap operas on television, she realized how important the mortals viewed this feeling.

Could she love like that? With a fierceness that filled her life? Would she love her child?

She cared about it. She needed it, almost as much as it would need her.

But something was missing.

Was it this elusive, powerful human love?

A knock at the door jerked her from her musings and she approached it hesitantly. Should she answer it?

"Ariel?" She'd heard the voice before. "It's Lizzie."

Ah, Rand's sister. Well, Ariel no longer had a reason to hide from his family now that his mother knew about her. Ariel opened the door to see Lizzie standing on the doorstep. "You just missed Rand."

"I know. I waited for him to leave. Tammy called him on purpose." Her grin held a hint of mischief. "I need you to come with me."

"Why?" Why would Rand's sisters lure him away? Ariel studied Lizzie, but found only a warm smile.

"It's a secret." Lizzie grinned, mischief dancing in her eyes.

Ariel hesitated, torn between discovering the secret or staying put. "I told Rand I'd stay here."

"Leave him a note. He won't worry if you're with me."

True enough. Rand trusted all his sisters. And Ariel's curiosity insisted she had to know about the secret. "Give me a moment then." Ariel scrawled a note and left it by the doorway, then slipped into her coat and followed Lizzie to her car.

Oddly enough, the metal beast didn't create the same aches Ariel usually experienced. Well, it was a small vehicle. Perhaps it didn't contain as much metal.

"How's Sequoia?" she asked as Lizzie set the car into motion. She wouldn't mind more time cuddling the infant.

"She's fine. She'll be there when we arrive."

"Where are we going?" Why was Lizzie being so mysterious?

"To Mom's house. She's having a family meeting."

"And I'm part of the family?" That thought warmed Ariel.

Lizzie sent her an amused smile. "You will be if Mom has her way."

"What does that mean?" Ariel's sense of unease grew. Maybe she shouldn't have come so willingly.

"We're all uniting around a common subject." Lizzie stopped at a red light and turned to look at Ariel. "You."

Fourteen

~

"Me?" Butterflies of trepidation danced in Ariel's belly. Meg had been angry with her the other night. Did she mean to cause Ariel harm?

No, Ariel couldn't believe that. The woman exuded caring.

"About what?" she asked.

"You and Rand." Lizzie aimed a significant glance at Ariel's belly. "And the baby."

"I think that's something for Rand and me to decide." Ariel had the unnerving sense of being led to her doom. Was this what family did? Interfered with another's life?

"Sorry, not with a baby involved." Lizzie sent Ariel a piercing look. "You don't mess with the Thayers and children. We take that personally."

"It's *my* baby." That was all she wanted—a child of her own.

"And Rand's. That makes it a Thayer."

Ariel shook her head. Though Lizzie's tone was friendly, it was also firm. What did this family intend to do? "You can't have my baby."

Lizzie didn't reply. Instead she pulled to a stop before Meg's house. "We're here. Come on."

Ariel thought about remaining in the car. They couldn't force her to do anything.

Lizzie opened the passenger door, a twinkle in her eyes. "Afraid?"

The Fae feared nothing. Ariel climbed out and met Lizzie's gaze in defiance. "Should I be?"

Rand's sister grinned. "I can tell you haven't dealt with Mom before." She linked her arm through Ariel's. "Don't worry. She'll feed you before she attacks."

That thought didn't provide any comfort.

Ariel preceded Lizzie inside, then froze as nine sets of eyes focused on her. All of Rand's sisters except Stephanie sat in the living room. Ariel's throat closed. She wasn't afraid. No, it was simply caution.

"Everyone here?" Lizzie asked as she closed the door behind her.

"All but Stephanie. I asked Dean to get her." Meg came to greet them. "Since the school doesn't have classes today, I believe she's home."

Meg motioned toward an empty chair. "Come, have a seat, Ariel. Would you like some tea, a homemade cinnamon roll?"

Ariel sank into the chair gratefully, uncertain if her wobbly knees would hold her much longer, and resisted the urge to squirm beneath the steady gazes of Rand's sisters. As she realized Meg was waiting for her answer, she recalled Lizzie's words. If Ariel didn't eat, would she be spared an inquisition?

Probably not. Besides, the smell of the cinnamon rolls made her mouth water even after a big breakfast. "I would love a roll, thank you," she said.

Meg vanished into the kitchen and Ariel studied each of the sisters. She'd met them all on Halloween and they'd all been friendly. Now they looked at her with a variety of expressions—from amusement to interest to anger.

A sense of dread filled her chest, adding to her discomfort. Perhaps she didn't want the cinnamon roll after all.

But Meg handed it to her on a small plate, along with a steaming cup of herbal tea. "Eat up," she said, her smile tight. "Once Stephanie gets here, we can begin."

Ariel could only stare.

She didn't need magic to know this was going to be bad. Very bad.

"Yes, I have the day off, but that doesn't mean I don't have things to do." Stephanie faced Bob across her small living room. "I have papers to check and assignments to prepare." She'd just seen him two nights ago. Surely he could wait until the weekend to arrange another date.

"We don't have to do much." He gave her a beguiling smile that added to his good looks. "Maybe we could hang out with your brother."

"Rand?" Where had Bob gotten that idea?

"Sure. I really liked him."

Stephanie wasn't so sure that feeling was mutual. Besides, she didn't want to endanger Ariel. Though she resented Dean's interference, he'd had a point. Ariel was too unpredictable for casual company.

"I'm sure Rand and Ariel prefer to be alone right now," she said firmly. "The baby's due soon, you know."

"Is it? When exactly?"

Good question. "Around the end of the week, I think." With Ariel, anything could happen.

"I see." Bob remained silent for several moments, then he smiled again. "Fine, we can just hang out here."

"Bob, I appreciate that you want to be with me, but I honestly have work to do. It'll be boring for you and frustrating for me to work with you around." Togetherness was one thing. Too much togetherness was another. "We can do something on Friday. How's that?"

"That will have to do." Bob cupped her chin in his hand. "I miss you when you're not around."

"I'm usually not far." Why couldn't she summon up

the same enthusiasm for him? She was actually getting so she liked the time she had away from him.

"Fine." He dropped his hand and headed for the door. "I'll call you later, okay?"

"Okay." She'd probably still be working. With the holidays approaching, she had tons of lessons to prepare.

Bob stepped out onto the porch, then turned back to face her. "I'll miss you." He drew her into his arms for a lingering kiss.

He was a good kisser. Steph had to admit that. So, why didn't she feel even the tiniest bit of tingle when he did so? As soon as he raised his head, she eased out of his arms. "I'll talk to you later."

He headed for his car and she watched him go, torn by her conflicting emotions. Bob was a nice guy, good-looking, and obviously interested in her, but this wasn't going to go anywhere. She knew that already. There was no spark, no passion.

Yet it was nice to have a man see her as an attractive woman for a change. She certainly never got that from Dean.

"Nice show." Dean appeared on the porch and she jumped. "Do you sell tickets?"

Heat rose in her cheeks against her will. "What are you doing here?"

"Your mom sent me to get you. Something about an important family meeting." He came to face her, his eyes and expression dark.

"Why didn't she just call?" Steph struggled to keep her voice even despite the fluttering of her pulse.

"Apparently, your phone's not working."

"It's not?" She turned inside, sensing Dean as he followed her. "It worked last night." She picked up the receiver only to hear nothing. Even after she jiggled the button, the silence remained. "Well, darn. I wonder if it's just my phone or the entire building."

Dean shrugged. "You can call it in from your mom's. She's waiting on you."

"Fine. Thanks for delivering the message." His abrupt appearance had set her nerves on edge. "I can get there on my own."

"Nope. I need to ensure you make it."

"Mom told you that?"

His gaze flickered. "Yep."

Unusual. Didn't her mother trust her to show up? Though Stephanie had a lot of work, a family meeting was not an everyday occurrence. It usually meant something important had happened . . . or was about to happen.

"Let me get my coat." She pulled it on and followed him outside. "Why didn't Mom send one of my sisters?" Anyone but Dean.

"I live closest and she knew I'd be leaving for work about now." Dean wrapped his hand around her arm, startling Stephanie. She could feel the warmth of his fingers even through her down jacket. "I'll drop you off and one of your sisters can bring you back."

"That's not necessary. My car's working fine now."

He hesitated in the parking lot, his expression unreadable. "It is necessary." He led her to his BMW and settled her in the passenger seat.

Stephanie forced herself to relax. Fine, she'd ride with him. She loved this car, though she'd only ridden in it twice before, and then always with Rand along.

"Thanks for coming to tell me," she said as he slid into his seat and started the car.

"Not a problem." He waited until he entered the heavy morning traffic before he spoke again. "Did he stay the night?"

"What?" His change of subject left her confused.

"Bob was just leaving your apartment. Did he stay the night?"

"That's none of your business." Yet she couldn't keep the warmth from surging to her cheeks again.

"Yes, it is. I consider myself a friend of the family and that guy is going to hurt you, Steph." Dean sent her a glance that made her heart skip a beat.

"I think I can take care of myself." She'd handled men before.

"Can you?" Dean asked softly.

Blast him, why did she let him under her skin? He made her feel guilty, like a child, when she hadn't even done anything. "All right, fine. No, he didn't stay the night. He's not done anything more than kiss me."

"I give it a three."

"Excuse me?" What *was* he talking about?

"Your little kiss with the jerk. A three. Tops."

Stephanie gaped at him. He was rating her kiss? "Out of what?"

"Ten."

"A three out of ten?" What gave Dean the right to make that kind of call? Even if he was mostly right.

"Yep, no passion, no touching. You could've been kissing your brother good-bye."

"I doubt that." A kiss for Rand would probably have more enthusiasm even if only on his cheek. "Besides, we were in a hurry. I had work to do."

"Even that monkey man you dated a couple years ago kissed better than that."

"Monty?" Steph could barely remember him. She had liked him, but, again, never found any passion for the man. "How would you know?"

"I can tell. I'm a connoisseur, you know."

He had to be kidding, but when Steph looked at him, he wasn't smiling. "Oh, right," she said. "Like you're the best kisser on the planet. Do you think all your kisses are tens?"

He shot her an enigmatic glance. "You tell me."

"I wouldn't know." She wasn't going to give him the satisfaction of admitting no kiss had lived up to his.

"I kissed you once." A strange note entered his voice.

"Did you?" She stared out the window. "I don't remember." As if she'd ever forget.

"On your sixteenth birthday."

"Oh, that." She waved a dismissive hand. "That was so

long ago, I'd forgotten." Or wished she could forget. Then maybe she wouldn't continue to compare every man she met to him.

Dean didn't respond until he stopped before her mother's house. Several of her sister's cars were already parked there. Before she could open the door, he came around and pulled it open.

She stood only to find herself trapped against the car as he placed an arm on either side of her. "What are you doing?" Her pulse leaped into overdrive.

"Refreshing your memory."

Before she could react, he kissed her, his lips as firm and possessive as she remembered. He cajoled, he teased, he sent fireworks throughout her system. Stephanie responded, softening beneath his mouth, and wrapped her arms around his neck.

He enfolded her in his grasp, holding her so close she wasn't sure where he ended and she began. Even her fantasies hadn't been this wonderful.

Her blood heated to boiling as her breasts swelled against his firm chest. Still he claimed her mouth as if branding her. And she let him. More than that, she gave as good as she received, her pulse hammering in her ears, her head spinning. Was this all another dream?

Abruptly he released her and stood back, his breathing as unsteady as hers. Stephanie could only stare at him. What had just happened here?

"Now rate that," he said finally.

She flinched, then brushed past him toward the house, unwilling to let him see the tears welling. Blast him. Once again, he'd shown her a slice of heaven and taken it away.

"Stephanie," he called after her, but she ignored him, almost running to get inside the house where she could safely slam the door to shut him out.

Everyone in the room turned to look at her, but Stephanie centered on one especially stricken gaze. Ariel.

Stephanie surveyed the room. They were all here. Every sister. Only Rand was missing.

Merciful Mother, what was going on? And how did it involve Ariel?

"Have a seat, Stephanie." Meg remained standing as Stephanie complied, adding to Ariel's nervousness. Though Steph had given her a look of sympathy, no one else had shown much support.

Her cinnamon roll remained uneaten on her plate. Despite the wonderful aroma, Ariel's throat was too tight to allow a bite to pass through.

"Now we can begin." Meg turned to face Ariel. "Ariel, dear, don't look so frightened. I just want to understand this situation better."

"I explained as best I could." She didn't dare tell them the truth.

"I'm sure you did, but I still have some questions and Rand's sisters deserve to know about this, too." Though Meg's tone held kindness, the determined glitter in her eyes told Ariel she had plans.

"Deserve to know what?" Stephanie asked.

"That Ariel intends to leave once her baby—*Rand's* baby—is born and take the child with her."

Several sisters broke out in protest and Ariel exchanged glances with Stephanie, who returned a dry smile. "I explained it already," Ariel said. "My life is too different from Rand's. We can't make a life together."

"You're living together now, aren't you?" Louise asked gently.

"Yes, but—"

"Don't you like Rand?" another sister asked.

"Of course I like him." She wouldn't have invited him to the magical realm if she didn't.

"Then what's wrong with him?"

"Why do you have to go away?"

"Have you tried counseling?"

The questions flew at her faster than she could answer them. Ariel hesitated before each answer, choosing her words carefully. "Nothing's wrong with Rand. He's wonderful." He was all she'd hoped he'd be and so much more.

Why wasn't he here now? He'd know how to defend her.

"Why do you want to leave him?" Lizzie asked.

"I don't want to leave Rand." Ariel froze as the words emerged from her mouth. In truth, she *didn't* want to leave him. She'd come to care for him as much as she could care about anyone. "But my world and his are too different."

"World?" Kathleen sent her a puzzled look. "You make it sound like you're from another planet."

"No." Not another planet, another realm.

Meg pulled a chair up beside Ariel and settled onto it. "I understand. Things are different here from your home and that frightens you."

"Yes." Exactly. Finally, someone who understood.

"And now, with the baby coming, it's even more confusing. I have no doubt you're the type of woman who will be a good mother and believes in the family unit."

Ariel blinked. Family unit?

"A child needs a mother and father, don't you agree?"

"I—" Her experience with this was nonexistent. What could she say?

"A stable home," Meg continued. "A loving relationship."

Ariel remained silent. From watching soap operas, she knew those things were difficult to attain.

"I'm sure you know Rand is a good man."

"Oh, yes." That she could answer truthfully.

"And he'll be a supportive, loving father."

"Yes." Ariel never doubted that.

"And you probably think marriage is merely a formality to solidify the relationship you already have." Meg patted Ariel's hand, her smile containing honest warmth for the first time that morning. "I'm sure this is all just a misunderstanding on all our parts and you really do intend to do the right thing."

"I'm trying—"

"Excellent." Meg enveloped Ariel in a hug. "You're under enough stress right now. Why don't you let us take care of all the arrangements?"

"Arrangements?" Somewhere along the way, Ariel had lost track of this conversation, but Meg's hug still felt good.

"Don't worry about a thing. We can handle it." Meg stood and surveyed her daughters. "Can't we, girls?"

A variety of affirmatives answered her. Immediately, Ariel found herself hugged by first one, then another sister. She didn't understand it, but she wasn't about to complain. This was much preferred to what she'd expected.

When Stephanie reached her, she clung to Ariel for a moment longer. "Are you certain about this?"

"About what?"

Before Stephanie could answer, Lizzie took her place, her hug enthusiastic. "I knew it would work out," she exclaimed.

What solution did they see that Ariel had been unable to find? "I hope so." Family was important. She saw Rand's side of things better now. His family cared about him. They created a tight-knit group and had brought her into it.

For a moment tears threatened, but Ariel blinked them back. No tears. Not here.

Even as Queen of the Pillywiggins, she'd never felt like she belonged, not like this family made her feel. They welcomed her, accepted her, despite her determination to make a life for herself and her baby. Ariel hadn't expected that.

"There's more coffee and cinnamon rolls in the kitchen," Meg announced. "Then we can start planning."

Planning? For the baby's birth, no doubt.

Ariel accepted a fresh cinnamon roll and devoured this one easily, her tension gone. Everyone was treating her as warmly as on Halloween night.

Kathleen paused beside her. "I didn't realize you were

so far along. Your costume hid it well on Halloween."

"I—" Ariel swallowed hard. "Yes, it did." Though she hadn't had nearly as much to hide at that point.

"I'm so glad Rand found you." Kathleen dropped her voice. "I didn't think he would ever settle down."

How to respond to that? "Thank you."

"So when is the baby due?"

"Around the end of this week."

"The end of this week?" Kathleen's head snapped up. "Mom, she's due at the end of the week."

"Then we mustn't waste any time." Meg grabbed a tablet and pen and resumed her seat. "How old are you, Ariel? We should know that, at least."

Ariel hesitated. She couldn't answer that. She simply didn't know. She'd always existed. The years were too many to count.

"She's twenty-five, my age," Stephanie said quickly from where she stood by the staircase.

Ariel shot her a grateful look. Apparently that satisfied everyone.

"And your favorite color?"

Ariel paused. Why did that matter? "I like them all." How could a person choose one color out of the myriad of nature? The rainbows, the flowers, the mountains. Each offered a special beauty.

"Well, if you had to pick," Allison, one of the twins, added.

"Yellow and green," Ariel said. The color of her buttercups.

"Fine. Fine." Meg scribbled on the tablet as she nodded. "Any family or friends we should know about?"

Family? What was Meg planning? "No, there is no one." The pillywiggins had not fought for her when Titania dismissed her. In fact, Ariel couldn't think of anyone in the magical realm who would even miss her.

"Oh, that's terrible," Lizzie said. She hurried to give Ariel another hug. "Well, you have a family now."

Ariel's chest tightened. A family. People who cared

about her. Who *needed* her. Could it be true?

The other twin, Amanda, spoke up. "She'll need a shower."

A shower? Ariel drew back startled. She had showered that morning.

"A baby shower first, I think," Meg replied, still writing on her pad of paper. "What do you have for the baby already?"

Have? What did a baby require? "I . . . nothing."

"Nothing?" Meg's tone implied Ariel had done something wrong. "We'll definitely have to hold a baby shower then."

Ariel only nodded, not completely certain of Meg's meaning. The baby had no need of anything. Once Ariel's magic returned to normal, she could supply anything they needed.

"Hmm." Meg stared at what she'd written, tapping her pen against the pad. "The license will determine the when of it. Tammy, I want you to look into that this afternoon."

"Yes, Mom."

"Louise, check with Father David about his availability."

"Yes, Mom."

As Meg issued orders to her daughters, they dissolved into chatter, sentences overlapping each other until Ariel was completely confused. What was going on?

"Ariel?"

She looked up to see Stephanie beckoning her toward the steps. When Ariel reached her, Stephanie took her arm and pulled her upstairs to an empty bedroom.

"What is it?" Ariel asked. Stephanie's alarm was palpable. Had Ariel done something wrong?

"Do you know what's going on down there?"

"Your family is planning something. Another party, perhaps?"

Stephanie rolled her eyes. "I knew you didn't understand. It's worse than that, Ariel. Mom bamboozled you."

"Bamboozled?"

"Conned you. Tricked you." Stephanie shook her head. "Ariel, listen to me carefully." She sighed. "They're arranging your wedding. To Rand."

Fifteen

~

"Wedding?" Ariel hesitated. No wonder she'd been confused. Now Meg's words made sense—in a mixed-up, mortal kind of way. "But I'm not marrying Rand."

Though she had to admit the thought didn't bother her as much as it once had. To spend more time with Rand . . . to lie in his arms . . .

"Well, Mom and company think you are." Stephanie gave her a wry smile. "Don't feel bad. Few people have been able to escape Mom when she sets her mind on something."

Ariel turned toward the hallway. "I have to tell them to stop." She couldn't allow them to believe in something that wouldn't happen.

"It's too late." Stephanie touched her arm in a warm gesture. "She's not going to hear anything but what she wants to hear."

"But I can't—"

Stephanie studied Ariel, her gaze appearing to look deep inside. "Would it be so bad to marry Rand?"

"No." That wasn't the point. To marry Rand, to remain

in the mortal world, meant giving up so much. Ariel might be a banished faery, but she was still a faery. "But I can't stay here."

"Is your world so great?"

That made Ariel pause. Not so long ago, her answer would've been an immediate yes; but, after spending time in this realm, becoming friends with Stephanie, meeting the Thayer family, learning to survive, she'd discovered this life wasn't as horrible as she once believed. Living here was different—challenging. It was dark in some ways, yet bright in others. Still, this world wasn't the magical realm.

"It's my home," she said finally.

Stephanie sighed. "I can't argue with that." She gave Ariel a quick hug, sending a warm rush of emotion through Ariel. "Come on. Let's get you out of here."

Ariel nodded. She was all for that. As much as she enjoyed Rand's family, they could be overwhelming. She grinned. She should invite his family to Titania's court. Now that would be a sight to see—the imperial Titania and the family-oriented Meg. If not for her magic, Titania wouldn't stand a chance.

"Hey, Ariel and I need rides home," Stephanie announced as they rejoined the chattering crowd in the living room.

"I'll take you," Lizzie said.

As Ariel donned her coat, Meg embraced her. "Don't worry about anything now, dear. We have it under control."

"Meg . . ." Ariel swallowed the words that would shatter the woman's radiant smile. "Thank you."

During the ride to Rand's house, Ariel replayed the hectic scene in the Thayer home. Would Meg be so quick to accept Ariel if she knew the truth of her origins? Recalling the woman's warm acceptance of her at Halloween, Ariel had to believe Meg would. A faery queen stripped of her crown would be just as welcome as a normal woman . . . provided she was good enough for Rand.

Good enough.

Ariel propped her chin in her hand and leaned her elbow against the doorframe. Though she'd learned to cook, she still wasn't what Rand wanted. He wanted a woman-free, child-free existence—a boring life. His proposal had been nothing more than a way to fulfill his sense of responsibility for the baby. It had nothing to do with how he felt about her.

And that mattered. A heavy weight settled in Ariel's chest. To her surprise, it mattered a lot.

What was happening to her?

Rand ran out to greet her as soon as Lizzie pulled into the driveway. The worry on his face added an extra beat to her heart.

"I'm fine," she said the moment she stepped out of the car.

"I thought maybe the baby had decided to come." The huskiness of his voice touched something deep inside her.

Ariel gave him a warm smile. "Not yet." She glanced down at her burgeoning belly. And it couldn't come soon enough. She was tired of being round. How did mortals do this for a full nine months?

As they met, he wrapped his arm around her shoulders. "Where did you go?"

"Lizzie had something to show me." Ariel waved farewell to Lizzie and Stephanie as they left. Thank the Stones. Ariel didn't need him talking to them right now.

To tell him of his mother's plans would only give him hope where there was none. Ariel would still leave. Nothing had changed that, no matter what Meg planned.

An all-too-familiar guilt seeped through Ariel's veins. She didn't want to deceive Meg and her family, yet Ariel had been . . . bamboozled, as Stephanie put it. The wedding wasn't Ariel's decision, it was Meg's. But telling herself that didn't make the uncomfortable, achy feeling disappear.

Once inside, Rand hung up Ariel's coat, then returned to cup her face in his hands. As she stared at him, her throat tightened. Somehow he'd become even more handsome. Perhaps because she now saw even deeper than his outward appearance.

"Are you sure you're all right?" he asked. "You look pale."

"Do I?" A confrontation with his family could do that. "Just tired, I guess." Which was true. Lately the weariness had become constant.

Brown eyes dark, he stroked his broad thumb over her cheeks, and Ariel softened and swayed toward him. Would she never cease wanting this man? He only had to touch her and her body responded.

She leaned closer, lifting her lips for his kiss. Instead of placing his lips on hers, Rand dropped his hands. Ariel stared at him, aware of her intense disappointment. Though the fire still flickered in his gaze, his fists coiled at his side and a muscle jumped in his jaw.

With a sigh, she turned away. He might want her physically, but he wasn't willing to share anything more with her.

And oddly enough, she wanted more.

Their first and only joining had been beyond her expectations—a passionate sense of belonging she'd never experienced before. What would it be like with emotions involved? With love?

She shook her head. *Enough of that, Ariel.* She was starting to think like a mortal, too.

"Kate Goodfellow called," Rand said, following her.

She turned to glance at him. Kate? Oh, Robin's wife. "Yes?"

"I guess Steph mentioned to her what a rough time you've had lately. She invited us for dinner tomorrow night."

Dinner with Kate . . . and Robin? Ariel smiled. Robin had lived among mortals for his entire life. He would have the answers to her questions, to these strange feelings affecting her. "I'd like that."

"Good." Rand gave her a sheepish grin. "I already told her we'd be there."

Ariel cocked her head. "What if I hadn't wanted to go?" She kept her tone light so he would know she was teasing.

"Then you'd miss a great meal." Mischief twinkled in his eyes. "One you didn't have to cook."

Ariel laughed. "How can I resist that?" As she looked at him, his face alight with good humor, her chest grew tight.

More importantly, how could she resist him?

Kate greeted Ariel and Rand at the door of the Victorian house, her smile welcoming. "It's good to see you again."

"And you." Ariel couldn't help but return the greeting. Kate's happiness flowed off her in steady ripples like the mystical stream through the magical realm. "How is Brandon?"

"Growing by the day." Kate motioned them forward. "He's in the living room with Robin."

Ariel's gaze went to Robin as she entered the room. Though now completely mortal, he still possessed a presence that would make even a blind woman notice him. It wasn't so much his appearance, though that was devastating enough—handsome even by Fae standards with black hair and dark eyes and a smile that could send pixies into a swoon—Robin radiated charm and overwhelming maleness.

"Ariel." Robin came to greet her, his infant son in his arms. "You're still as beautiful as ever."

"Even pregnant?" she asked. How could anyone overlook that?

"Especially pregnant." Warmth lingered in his gaze, then grew more heated as he looked toward Kate. "I hadn't thought Kate could be more lovely until she was carrying Brandon. She was extraordinary."

Heat warmed Ariel's cheeks as Robin and Kate exchanged glances. The passion between them simmered like a physical force. Suddenly, Ariel wanted to experience something like that. Only the night she'd shared with Rand had come close.

Turning toward Rand, she found him watching her closely, his expression unreadable. Did Robin and Kate's display of emotion bother him? Or did it stir him to seek something more, as it did Ariel?

Robin passed the baby to Kate, then faced them. "Can I get you something to drink? Coffee, juice, Coke?"

"Coke for me," Rand said.

"Juice," Ariel answered. She'd tried Coke once and didn't like the giddy feeling it gave her.

"Be right back." They sat while he disappeared into another room, then reappeared with a tray of glasses. "How are the pillywiggins doing?" he asked as he handed Ariel her drink.

She started. He didn't know. Of course, he wouldn't know. He'd been trapped in a portrait by Titania during the time when Ariel lost her position. "I don't know." Her voice dropped low, pain filling her afresh at that admittance. Would she ever be among the pillywiggins again?

"Don't know?" Robin's expression was puzzled. "But you're their queen."

"Not any longer." A waver entered Ariel's voice despite her attempt to contain it. Admitting this to Robin, who had known her as queen, reopened her barely healed wound. "Titania banished me from her court."

"Banished you? But why?" Robin looked toward Rand. "Did you know this?"

Rand nodded. "She told me that when she first admitted she was Fae."

"Why didn't you mention it when we talked?"

"I didn't think it was important," Rand admitted.

"Of course it's important. Ariel has been the pillywiggins' queen since the dawn of time." Robin knelt in front of Ariel, the concern on his face warming her. "What happened?

Ariel forced a wan smile. "I . . . ah . . . said something I shouldn't have and Titania took offense." She couldn't tell Robin she'd been defending him. Even knowing the ultimate outcome, she would do the same again. He hadn't deserved Titania's harsh treatment. Thank the Stones he had managed to find happiness despite the Fae queen's hatred of him.

"What could you have said to offend Titania that deeply? True, it doesn't take much, but to remove you as queen . . ."

Ariel refused to meet his inquiring gaze. Even as a mortal, Robin was too perceptive.

He stiffened and rose slowly to his feet. "You were one of my few friends in the realm. Did you come to my defense?"

Ariel hesitated as Kate came to Robin's side and touched his shoulder, her face solemn. "I . . ." Ariel swallowed and started over. "I told her what she'd done was wrong. Titania's spell trapped your essence in your portrait for eternity. You didn't deserve that."

"It *was* wrong," Kate said, a fierceness in her voice that startled Ariel.

"I agree, it was wrong, but Titania wouldn't have wanted to hear that." Robin placed his hand over his wife's, then gave Ariel a sad smile. "I'm sorry."

She raised her shoulder in a mortal shrug. What was done could not be undone. "I'll survive." Once the baby came, she wouldn't be alone in the realm any longer.

Robin didn't respond, but Ariel sensed he wanted to. What more could he say? The fault had been hers entirely for speaking so boldly to the easily irritated Queen of the Fae.

Kate squeezed Robin's shoulder. "I think the baby's finally asleep. Will you put Brandon to bed while I get dinner on the table?"

"Gladly." Robin's smile brightened at once as he accepted the child. He paused only to shoot Ariel and Rand a quick smile. "Excuse me. I'll be right back."

Kate headed for the other room. "Make yourselves comfortable. It won't be long."

Ariel rose to her feet. "Can I help?" Her emotions were too stirred to remain still.

"No need. There's not much left to do." Kate left and Ariel stared at the doorway, feeling suddenly bereft. Robin's concern had brought back the full impact of her dismissal—the sharp pain, the sudden shock, the overwhelming loss, and utter loneliness.

She jumped when Rand stepped behind her and enveloped her in his arms. "I'm sorry," he murmured against her ear.

"Sorry?" She twisted to look up at him over her shoulder. "For what?"

"I didn't realize until this moment how awful it must've been to lose your position like that. You never said much about it."

His caring was her undoing. A tear slid from her eye to trace a path down her cheek, then landed on the carpet where it eventually formed a tiny opal. "There was nothing to say." Tears clogged her throat.

Rand gently turned her to face him. "If I hadn't been so distrustful, so unbelieving, you might've trusted me enough to tell me more."

Ariel buried her face against his chest, reassured by the rhythmic beat of his heart, the strength of his arms around her. "I'm alone," she murmured, the words escaping without thought. "So totally alone. No one needs me anymore."

"Surely you have friends . . ."

"We don't have emotions as intense as you do." Ariel dared to look up and meet his steady gaze. "Friendship is fleeting at best. No one demanded that I stay as queen."

"Then they're all fools," he said softly.

More tears escaped. "That's why I need this baby, Rand. Don't you see? It's all I have left."

He stilled, but kept holding her. "Dear God, Ariel . . ." A raw note colored his voice.

"I'm back."

At Robin's pronouncement, Rand released Ariel and

she swiped quickly at her face to erase the telltale tracks. Robin hesitated in the doorway, his gaze lingering on them, then dropping to the scattering of opals on the floor.

"Faery tears become opals?" He bent to scoop them up and examined them in his palm. "I didn't know that."

"That's because faeries don't cry." Ariel tried to smile. "Unless they're pregnant."

"I see." Robin handed the opals to Rand who slipped them into his pocket. "I'm afraid there's a lot about the Fae I don't know."

"That's because you've always lived among mortals," Ariel said, lightening her tone.

He grinned. "I like mortals better." Robin crossed the room to stare up at the portrait of himself that had once been his prison. "I prefer them."

"Is that you?" Rand asked, going to Robin's side.

"It was. A long time ago."

He sounded so matter-of-fact. Ariel frowned. Didn't he resent Titania trapping him in there? "Titania put a spell on Robin to imprison him in that portrait for eternity," she told Rand.

Rand blinked, looking from Robin to the portrait, then back. "How did you get out?"

Robin's smile lit the room. "Kate freed me." He turned toward the door as if he'd known she would chose that moment to emerge. "My beautiful, sweet Kate."

He crossed the room and kissed her with such tenderness that Ariel ached. Nothing in her lifetime could equal that.

Kate emerged from the kiss, her cheeks flushed. "Wow, you must be hungry. Dinner is ready."

Robin put his arm around her shoulders to lead the way. Rand followed suit, wrapping Ariel close to his side as they followed. She nestled close to him, enjoying the heat of his body, the familiar scent of his masculinity.

The meal passed quickly as they covered more mundane topics—the work Robin and Kate did at the school where Stephanie worked, Rand's handyman business, and, of course, Brandon.

"How do you know what to do?" Ariel asked. Though growing more experienced with children through Rand's nieces and nephews, she would never learn all she needed to know to be a good mother.

"Read books. I have some I can loan you," Kate replied. "And practice. I'm not perfect. Every day is a new experience."

"A new adventure," Robin added. "No one—mortal or Fae—knows everything about children. The secret is to love them."

Love again. That enigmatic, elusive mortal emotion. Would Ariel ever completely understand it?

Following an excellent dinner, they resettled in the main room, a fire burning in the fireplace. Ariel excused herself to visit the bathroom, then paused by the open door of Brandon's room on her return.

She stepped inside quietly to peer down at the slumbering infant. He had grown since she'd first seen him, but he was no less cuddly, no less needy. Oberon's grandson—a helpless mortal and perhaps stronger because of that.

Sensing someone behind her, she turned to see Robin by the doorway. He smiled as he joined her. "Thinking about your baby?"

Ariel rested a hand on her belly. "It was while admiring your son that I decided to have a baby of my own."

"To be honest I didn't know faeries could get pregnant." Robin's eyes twinkled in the dimly lit room. "I've never seen one pregnant before."

"Neither have I, but I wanted a child so badly. I had to feel needed again." She stopped abruptly. She hadn't meant to tell him that.

"I'm sorry." He paused, then continued. "I'm sorry about Titania, about your loss."

Ariel only nodded.

"But do you think a baby will suddenly make things all right?"

She jerked and met his gaze. "What?"

"There's more to having a child than just being needed, Ariel." Robin bent to lay his hand on Brandon's back. "And I don't know that I can explain it."

"It's complicated," she said, understanding his difficulty. So much in this world was. She watched him, so comfortable with himself, with this realm, as he straightened the blankets around his son. "How do you survive here?"

"The life is harder," he admitted. "To exist as a human requires work, but I find it more rewarding as well. People here are more honest in their feelings than among the Fae. And they feel so much more intensely—for good or bad."

Ariel agreed with that. Though she'd had a familiarity with most emotions, she'd never experienced them much herself until her extended visit here. "Do you regret giving up your magic, your immortality?"

He faced her, his expression solemn but the light in his eyes bright. "Not for a moment. I have Kate, I have Brandon. I have a job I enjoy. Friends. I wouldn't change it for any amount of magic."

"But why?" What could make someone give up that essential part of his being?

"I love Kate. I want to be with her more than I want anything else."

"I don't understand this human love." So much revolved around it—couples, families, lives. This single emotion held as much power as all the magic in the realm.

"That's difficult to explain." Robin grinned. "I had thought I couldn't love, but then I met Kate and that made all the difference. I'm incomplete without her."

"But what does it *feel* like?"

He hesitated, obviously lost in thought. "It's wonderful—a warmth that fills your entire being, a sense of belonging with another person, a wanting to be with that person all the time. It's being sad when she's sad, happy when she's happy. It's wanting to make her happy. It's wanting to touch her, to kiss her, to grow old with her, to share all the days and nights of our lives."

Ariel couldn't breathe. So much of what he said explained the unusual feelings inside her. Could she be in love with Rand?

Robin evidently misunderstood her silence. "Sorry. Don't get me started. Kate's my favorite subject." He touched Ariel's arm. "Let's rejoin the others."

As they entered the main room, Rand and Kate were laughing and Ariel focused on Rand's animated face, only to experience the all-too-familiar tightening in her chest. Did she love Rand? Did that explain the uncertainty of her feelings?

No, impossible. Robin had said love was wonderful. If anything, she experienced torment around Rand. The wanting, the needing, the guilt. That wasn't love.

This emotion came from nothing more than a forgotten faery lost in a mortal world.

"I enjoyed that," Rand said as he seated Ariel in his truck. Though she'd been quiet after returning to the living room with Robin, she'd also laughed and joked with the other couple, the first time he'd seen her so relaxed.

Of course, Robin had once been Fae—something Rand still found unbelievable. If ever a man was *not* a faery, it was Robin Goodfellow. But Robin had related to Ariel in a way Rand hadn't yet managed. Even with Robin's obvious love for his wife, Rand had had to fight back rising feelings of jealousy.

"I learned more tonight about your world than you've ever told me," he said, climbing into the driver's seat.

"Robin has only been there a couple times. His perspective is different." Ariel didn't look at him as she spoke.

He started the truck and headed for home. "Sounds to me like he prefers it here."

"Yes, he does."

Her agreement startled Rand but when he glanced at her, he found her staring out into the darkness. "What did you two talk about?" He hadn't meant to ask, but the question sneaked out. "Upstairs?"

Ariel hesitated. "Many things. Babies and ..." She trailed off. "Babies."

"Blast it, Ariel." She was keeping something from him. "Can't you talk to me? I'll understand."

"You'd try." She looked at him then. "Just as I'm trying."

"What?"

"Robin gave up everything—his magic and immortality—to be with Kate."

Ah, now he knew. "That frightens you, doesn't it?"

"I ... yes, I guess it does." Ariel pushed her hair back from her face. "Robin was only a few hundred years old, yet he'd had his magic all that time and he gave it up for love."

Something in her voice touched Rand deep inside—fear, panic, awe? "And what frightens you more—that he gave it up or that he fell in love?"

When her eyes widened, then shuttered, he realized his question had had more impact than he'd expected. "Love does not exist in my world," she murmured, returning her gaze to the outside.

"Your loss," he replied. What was a world without love? Rand grimaced. Hadn't he been avoiding that same emotion himself? No women, no entanglements. That had been his plan.

And now look where he was—knee deep in both.

What could possibly happen next?

Sixteen

~~

The answer to that question rapped on his door late the next afternoon. Opening it, he found his sister Kathleen standing there.

"What are you doing here?" The interruption had dragged him away from Ariel. He'd been showing her how to play cards, a game she'd picked up quickly. So quickly, in fact, she was kicking his butt. Maybe she had more magic left than he suspected.

Kat waved a small tablet in front of his face. "I just wanted to give you two the updates on everything."

"Updates?" On what?

"That's not necessary." Ariel spoke quickly from behind him, triggering an uneasy chill over his skin.

"Updates on what?" he repeated more firmly, not taking his eyes off his sister.

Kat glanced from Rand to Ariel, then back, her lips pressed tightly together. "Didn't Ariel tell you?"

"Tell me what?" And why did he have the sinking feeling he wasn't going to like it?

"There's nothing to tell. Good-bye, Kathleen." Ariel

brushed past him, trying to shut the door, but Rand snared her elbow.

"Tell me *what*?" he demanded. What had his well-intentioned destroyer faery done now?

Kat hesitated, then presented him with a brilliant smile. "That the two of you are getting married."

"We're getting married?" he echoed. The last he'd known, Ariel had refused him. "Do I know when?"

His sarcasm went over Kat's head. "Next week, I think. We're making all the arrangements, but it still takes some time."

"I imagine it does." He glanced at Ariel, but she refused to meet his eyes. Damned straight. What kind of trick was she playing now?

His pulse quickened. Or did she really intend to marry him?

Kat evidently sensed the rising tension for she backed away. "I think I came at a bad time. I'll talk with you two later."

"That might be a good idea." Rand had some talking of his own to do.

He waited for Kathleen to leave, then released Ariel's arm. "Well?"

"It's not my fault." She stalked to the middle of the living room before spinning to face him.

"I've heard that before." Almost continuously since her arrival.

"It's really not."

Rand remained in the archway. "Tell me this—are we or are we not getting married?"

Ariel hesitated. "We're not."

Her voice was so quiet he had to strain to hear and her words acted like a drop-kick to his gut. "Then why does my family think we are?" He spoke coolly, fueled by irritation—at himself when he should know better, and at Ariel for keeping him in the dark.

"It's your mother. She bam . . . bamboo . . . bambuzz . . . tricked me."

Now *that* he'd believe. Rand crossed his arms. "What happened?"

Ariel paced the room, her long hair flowing behind her. "When Lizzie took me on Tuesday, it was to a family meeting at your mother's."

A family meeting? Without him? Poor Ariel. She hadn't had a chance. "And?"

"We were talking." Ariel bit her lip. "Actually, your mother was talking and the next thing I knew she was planning our wedding. I never agreed to it."

"But she evidently thinks you did."

"I know." Ariel stopped, her hand going to the small of her back.

"And when did you plan to tell me about this?" He could understand his mother's methods, but keeping this a secret was asking for trouble.

"I . . . I didn't."

"You didn't?" Rand stared at her. Did he really know this woman at all? "Didn't you think I'd find out?"

Her gaze dropped. "Not while I was here."

Realization dawned. "You intended to have the baby and disappear and leave me to face my mother and sisters?"

The color drained from her cheeks. "I wanted to stop her, but Stephanie said it would be useless."

"That doesn't mean you couldn't tell me." He advanced on her, his fists clenched, resisting the urge to shake her. His imagination conjured up the scene in which he'd have to tell his mother his bride-to-be had split . . . with their child. Damn her.

"I thought . . . I . . ." Ariel shook her head. "I don't know what I thought."

"You didn't think about anyone but yourself. That's for damn sure." Rand struggled to keep his voice even but couldn't shake the ache in his gut. She intended to leave him . . . no matter what. "You really are heartless, aren't you?"

She flinched and he immediately wanted to take back his words.

"I guess I am." She straightened to her full height, little as that was. "But you already knew that, didn't you?" Her eyes sparkled but no tears fell.

Rand grimaced. *Think before you speak, man.* "Ariel, I didn't—"

She stalked toward the front door. "I need to be outside."

The door slammed after her and Rand groaned. He'd botched that for sure, but knowing she intended to leave, to take their child . . . He'd hoped to change her mind, to convince her to stay with him.

Fat chance now.

Ariel stormed outside with no destination in mind. She just had to get away before she revealed her weakness. Rand's words had hurt as much as if he'd slapped her. She wasn't heartless.

Or was she?

She had been thinking of herself, especially since Meg wouldn't accept that Ariel didn't intend to marry Rand. What more could she do?

She should've told Rand. He could've taken care of it. But he'd been taking care of her too much lately. No wonder she found it difficult to think of leaving him.

"Stones." When had her life become so complicated?

She froze on the sidewalk as Stephanie and Bob drove up in a battered blue car. Perfect. A chance to get away on her own for a while.

Before Stephanie could step out of the car, Ariel yanked open the back door and slid inside. "Take me with you."

Stephanie dropped back onto her seat and turned to look at her. "We were coming to see you and Rand."

"I don't want to be here right now." Ariel swallowed the thick lump in her throat. "Take me with you. Anywhere. Just not here."

Stephanie glanced at Bob, who shrugged and started

the car again. They were on the road before Stephanie spoke again. "What happened?"

"Rand is angry with me." And she didn't want him to be. They'd been laughing during the card game, sharing a closeness that made Ariel's chest ache. Now it was all gone.

"Why?"

"I didn't tell him about your mother and her plans for us."

Stephanie blinked. "Why not? Doesn't he deserve to know?"

"Yes, he does." Admitting it only added to the ache in her chest. "But I was afraid." Another new experience. "I . . . I didn't want to disappoint Rand or your mother."

And she would've done both by explaining. The betrayed look in Rand's eyes when she'd told him there would be no wedding was exactly what she'd hoped to avoid. Ariel closed her eyes. Now she was a coward as well. Her time in the mortal realm was certainly not making her a better person.

"I don't think there's any way to avoid disappointing someone, Ariel. Not if you intend to take the baby and go . . ." Stephanie gave Bob a quick glance. "Home," she finished.

"And where's home?" Bob asked.

"Far from here," Ariel murmured. At the moment the magical realm felt like an eternity away.

"Like Mars, perhaps?"

Ariel started. "What?" Wasn't Mars a glowing dot in the heavens?

"Or maybe some other planet?"

Ariel exchanged puzzled glances with Stephanie. What did he mean? "I'm—"

"You're not human. I know that."

Ariel's heart skipped a beat.

"Of course she's human," Stephanie said. "Where did you get such a ludicrous idea?"

"From this." Bob reached into his pocket and pulled

out a single gleaming opal and laid it on the dashboard. "She cried and it turned into this." His smile held no warmth. "I never saw a human do that."

Fleeting panic crossed Stephanie's face, adding to Ariel's tension. "You must be mistaken."

"I don't make mistakes about things like this." He touched the opal. "I had this appraised. You have any idea how much this is worth?"

The stone held no special value in the magical realm, but here . . . Ariel wrapped her arms around herself. Here things were different.

Abruptly Bob pulled off the road, sliding to a stop by a small park. "Out." He looked at Stephanie as he spoke.

"Sure. Fine." She opened her door, then extended her hand toward Ariel. "Come on."

"No. She stays."

The flat chilling tone sent shivers over Ariel's skin and she reached for the door handle.

"Don't even think about it."

She found herself facing a gun. Even without its poisonous lead, it looked deadly. She froze and met Stephanie's stricken gaze.

"Close the door and get away from the car," he ordered. When Stephanie hesitated, Bob waved the weapon toward her. "Now."

"But, Ariel—"

"She won't get hurt as long as she does what I want." The calculated gleam in his eyes didn't reassure Ariel. "Close the door. Now."

As soon as Stephanie swung the door closed, he pulled back into traffic, heading for the highway. Ariel glanced back, catching a brief glimpse of Stephanie running after them until she fell too far behind.

Her heart filled her throat. "What do you want from me?"

"I want a bunch of these opals." Bob merged the car into the freeway traffic. "And more. I figure if you can do this, who knows what else you can do?"

It all came down to wealth. Ariel had encountered mortals like this before, and avoided them. But now she had limited magic and a baby to protect. By the Stones! At this point, she was practically mortal.

What *could* she do?

The tightness in her chest made it difficult to breathe. This would be a good time to let Rand take care of her. . . .

If only he could find her.

Stephanie collapsed against a car, her chest heaving, unable to catch her breath. She couldn't catch them. Then again, what could she do if she did? Merciful Mother, Bob had a gun.

Why hadn't she broken up with him like her instincts had told her? She'd planned to wait until their date on Friday, but he'd shown up tonight wanting to take a drive. She'd accepted, figuring what harm could that do?

Plenty.

She straightened. She had to find a phone. Rand would know what to do.

Spotting a convenience store on the next corner with a phone, she raced toward it. She scooped some change from the bottom of her purse and dialed.

The phone rang. And rang.

Blast Rand. He'd been there only moments ago. Where could he have gone?

She rested her forehead against the cool phone. What now? Who could she call? Her mother? Her sisters? And how could she explain why Bob had taken Ariel?

The police? No, they'd ask questions she didn't dare answer.

Or she could call Dean. After their last encounter, she'd wanted to avoid him—preferably for the rest of her life. But this was more important than pride.

He picked up on the second ring. "Hello?"

"Dean, I need your help." Stephanie had to pause to gasp for air.

"Stephanie?" His voice held concern. "Stephanie? You there? What's wrong?"

"Bob, he . . . he . . ."

"Did he hurt you? I'll—"

"No." She drew in another breath. "He took Ariel. He knows."

A moment of silence answered her. "Where are you?" She told him.

"I'll be right there."

She paced the parking lot until she spotted Dean's BMW. By the time she reached it, he was already outside. He grasped her shoulders. "Are you all right?" he demanded.

She nodded. "Just scared." She met his gaze. No matter what, she knew she could trust him. "He has a gun."

"Good God." Dean wrapped her in a hug and for a moment Stephanie enjoyed it. She felt so at peace, as if she belonged in his arms.

But she couldn't escape reality. "We have to tell Rand. I tried to call him but got no answer." She looked up. "I know he was just there."

Dean released her and she fought back the urge to cling to him. "Did you call the police?"

"No." She grimaced. "I wasn't sure what to tell them about Ariel."

"We'll call them from Rand's. Tell me everything on the way there."

She did, the full horror of the situation filling her as she spoke. "I should have stopped him, done something." Bob could hurt Ariel and it would all be her fault.

Dean reached out to squeeze her hand. "There was nothing you could've done. If you'd fought him, you might have both been killed."

"But now he has Ariel." Her voice quavered. "What if he kills her?"

Cold resolution filled his face. "We won't let that happen."

"Promise me." She was irrational but at the moment

she felt like the child he'd always treated her as.

A corner of his lips lifted and he took his eyes from the road to give her a reassuring smile. "I promise."

And she believed him.

Where could she have gone? Rand circled the block for the third time searching for Ariel. She hadn't had that much of a headstart on him. He should've found her by now.

He pushed his fingers through his hair. Why hadn't he thought before he spoke? *You, Thayer, are an idiot.* He knew what his mother was like when she made up her mind. Ariel had been sentenced before she'd ever spoken a word.

Mom wanted him married. She'd made no secret of that for the past several years. And apparently Ariel met with her approval.

No doubt because of the baby.

Rand paused to stare into the gathering dusk. Where was Ariel? She met with *his* approval for so many reasons—only one of them being the baby.

Damn, he wanted her, wanted to be with her, wanted to see her smile.

So, of course, he'd done his best to scare her away.

And succeeded.

Where could she be?

His steps lagged as he returned to his house. Maybe she had come back while he was searching for her.

But the house was empty.

Had she gone to stay with someone else? Who?

He froze. Of course, Robin and Kate.

Before he could reach for the phone, his front door swung open and he turned, relief flooding him. "Ariel—"

He took two steps, then stopped at seeing Dean and Stephanie, their expressions deadly serious. "What happened?"

"It's Ariel." Stephanie's cheeks bore tear tracks.

"Is she all right?" Rand suddenly found it hard to breathe. "Where—?"

"Bob kidnapped her," Dean said.

The words took a moment to register. "What?" Rand stared at them. "That's impossible. Why?"

"He knows about her." Stephanie approached him, her eyes wide in her pale face. "He saw her crying at the mall."

No, this couldn't be happening. Kidnapped? Ariel? *His* Ariel? Rand seized Stephanie's arms, his grip fierce. "Tell me everything."

"Let her go and she will." Dean eased Stephanie from Rand's hold and guided her to a chair where she sat, burying her face in her hands.

"I should've known," she muttered. "I should've known."

"Known what?" Rand stalked over to look down at her. He was in no mood for word games.

"That Bob wasn't really interested in me." Steph gazed up at him, appearing fragile for his normally self-assured sister.

Rand dropped to one knee before her and took her hands in his. "Tell me, Steph." He gentled his tone despite the insistent urge to do something. "I need to know."

As she explained about Ariel jumping into Bob's car and his use of a gun to force Stephanie out, Rand's gut twisted into a cat's cradle. He had to find Ariel. And soon.

"Where would he have taken her?" he asked. "Do you have any idea?"

Stephanie shook her head. "I don't know."

"Think, Steph." Rand couldn't contain his anxiety. "Think."

Dean stood behind the chair and rested his hand on Stephanie's shoulder. "Take a moment, Steph, and try to remember the places he's taken you."

"I've only known him a week." Tears made her voice thick.

"Sometimes that's enough." Dean spoke gently, obviously using his best bedside manner. "Draw a deep breath and go over your time together."

Steph bowed her head, the silence growing interminably long. Rand fought to restrain his sense of urgency. He needed to do something. Now.

"I know where his apartment is," Stephanie said abruptly. "I know where he works. I know where he likes to go drinking."

"That's good." Dean squeezed her shoulder as he met Rand's gaze. "We can start there after I call the police."

Rand extended his hand before Dean could move. "No. No police."

"The man has a gun, Rand," Dean said.

"If we don't find her in a couple hours, then we can call them. I think they'll make it worse instead of better." He didn't want to waste time explaining this to someone or filling out forms when he could be searching for Ariel. She'd been in his care. He had to find her.

Dean frowned. "Are you sure?"

"I'm sure." Rand glanced toward his sister. "Give me a description of the car."

Stephanie did as they hurried for the door. Rand froze on the steps and stared up at the softly falling snowflakes. "Great." Rand clenched his fists. Just what they needed. Treacherous roads on top of everything else.

He started forward, but Stephanie caught his arm. "Wait, I remembered something else."

He glanced at her, waiting.

"Bob has a cabin between Divide and Cripple Creek. He mentioned going up there to hunt."

A cabin. The perfect place to hide. "He's probably there."

"Would he go there tonight?" Stephanie looked up into the sky. "The weathermen predicted heavy snow for the mountains."

"I don't know what he'd do." But Rand had to check. "Do you know any more of the cabin's whereabouts than that?"

She started to shake her head, then stopped. "It's not too far from Mueller State Park."

"That'll have to be enough." Rand would find it—one way or another. "But in case I'm wrong, I want you and Dean to search all the places here in town."

Dean nodded. "We'll find her, Rand."

"We have to." Rand hurried for his truck, trying not to think of his little lost faery with a crazed kidnapper.

He had to find her. He had to keep her safe.

Or he would be the one lost.

Seventeen

Snow fell steadily as Bob wound his way through the pass, the flakes piling up on the white coating already on the ground. The car slipped several times as he raced along the highway, but he didn't slow.

Ariel didn't release her breath until he paused by a small cabin hidden in the snow-covered pines and aspens. She flinched as Bob waved his weapon at her and forced her from his car into the building.

She shivered from fear as much as from the cold wind. She was alone in this. Rand had no way to know where she was. If she was to survive this without her magic, she would have to use other skills—like her mind and mortal ingenuity.

The interior of the cabin was dark and cold with little furniture. A double bed occupied one corner, its blankets tossed in a heap, and a battered table and chair dominated the middle of the room. Bob motioned Ariel into a chair and she swallowed hard to keep from gagging. A plate with food encrusted on it still remained on the table. Did this man have no sense of cleanliness?

A wood stove near the sink evidently doubled for cooking and heat, for Bob lit it immediately, then came to face her.

"What are you?" he demanded.

Ariel didn't answer. He didn't deserve to know.

"Why do your tears turn into opals?" His expression darkened at her continued silence. "What else can you do?"

Ariel merely stared at him, fighting down the rising waves of terror. She could handle this . . . somehow. If she had her magic full strength this beast would already be a toad.

Covered with warts.

"Look, I don't want to hurt you, but if you don't cooperate I may have to." Bob drew closer, his grip firm on the gun.

Ariel watched the gun closely. Though she didn't feel the ache iron usually produced, she did experience a painful terror deep down inside. She had to do something—for herself, for her baby.

"I can do nothing for you," she said finally. "I'm afraid you've made a big mistake."

"This is no mistake. I saw you at the mall. You were crying and your tears changed into opals. Stephanie grabbed them, but she forgot one on the floor." Avarice gleamed in his eyes. "You don't find opals very often, especially ones as pure or as large as this."

Ariel bit her lip. Now would be a good time to be able to lie.

Well, why couldn't she? Among the Fae, lies served no purpose, for the truth was always known. But among mortals, lies fell from lips as easily as truths. And now with her magic so depleted, she was more mortal than not.

"It was . . . it was . . ." She had to force the words from her mouth and discovered she still couldn't avoid the truth entirely. "Magic. A trick of magic. A . . . an illusion."

Bob grimaced, his disbelief obvious.

Okay, so she wasn't a good liar.

"I know what I saw." Bob leaned over the table toward her and Ariel drew back. "Now cry for me."

"I won't." She had no intention of producing opals for him.

He slapped her with such viciousness, she nearly tumbled from the chair and had to grab the table to stay upright. Ariel raised her hand to her cheek, blinking back the tears that threatened to rise. She'd never experienced pain before—not like this.

How dare he? She'd never harmed a living creature in her life and did not deserve this.

Ariel knocked over her chair as she pushed it back and rose to her feet, her fear overridden by a new emotion—anger.

"You will not touch me again." She heard the power in her voice. Her magic might be diminished, but not the rest of her. "You are nothing but a mere mortal."

Bob recoiled, his eyes widening. "Wha . . . what?"

"You want to know who I am . . . *what* I am?" She clenched her fists to contain the tremor through her body. "I am Fae. I am Ariel, former Queen of the Pillywiggins and you, Bob Harris, have chosen the wrong faery to intimidate."

"Ah, um, just give me the opals and you can go." He waved the gun, but his poise was shaken. Uncertainty lingered in his eyes.

"Do you know what my magic can do to you?" Ariel slowly advanced around the table toward him. "With it, I can turn you into a dog, or a toad, or, more appropriate, a worm."

Though Bob stood several inches taller, he backed up as she approached.

"My magic can transport you to the middle of the ocean where you will surely drown." Ariel kept as close to the truth as she could. She didn't need to lie about this. "My magic can destroy this cabin around you or inflict you with such ailments that you'd wish you'd never been born."

Bob paled and his gun hand dropped. "Look, all I want are the opals. You don't need them. Why can't I have them?"

"Because you don't deserve them. Have you ever gone out of your way to help someone with no thought of reward? Have you ever given to someone less fortunate?"

Mixed emotions crossed his face, providing her with the answer. This man had never thought of anyone but himself and his wants. He was as far removed from Rand and his family as the east was from the west.

"What you did to Stephanie was despicable. You used her, toyed with her emotions." Ariel wanted to produce a ball of fire in her palm but decided against it. That was one spell she didn't want to go out of control.

"I didn't hurt her. She wasn't really interested in me." Bob stood his ground near the door.

"Perhaps not." Ariel suspected Stephanie's interests lay in a different man. "But you couldn't have known that when you first approached her."

"Hey, I let her go." Bob scowled and pointed the gun at Ariel. "Now give me the opals and you're free."

Ariel allowed her disdain to show on her face. "You think your puny mortal weapon can hurt me?" Actually, being made of iron it could kill her, especially in her weakened state, but he didn't have to know that. "I am immortal. I have existed since the dawn of time and I will continue to exist long after you are nothing but dust."

For a moment Bob wavered, obviously torn between his fear and his greed. His greed must have won for he straightened, defiance in his gaze. "If you're so powerful, why haven't you disappeared from this cabin already? Why are you living with Rand?"

Logic. Ariel bit back a curse. She hated dealing with logic. "Because I prefer to teach you a lesson." Not entirely true, but close enough.

"If that were true, you would've done something already, before we ever got here."

And so she would have—if her magic had been working.

Bob started toward her, but she refused to retreat. She would not show fear. "Maybe the only thing you *can* do is cry opals." He gripped her shoulders, his fingers biting into her flesh. "And you're going to give them to me or I'll . . ." He paused and an evil smile lifted his lips. "Or I'll give you to the scientists to study. I imagine they'd be thrilled with a real live faery."

Ariel felt the blood drain from her cheeks. She couldn't control it. But the thought of scientists terrified her more than anything this man could do. She'd lived long enough to know that mortals with their insatiable curiosity could do far more damage to one of her kind than those obsessed with financial gain.

She lifted her chin defiantly. "No scientist could trap me." If she had her powers.

"Oh, no?" Bob shook her. "I have."

Before Ariel could think of a suitable response, the door flew open and Rand burst inside. "Take your hands off her, you sorry son of a bitch." The growl in his voice sent a tremor of fear through Ariel. She'd never seen his expression so violent before.

As Bob released her to whirl around, Ariel seized his wrist and twisted until the gun clattered to the floor. He pushed her so that she stumbled against the table while he launched himself at Rand.

Rand appeared to expect this, for he ducked and punched Bob's chin. Bob staggered back a few steps, then steadied himself and ran at Rand again.

The small cabin became a battleground with both men swinging at each other. The impact of fists against flesh made Ariel wince. She'd experienced this mortal brutality before but never so closely. Of course then she hadn't cared about the outcome.

As the men fought, she examined the bare furnishings for something to use as a weapon. The gun remained on the floor. She could not . . . would not touch that.

As she found a lantern by the bed and lifted it, Bob managed to land a hard fist on Rand's jaw, knocking Rand to the floor, his head hitting the corner of the cupboards. Ariel cried out, dropping the lantern, as she rushed to his side.

Rand remained unmoving, blood pouring from the gash in his skull.

Ariel grabbed a towel off the counter and pressed it against his head, then glared at Bob, who stood by the door, his eyes wide. "You are a doomed man," she told him. Once her magic returned, she would put a spell on him to plague him for the remainder of his life.

His gaze flitted between her and Rand's bloody head. With a choked cry, he yanked open the door and ran outside.

Ariel ignored him. Rand was more important than revenge. Her heart filled her throat as she cradled his head on her lap. A pulse still beat in his throat, but she had no idea how badly he was hurt.

The towel soaked through and she rinsed it in the pumplike sink before reapplying it. Was the blood flow easing?

If only she had her magic. Ariel searched deep inside. A small core of power remained—dim and unreliable— but it was there. Could she heal him, save him? Or would she do more harm than good?

"Rand, Rand, please, don't die." She could not bear to lose this man. Her existence would mean nothing without him.

Ariel gently pushed a lock of hair away from his face— a face she never tired of seeing, a face so full of expression and warmth it brightened her day, a face belonging to the man she loved.

To dispute it any longer was to lie to herself. She loved Rand Thayer . . . had probably loved him for a while and hadn't even realized it. Only this emotion was far more intense than Robin had described, or maybe it couldn't be described. It filled her, warmed her, and controlled her with her foremost thoughts being for Rand.

She couldn't lose him. No matter what happened in their future, she couldn't allow him to lose his too-short mortal life. She had to try what little magic she had remaining and hope it was enough.

The blood had nearly stopped and she placed her hand over the wound, reaching deep inside her, drawing on everything she had left. The power was there but so slight as to be nonexistent.

"Please work," she murmured. "By the power of the blessed Stones, please work."

Heat spread through her veins, down her arm and through her palm to Rand's head. But was it enough?

She bent to touch her lips to his. "I love you, Rand Thayer." As if the words had a magic of their own, power erupted from her, crackling in the air around them. Her palm burned until she could endure it no longer. Pulling away from Rand's wound, she found it knitted together, only the blood staining his hair a witness that it had even existed.

Incredible. Mortal love was more powerful than even her faery magic.

Darkness descended outside the tiny cabin, surrounding it with a snow-blanketed hush, as Ariel continued to hold Rand. His wound might be healed, but he still hadn't opened his eyes, though his chest rose and fell with even breaths. Had his injury been far worse than she'd thought?

She brushed her fingers over his cheek. "Rand, come back to me." She would not let him go into that realm where even faeries couldn't travel.

He expelled a heavy sigh as his eyelids flickered. After blinking several times, he met her gaze. "Are you all right?" he asked, his voice raw.

"Me?" She released a pained laugh. "What about you?"

"I have a headache and a half." He sat up slowly and Ariel kept her arms around him, offering support. Once upright, he placed one hand against his head, then drew it back to stare at the blood staining his palm. "Am I bleeding?"

"Not any longer." Ariel held up two fingers as she'd seen them do on the television. "How many fingers?"

Rand grinned. "Two." He struggled to his feet, using Ariel for balance, then glanced around the cabin. "What happened to Bob?"

"He left. I think he was scared when he saw you bleeding."

"Good." Rand looked at her, his gaze intense. "Did he hurt you?"

"No, I—" She stopped as Rand touched her bruised cheek with gentle fingers. "Oh, he slapped me once." She'd forgotten that in the ensuing battle.

Rand's eyes darkened. "He's going to pay for this."

"So he will." She owed Bob far more for hurting Rand.

Rand blinked as if surprised by the coldness of her voice, then placed a light kiss on her cheek. "All better?" he asked in that playful tone he used with his nieces and nephews.

"Much." The warm tingle his kiss sent through her removed all thoughts of lingering pain from her mind.

Turning away, Rand bent to retrieve the gun from the floor, then examined it. "Damn thing isn't even loaded."

"He said he didn't want to hurt me." At least Bob was only greedy, not dangerous.

"He still kidnapped you." Rand's voice cooled. "What did he want?"

"My opals."

"Jeez, I have a whole jar of the things at home. He could've had some if he'd approached this differently." Rand paused. "No, forget that. The only thing I want to give him is a fat lip."

Ariel lifted her hand to his cheek, reassured by his warmth. "Are you all right? Really all right?" She had come so close to losing him that she couldn't keep her hands off him.

Rand's smile turned her knees as wobbly as green Jell-O.

"As long as you're safe, I'm very all right." He hugged her close. "What do you say we go home and get out of this dump?"

"I would love that." She wanted nothing more than to be home with Rand, to hold him close.

Stepping outside, she gasped. The snow had enveloped the countryside in a heavy blanket of white, reaching as high as the bottom of the truck door. She had never seen anything like this before. "Can we drive in this?"

"We'll make it." But Rand frowned as he approached his truck and lifted his half-opened hood. "Damn it all to hell."

Ariel joined him in peering into the mass of machinery. Could he make sense of it? "What?"

"The jerk took my distributor cap." He slammed the hood down. "We're not going anywhere for a while."

"Are we trapped?" Ariel tried to summon up some fear, but as long as Rand was with her she didn't care how long they spent here.

"At least until morning." Rand reached inside his truck and pulled out his cell phone. "I can call Dean, but I don't want him driving up here in this. Not in the dark."

The mention of Dean reminded Ariel of Rand's sister. "Is Stephanie all right?"

"Blaming herself, of course, but physically okay." Rand produced a wry smile. "For once she and Dean were working together. I haven't seen them do that without bickering in ages."

"That's one good thing to come out of this." Ariel held out her hand to Rand to lead him back inside.

Dean and Stephanie together. If Ariel had truly sensed their emotions correctly, this had the potential to be mortal magic at work.

A very good thing, indeed.

• • •

Stephanie stood by Dean's side as they examined the interior of the dimly lit bar. Aside from a few curious gazes, the patrons ignored them, more concerned with their drinks than with strangers.

"They're not here," she muttered. Not that she had truly expected to find Bob and Ariel there. But where else could she look? Bob's apartment had been empty, his office shut up tight.

Dean touched her shoulder. "Give me a minute to talk to the bartender. I'll be right back."

He left her by the door and Stephanie continued to examine faces. No Bob. No Ariel. Merciful Mother, if anything happened to her friend . . .

"Hey, baby, how about I buy you a drink?"

Stephanie turned at the deep voice to find a heavy-set biker beside her in the traditional leather jacket and worn blue jeans. A heavy beard covered his face but his eyes examined her with more than a little interest.

She took a step away from him. "No, thank you."

"Come on. I'm just trying to be friendly."

"I said no, thank you." She didn't need this crap.

"She's with me." Dean stepped between them, glaring at the biker. Something in his expression must have reinforced his words for the man shrugged and turned away.

Dean touched Stephanie's arm, a dark gleam lingering in his eyes. "Let's get out of here."

She was all for that. Once outside, amid the falling snow, Stephanie drew in a deep breath, the cold stinging her lungs. Good, she deserved it.

"What are we going to do?" she asked as they paused by Dean's car. "I don't know where to look next."

"Maybe Rand already found her."

"But what if he hasn't?" Too many sordid scenarios filled her mind, none of them ending happily. "What then?" Her voice broke, and her throat choked with tears.

When Dean pulled her into his arms, she went without hesitation, burying her face against his shoulder. Here she felt safe, secure, as if Dean could make it all right. She inhaled his special scent—a mixture of soap and after-shave that she'd always associated with him.

"It's all my fault," she whispered. She'd been such a fool.

"No, it's not."

"Yes, it is. I knew Bob wasn't right for me, but I let myself believe he could be because he flattered me, because I could show you I wasn't a child any longer. How could I be so stupid?" All she'd done was make a mess of everything.

Dean continued to hold her, but he'd stilled, a sudden tension in his body. Stephanie glanced up at him to find his gaze dark. "What is it?"

"What do you mean, show me you're not a child any longer?" His voice held a note she'd never heard before, one that frightened her almost as much as it intrigued her.

Had she said that? She tried to recall her ravings. Oh, blast, she had. "I . . . you . . . you always treat me like a child and I'm sick of it."

"No, I don't." But he didn't sound convinced of that.

How could he deny it? "Giving me candy bars, patting me on the head, calling me Steve, which I haven't answered to since I was twelve. What do you call that?" She wrenched from his hold, but he caught her arm before she could stalk away.

"I like to tease you." He turned her to face him but she wouldn't meet his probing gaze. "You always react with such fire."

"Well, I'm not a child any more, Dean Carstensen. I'm twenty-five. I'm a woman and have been ever since I was sixteen and you—" She caught herself before she could reveal any more. Her foolish tongue had already said more than she'd wanted him to know.

"What about when you were sixteen?" A deadly calm entered his voice.

Stephanie shook her head. "Nothing." She tried to pull away, but he only tightened his hold.

"Stephanie, be honest with me." He drew her close until

she had to lift her head to see his face. "For once in your life, be honest with me."

Honest? She'd give him honest. "What do you want? You want me to admit it? Fine. I fell in love with you at sixteen and I haven't been able to stop. Does that make you happy?"

She closed her eyes at the end of her outburst, heat filling her cheeks. *Oh, that was incredibly stupid.*

He murmured something. Was it "very"? Before she could open her eyes, his mouth found hers as he pulled her against him.

She melted. How could she resist? He kissed like he did everything else—with skill, with passion, with a style that was definitely Dean. He kissed her as if tomorrow would never come and right now she didn't want it to. She wanted this moment to never end.

Her pulse raced, her breasts swelled as he continued to claim her lips, to plunder and seduce with such ferocity that she couldn't help but respond, couldn't stop herself from wrapping her arms around his neck.

No wonder no other man had ever touched her heart. No other man could be Dean.

When he finally lifted his head, he gave her such a loving smile that her stomach knotted. "It's about damned time," he said.

"What?" She moistened her tender lips with her tongue, an action he followed closely. They might be swollen from the passion of his kiss, but she didn't mind, not for a moment.

"It's been hell waiting for you to give up your independent, I-don't-need-a-man outlook on life, then when you showed up with this Bob character . . ." Dean shook his head. "I was going crazy."

Stephanie's heart leaped. "You mean you . . ." She couldn't finish. Her lungs could barely draw breath.

"I mean I love you, Stephanie Thayer." He cupped her cheek in one broad palm. "You knocked me for a wallop when you were sixteen and I haven't been able to think about anyone else since."

"But you kissed me, then patted me on the head like a child."

He grinned. "I thought you didn't remember it." She ducked her head, remembering her blatant lie, but he lifted her chin. "I knew then I liked you, that you were special, but until you kissed me I hadn't realized how deep it went." He ran his thumb over her lips, adding to her inner tension.

But she didn't speak. She could only stare. All this time? All this time he'd loved her?

"It scared the hell out of me so I patted you on the head."

"But why didn't you say something later?"

"I was nineteen, going away to college, and you were only sixteen. At that point you *were* a child, Steph. I couldn't deny you the chance to grow up into the woman I knew you'd become." His lips twisted in a smile. "I'd planned to approach you once I graduated, but by that point you would barely give me the time of day. All I heard was how you were following Rand's credo—no marriage, no love, no involvement."

"You hurt me," she said softly. He winced. "If love hurt that much I didn't want anything to do with it. Then I discovered I couldn't love anyone else because I kept comparing them to you."

Dean drew a gentle kiss from her lips. "I'm sorry. I never meant to hurt you. I was trying to do what I thought was best at the time."

"I hate magnanimous men." She spoke without inflection but gave him a slow smile. "However, I'm willing to let you make it up to me."

"Oh, I intend to." He dipped his head toward hers again. "For many, many, many years to come."

This kiss was even better than the first, if such a thing was possible. Gentle, filled with promises, and containing more love than Stephanie had ever expected to know.

Whoever said dreams couldn't come true?

The shrill ring of Dean's cell phone broke them apart, shattering the illusion as reality rushed back. How could she have forgotten about Ariel?

Dean answered the phone, keeping one arm firm around her shoulders. "Yes?" He listened for several moments but his face brightened. "Great. Okay, in the morning."

He closed the phone then ran his finger down Stephanie's nose. "He found Ariel. She's okay."

Relief weakened Stephanie's knees and she leaned into him. "Thank goodness."

"However, Bob stole his distributor cap before he left so he wants me to bring out a new one once the snow stops."

"Okay." Stephanie peered up into the night sky. The snow showed no sign of stopping any time soon. Mischief made her speak. "What do we do in the meantime?"

The look in Dean's eyes answered her. "Come home with me," he said, his voice husky.

"I'd like that." Stephanie snuggled against him.

She'd like that very, very much.

Eighteen

Once inside the cabin, Rand didn't want to release Ariel, needing to reassure himself she was okay. He'd experienced anger before, but nothing like the blind rage that had driven him at seeing Bob's hands on her. He'd wanted to kill the man.

Perhaps it was best he had been knocked unconscious. He might have actually succeeded. He gingerly touched the back of his head. Aside from some tenderness, he felt fine.

Only one problem remained—he was stuck overnight in a tiny one-room cabin with a woman he wanted beyond reason. Outside, snow continued to fall, slower now, but still creating a sense of isolation—and the impression that he and Ariel were the only two people alive. Night had arrived, turning the trees outside to shadowed guardians.

He ran his hand over Ariel's hair, breathing in her special scent. If he lived to be two hundred, that smell would always remind him of her. And no doubt would induce the same physical reaction—hammering pulse, rushing blood, and a hard-on that strained against his pants.

He could list a hundred reasons why he should relax—she'd just been traumatized, she was near the end of her term, she had used him once long ago and intended to ditch him as soon as the baby was born, leaving him to his mother's wrath; but none of that mattered. The light in her eyes when she looked at him set his blood on fire.

He'd almost lost her. He never wanted to lose her again.

When Ariel eased out from under his arm, the sense of loss was immediate. "Where are you going?"

"I thought I'd make you some coffee if there is any." She opened the cupboards and peered into them.

"I don't need coffee." Besides, Rand didn't trust any of the dishes here to be fit for human use. He crossed to behind Ariel and ran his hands down her arms. "I need you."

She stilled. "What?"

He turned her to face him and found her eyes wide and wondering. "I need *you*." God help him, she had gotten under his skin and stayed there.

The smile she gave him lit up the room brighter than the lantern on the table. "I'm here."

She placed her palms against his chest, her touch warming him even through his clothing. Rand didn't bother to think, to rationalize all the reasons why this was a bad idea. He simply bent and kissed her.

Her lips softened beneath his, then parted, inviting him to explore, and he did. Her mouth held a magic all of its own—soft, sweet, and very, very hot. Rand had to force himself to concentrate on just the sheer pleasure of Ariel's lips.

He could kiss her for hours.

He drew her as close as her belly would allow. Seeking entry, he dueled with her tongue. She gave as good as she received, answering him kiss for kiss, clutching the front of his shirt with her fists.

And he wanted more.

Even pregnant, she fit within his arms as if designed

for them. When she released a small sigh of contentment, it added to the ache deep within him.

He left her lips to blaze a trail along her jawbone, to nuzzle the tender flesh beneath her ear, and her sighs gave way to moans, her breathing ragged. "I want you," he whispered against her ear.

"Oh yes," she murmured. "Please, yes."

To hell with the past, to hell with the future. All that mattered was now and the woman in his embrace. Tonight they belonged together, his worries forgotten.

Finding her lips once more, he cupped her breast, the flesh so full it filled his hand. Her nipple hardened beneath his thumb and Ariel breathed a moan into his mouth.

Desire raced through his veins, a mixture of pain and pleasure so intense he knew nothing but the satisfaction of Ariel. The softness of her lips, the fullness of her breast, the eagerness that matched his own.

He only lacked the feel of flesh against flesh. Tugging at the edge of her sweater, he pulled it over her head, then released the clasp on her bra to remove it. Her breasts jutted free, the areolae darker, the nipples taut peaks begging for attention.

Attention he was more than willing to give.

He led her over to a chair and straddled it, then pulled her down to sit across his lap facing him. His erection strained against his pants, her inviting heat so close.

Claiming her mouth, he caressed her breasts, gently at first, then more firmly as her moans turned into small cries. By the time he left her lips, her nipples had become tight pebbles and he drew one peak into his mouth.

She squirmed against him, inciting him even more. Rand shifted. There would be time soon enough. He wanted to savor this pleasure, the unique scent and flavor of Ariel. He had denied himself this for far too long.

He left her breast as she tugged off his sweatshirt, but returned to love the other while she ran her fingers through his hair, her head thrown back and breath coming in gasps. She rocked against his erection until he could barely stand it.

Rand stood her on her feet and shucked his jeans and underwear in record time. Ariel's eyes widened as he sprang forth, ready for action.

Grinning, Rand reached for her pants, but she abruptly brushed his hands away. "I'm grotesque," she protested. "I'm so big."

"You're not grotesque." Rand slid her pants and underwear off, revealing her swollen belly. Yes, she was large, but she carried a child in there . . . their child.

He dropped to his knees to place tender kisses over her abdomen. "You're beautiful," he murmured, "in every way."

"Rand." Her voice held tears and he glanced up to see them glistening in her eyes. "I want you inside me."

"Soon." He touched her, finding her already moist nub, and caressed her there until she dug her fingernails into his shoulders.

"Please, Rand."

He stood slowly, kissing a path up to her lips. He'd never made love to a pregnant woman before, which called for slight modifications. Perhaps sitting had been the right approach all along.

Taking his place on the chair, he drew her down over his erection so that he entered her slowly. Her tight opening wrapped him in ecstasy. He groaned as he filled her completely, then he reached to hold her bottom and guided her to meet his thrusts.

Only with Ariel had making love been so satisfying. Only with her did he feel as if he was joining with his soulmate.

Her breasts moved before his face and he found one with his mouth. His hands might be busy, but this method certainly had other advantages.

Ariel gasped, but didn't slow her pace, her hips moving rhythmically. Her gasps quickened until she pulsed around him, sweetening his pleasure.

He exploded as her climax eased, finding release so close to heaven he could've died and not known the difference.

They stilled, but remained wrapped around each other, the only sound that of their erratic breathing.

He stole a quick kiss, then met her gaze. "You know, for a faery, you're pretty good."

She smiled and swatted ineffectually at his chest. "And here I was going to say the same thing about you being a mortal."

"I guess we deserve each other." Even as he said the words, they echoed in his head. Did that contain more truth than he'd intended?

Her eyes darkened in intensity. "I guess we do."

His heart gave an extra beat. Was she reconsidering her decision to stay with him?

She shivered despite the heat pouring from the wood stove and Rand eased her to her feet. "Let me fix up the bed." He managed to find clean sheets in a box by the bed and remade it in record time, his glance constantly straying to the enticing figure of his pregnant faery.

By the time he pulled back the covers and waved her forward, he had decided he could handle another round. Ariel eyed his erection as she climbed into the bed, then stroked him, wrenching a groan from Rand's throat.

"Maybe you're *not* just a mere mortal," she said, mischief dancing in her eyes.

"Mere mortal? Me?" Rand wrapped her in his arms and rolled her onto her back. "We've only just begun, m'lady."

He made love to her again, slower this time without the fierceness of their first union but equally as intense. Her touch, her cries drove him to heights he hadn't imagined. Amazing what making love to the right woman could do.

The right woman.

That thought sent shivers along his spine. What had

happened to his plan to avoid women, to remain single for the rest of his life?

He grimaced. Ariel had dropped into his life, that's what.

She snuggled against him, and he wrapped his arms around her as the wind howled outside the cabin. If the snow didn't die down soon, they might not be able to leave tomorrow, either.

He didn't mind that at all.

Making love to Ariel was heaven. Their first joining had been from lust, but this . . . this was a sharing of not only bodies, but souls. For the first time in his life, he'd felt like more than a physical participant in the act.

He leaned forward to kiss her forehead, then jerked as a rose dropped from the air to land on the blankets. As he sat upright, Ariel giggled.

Picking up the flower, he turned to look at her. Humor lit her eyes. "Changed to roses, have you?"

"It's not me." She took his hand and placed it against her prominent belly. "The baby has the hiccups."

He actually felt the next little hiccup inside her followed by another rose that hit his head on the way down. He couldn't help but smile. "Looks like we have another flower faery."

"I expected as much." Ariel laughed as more flowers fell, following a succession of hiccups. "Too bad this didn't happen when Bob was here. I really would've scared him then."

"Scared him?" His petite Ariel couldn't scare a mouse.

"I had him terrified for a while." Ariel's gaze fixed on something only she could see. "But I didn't have the magic to see it through."

At the sadness in her voice, Rand lay down and cuddled her closer. "What did you do?"

"I told him all the things I could do to him—turn him into a toad, drop him in the middle of the ocean, plague him with ailments for the rest of his life." She sighed. "I still intend to plague him once my magic returns."

"Can you really do all that?" He'd had no idea her magic was that powerful.

"That and more." Ariel yawned suddenly and covered her mouth even as she closed her eyes and wrapped one arm over his chest. "You wore me out."

Rand grinned and kissed her. "Then sleep, my little faery. I'll be here to protect you."

Her eyes flickered open, the blue dark like a stormy sea. "I'm counting on it."

Within moments her even breathing signaled that she'd drifted into a deep slumber. Rand merely watched her, studying the arch of her eyebrows, the fine line of her nose, the curve of her cheek, the sensuous bow of her lip.

In the past two days he'd learned more about Ariel than in the three weeks prior. While she'd mentioned losing her crown, she'd never said it was because of her defense of Robin. And she'd never let on about her loneliness. No wonder she wanted a child so desperately.

Rand tightened his hold around her.

A child he was going to lose when he let her go.

He had to face it. Both Ariel and the baby were magical. For them to exist in his world was asking for trouble. There were too many people around like Bob, who were willing to take advantage of them. Rand had been lucky, locating Bob's cabin through a nearby store clerk, but what if their child had been kidnapped? A child too innocent to know not to use magic in front of others? What if Rand wasn't so lucky the next time?

Ice chilled his blood. He didn't dare take that chance. Ariel had been right all along. She had to return to her world . . . with the baby. For their own safety.

Sharp pain stabbed his heart. He closed his eyes even as he breathed in the buttercup scent of Ariel's hair.

Damn, he was going to miss her.

"Stop it, Ariel."

She laughed as Rand pulled her hands out from under his shirt. "But I like touching you." And she could never have enough. Sharing her body with Rand last night had been beyond anything in her experience, even more fantastic than their first union. This mortal love heightened everything to an incredible level.

"Dean could be here any moment. I don't want him walking in on you and me and . . ." Rand held her hands in his as he placed a lingering kiss on her lips—a kiss that said he wanted her as much as she wanted him. "We'll be home soon."

"Not soon enough, but it'll have to do." She nipped at his chin, then froze when she heard the sound of a motor outside.

Rand lifted one eyebrow. "See?"

She followed him as he crossed to the door and pulled it open in time to see an SUV slide to a stop beside his truck. "That's not Dean's car."

"Looks more like Jerry's," Rand said. "Susan's husband. It has four-wheel drive."

As Dean stepped out of the vehicle, Rand started out to meet him, then paused to point a finger at Ariel when she would've followed. "Stay here until I have the truck going. The snow's deep and you don't have any boots."

Ariel sighed and crossed her arms. Neither did he, but if he wanted to play the protective male she wasn't going to stop him. Today he could ask for the moon and she'd give it to him.

She smiled. That probably went for tomorrow, too.

She'd never imagined she could feel like this—as if she could fly without the aid of magic. Even nurturing a field of buttercups into bloom couldn't begin to compare.

Dean and Rand laughed as they worked together under the hood of the truck. Standing, Dean spotted her and trudged over, stomping the snow off his boots in the entrance.

"How are you feeling? No ill effects?"

Ariel couldn't keep a foolish smile from her face. "I'm wonderful."

A sly grin slid across Dean's face as he glanced from

her to Rand. "I imagine so. Maybe I shouldn't have gotten here so quickly."

She placed her hands on her nonexistent hips in mock ferocity. "Maybe you shouldn't have."

He laughed. "I'll remember that."

Ariel studied him. She wasn't the only one filled with good humor this morning. "Something is different with you."

"Is there?" Impish lights shone in his eyes. "You must be imagining things."

"I don't think so." She cocked her head. If her suspicions were true . . . "Where's Stephanie? Why didn't she come with you?"

"She was still asleep. I—" Dean cut himself off and gave her rueful smile. "Evil, aren't you?"

If her joy could be compounded, this news did it. "Just very, very happy."

"Yeah, me too." An emotion filled his face—an emotion she could now give a name. Love. "But don't tell Rand. I'll do that."

"I won't say a word." In fact, Ariel hoped words wouldn't be necessary for a long time after they arrived home.

Rand got the truck going and joined them. "That did it. Thanks, Dean."

"No problem." Dean turned toward the SUV. "I'm going to head back. Call me on the cell if you get stuck."

"I should be okay. The truck has four-wheel drive."

Dean climbed inside his vehicle and was out of sight in moments. Anxious to return to a certain sleeping someone, no doubt.

Rand motioned toward the truck. "Your carriage awaits, my queen." Before Ariel could move, he swung her into his arms.

She wrapped her arms around his neck as he waded through the deep snow. "You don't need to do this. I can walk."

"I know I don't have to do it." The warmth in his eyes

triggered an answering heat in her veins. "But I want to."

He rested her on one knee as he opened the passenger door. "I don't remember you weighing this much last time," he muttered.

She gasped. "Aren't you charming? I do happen to be pregnant, you know."

"Are you?" Devilish mischief played across his face. "I hadn't noticed."

She satisfied herself with tugging at a lock of his hair before he seated her inside. "I have ways to make you suffer for that," she told him, already imagining how she'd torment his body until he begged for mercy.

Then she would take him inside her.

Evidently Rand could read her mind, for he gave her a wicked grin. "I'm counting on it."

He drove slowly along the snow-covered road leading from the cabin, the only other tire tracks those from Dean's vehicle. Ariel glanced back at the cabin, oddly reluctant to leave it. For a short time the mortal world had been kept at bay.

If only it could continue to stay away.

The main roads had been plowed at least once so Rand picked up speed as they headed back toward Colorado Springs. Ariel watched the passing scenery, fascinated. The unblemished snow packaged the world in a sense of purity, of crystal beauty and winter magic. If she hadn't stayed in the mortal world, she would have missed this.

The evergreens lining the road emitted a joyous sonata, the rustling of their branches musical as they celebrated the new snowfall. Even the aspens, slumbering deeply, added to the melody, the last few leaves clinging stubbornly and dancing in the wind.

"This is so beautiful," she murmured. The magical realm had nothing like this.

"*You're* beautiful." Rand glanced at her with a slow, sensuous smile that tightened her breasts at once.

"I—" She didn't finish, aware of the tiny jerking within her. A fragrant red rose drifted to the seat.

When Rand shook his head in mock despair, she laughed. Her child was most decidedly a pillywiggins.

More roses littered the seat before the hiccups eased.

"What am I going to do with you?" Rand asked, his tone light.

"I can think of several things." All of which involved getting naked and spending many long hours with each other. She hadn't begun to explore his body, the solid muscle, the toned flesh, the velvet soft length of his masculinity. Even hours wouldn't be enough.

"I don't know." The corner of his lips lifted. "I wouldn't want to wear you out again."

"I dare you to try." She knew enough of that mortal threat to know most men could not refuse it.

"Dare me, eh?"

"Or are you afraid I'll wear *you* out?" Ariel slid her hand over his thigh and was rewarded by the tensing of his muscles.

Rand chuckled. "This is going to be a very interesting afternoon."

"You—" Ariel stopped as a sharp tension rippled across her belly, then faded away. "That was different."

"The baby?"

"Yes. It was similar to a growing pain, yet not the same."

The humor fled from Rand's face and the look he gave her held a hint of panic. "Are you going into labor on me, Ariel?"

"I don't think so. It was only once." She waited but the sensation didn't reappear.

"If it happens again, tell me." Rand's knuckles whitened on the steering wheel as he guided them through the winding curves of the pass. "Dear Lord, you could have the baby any time now, couldn't you?"

"It's possible." She had no real way of knowing how close she was to the end of her term other than her burgeoning belly. Though Dean's rough guess on her accelerated pregnancy set a date of this weekend—only a couple more days.

The solemn expression remained on Rand's face. "Ariel, I . . ." He paused. "I won't stop you from leaving after the baby's born."

Her chest grew tight. Didn't he want her to stay? Now, when she ached to be with him, he wanted her to leave? After what they'd shared?

He hadn't said he loved her. Perhaps for him, their joining had been nothing more than the pleasure of lovemaking. Her spirits sank and she turned away to stare unseeingly out the window.

He'd only asked her to marry him out of obligation. She'd known that at the time. Apparently he no longer felt that obligation.

That made him no different than most mortal men of her acquaintance. They showed little care for others. It shouldn't matter.

But it did.

Rand wasn't most mortal men. He was the man she loved.

Who no longer wanted her.

"Did you hear me?" he asked.

"I heard you." What could she say? What did he want her to say? "Am I supposed to be pleased to have your blessing?"

He snorted. "Yeah, right." His voice sounded bitter. "My blessing."

He said nothing more and the silence thickened as he completed the drive to his house. The magic had fled from the sunny day and she hugged herself to hold in the hurt. Robin had not told her loving could be exquisite pain as well.

"What the—?"

Ariel looked up at Rand's exclamation to see several cars and vans parked in front of his house and a group of men and women filling the yard. As Rand pulled into the driveway, the strangers turned as one and advanced.

He leaped from the truck. "What the hell is going on here?"

Everyone talked at once so that Ariel could barely understand them. One question came through clearly. "Are you Rand Thayer?"

"I am."

Ariel stepped out of the truck and walked around the front to join him. "Rand?"

At her voice, the pack whirled on her. She jerked back as a large black knob was stuck under her chin. "Are you Ariel?" someone asked.

She stared at the group, uncertain how to answer.

A man planted himself in front of her, his gaze intent. "Are you the so-called faery?"

Nineteen

~

Rand tried to reach Ariel, but the reporters swarmed around her. How—? Bob, of course. Since Ariel had escaped him, he no doubt intended to make her pay by revealing her identity. Recognizing the names on some of the nearby vehicles, he groaned. Sleazy tabloids. Only they would believe such a crazy story.

"You're a faery?"

"You have magic?"

"Do something for us."

"Where are your wings?"

"Can you fly?"

He paled. If she told the truth, this would turn into a worse circus than it was already. He had to protect her.

"I can't believe you're all falling for that nonsense," he shouted over the querying voices. A couple of reporters turned to look at him. "I had no idea our local media believed in faeries." More heads looked his way. "I guess that explains some of the articles I've read in the paper."

A man frowned at Rand. "Look, we got this information from a reliable source."

Bob? Reliable? "I'm sure it was. Did he also tell you to let Prince Albert out of a can?" Rand snorted with derision. "Come on. Do *you* believe in faeries?"

He caught a glimpse of Ariel, her eyes wide, and her expression concerned. *Don't say a word.* If he could get these newshounds out of here before she spoke, they might have a chance.

One woman, her hair long and stylish, persisted in tormenting Ariel when some of the others drew back. "I was told your tears turn into opals. Is that true?"

Ariel's unease showed on her face. "Leave me alone." She pushed against the swarm around her, but couldn't get through.

Rand's heart lodged in his throat. His worst nightmare had come true. How could he protect Ariel? He'd never felt so completely helpless.

He shoved through the crowd until he reached her and wrapped his arms around her. She snuggled against him, appearing even smaller than usual.

He glared at the reporters. "Look, are you done bothering a pregnant lady?"

"What kind of faery are you, Ariel?" the woman asked.

"Tell me, lady, do you believe in the Easter bunny, too?" Rand asked. He pushed his way toward the front door, taking Ariel with him.

"I'm following up on a lead." The reporter didn't appear fazed at all. Instead, she kept pace alongside Ariel. "Do you have magical abilities? Where did you come from? Why are you here?"

Ariel spun from Rand's arms to face the woman. "Go away. I'm not in the mood for this."

"Answer my questions and I will." The woman glanced down at her tablet. "Is it true you can turn someone into a toad?"

Tension reverberated through Ariel and Rand rested his hands on her shoulders. "Come on. Let's get inside."

But she didn't budge. She glared at the woman reporter.

"Don't you think if I could I would've done so to you already?"

The woman drew back at that, then her expression lit up. "She's crying."

Crying? Oh, Lord, no. Rand pulled Ariel toward him, but not before the reporter dabbed at the tears on Ariel's cheek. As the reporter studied the droplet of water on her finger, Rand pushed for the door.

"It's just water," the reporter said, her disappointment clear.

Rand looked around. Water? As he watched, the woman swiped her hand on her slacks, turning away, her expression disgusted.

"We've been had," she muttered.

"I tried to tell you," Rand called after the departing media.

He wasted no time getting Ariel inside. "Are you all right?"

"Angry, mostly." She slipped from his hold and hung up her coat. "What horrid mortals."

She stalked to the living room, then stopped, her head bowed. "My magic's gone," she whispered. "Totally gone."

Rand frowned. Had he heard right? "Gone?"

"I can't feel it within me any more." Her voice wavered.

That explained the lack of opals. He crossed over to her. "It'll come back when the baby is born." And that would happen all too soon.

"And once it does, I'm turning them all into toads." She turned to face him, her eyes ablaze.

Though he tried to stop it, a chuckle escaped him as he imagined the woman reporter hopping across the yard. "Not the best thing to do, I'm afraid."

"What do you care?" Defiance continued to tinge her words. "I'll be gone."

A sledgehammer impacted his chest. For a moment, Rand couldn't draw a deep breath. Yes, she'd be gone.

She had to leave. Today's display only reemphasized that.

But he didn't want her to go.

"Of course," he muttered finally. He paced away from her, unwilling to look into her face, for then he'd want to touch her, hold her, kiss her, and never let her leave him. "It'll be safer for you in the magical realm."

"Yes, it will." But she didn't sound convinced.

Rand drew in a deep breath. She had to go. After all his attempts to convince her to stay, he had to face what was right for Ariel, not for him. It wasn't safe in his world for her . . . or their child. "You need to go," he said, despite the agony of saying the words. What more could he say to persuade her to leave? "I certainly don't want any more reporters nosing around here."

"Don't worry." Ariel's chin lifted in her familiar gesture of defiance. "I'll have turned them all into toads."

"I think you'll be busy with other things." A fist squeezed his heart. "A crying, hungry baby for one." He stretched out his arms, trying to act nonchalant. "And I'll finally have peace and quiet."

She tensed, motionless, and moisture appeared in her eyes. Damn, he'd gone too far. Again. Rand took a step toward her, but she backed away.

"Don't worry." Ice layered her words. "I'll be gone as soon as possible." She whirled around and rushed upstairs.

Damn. Rand pulled his fingers through his hair. This wasn't the way he wanted it. If he had his way, he'd make love to her nonstop for the next several days, but if he did, he'd never let her out of his arms.

He heard her door slam and winced. After such a glorious night, who would've thought it could deteriorate into this?

Unable to stand still, he paced the room. He needed to do something—something to keep him from thinking of Ariel. Besides that, he wanted to smash his fist into someone. One of the reporters would do.

He stiffened. Or better—Bob Harris.

Time to let the police do something. Had Bob returned

to his apartment? Stephanie had given Rand the address. He'd stop by the police station and take them there. Whether the gun had been loaded or not, Bob had still kidnapped Ariel and hadn't been punished.

At the door, he paused and glanced upstairs. The reporters had left. Ariel would be safe enough in her room. Besides, Rand wouldn't be long.

But before he returned, Bob Harris would know never to mess with Ariel again.

Ariel sank onto her bed, wiping furiously at the tears that trickled down her cheeks. Normal, human tears.

Her world was falling apart—no magic and no future with the man she loved. Stones, she had been better off not knowing how to love. This internal, heart-wrenching pain was worse than any physical distress she'd ever suffered.

At least Rand had made his true feelings known before she admitted her love or agreed to stay here with him. She'd suspected all along he only wanted her to stay because of the baby. Obviously she'd been right. Now he didn't even want the baby.

She'd thought better of Rand than that. How could she have been so mistaken?

At the sound of the front door closing, Ariel rose to her feet and peered out the window as Rand climb into his truck and drove away.

Now he was deserting her.

Didn't he care whether the reporters had upset her? Ariel sighed. Truthfully, she'd been upset, but mostly angry. If she'd had her magic, she would've . . .

She turned away from the window. If she'd had her magic, that incident would never have happened. She could've disappeared or cast some glamour to influence their thinking.

Instead she'd been stuck with no options, feeling betrayed and helpless. And all she could think was how

Rand's life would be destroyed if the reporters actually discovered she was a faery.

Even knowing he wanted her out of his life didn't change her feelings. She wanted to hate him, wanted to plan a spell to torture him, but she couldn't. She was left with the feeling that a part of her had been ripped away.

A pox on the mortals and their emotions. A pox on the entire human realm.

She had thought herself lonely when she left the magical world on her mission for Oberon, but it barely compared to the desolation surrounding her now. Now she was truly alone—not a faery, not a mortal, not belonging anywhere.

All because Rand Thayer wanted peace and quiet.

Ariel froze in the middle of the room. He wanted peace and quiet? By the Stones, she'd give him peace and quiet.

Going to the telephone, she quickly dialed Stephanie's phone number. The woman surprised her by answering right away.

"Ariel, are you all right?" she asked once the hellos were spoken.

"I'm unharmed." At least, physically. "I need your help, Stephanie."

"All you have to do is ask."

"It involves Rand."

"I'm interested." Stephanie replied with more than a little curiosity.

"I need you to call a family meeting." Ariel hesitated. Was this the right path to follow?

Recalling Rand's earlier words, she winced. Oh, yes, definitely the right path. For the first time in his life, Rand would get exactly what he wished for.

Rand pulled into the driveway and switched off the motor. He made no move to get out of the truck, but glanced at his bruised knuckles. He'd managed to land one good one on Bob, before the police took him in for questioning, which had provided some satisfaction but still hadn't eased the ache in his chest.

All this had started with a sense of responsibility over a child he hadn't really wanted. Now the thought of losing Ariel and the baby tortured him. Somewhere along the way his priorities had changed, but he sure didn't know where.

He wanted Ariel to stay because she was Ariel, because she made him laugh, because making love to her was beyond anything he'd ever experienced or would ever experience. And she couldn't stay. As she'd told him over and over, she didn't belong in his world.

Especially with people like Bob and those reporters around.

Rand sighed and stepped out of the truck. Perhaps now Ariel would let him apologize for his earlier remarks. He'd only wanted to persuade her to leave, but his despair over doing so had made him speak more harshly than he'd intended.

With a grimace, he let himself inside a silent house. Evidently, she was still angry. However, he still needed to take her to the police station so she could give her statement and ensure Bob was officially arrested.

"Ariel?" He climbed the stairs, then paused outside her bedroom. Should he knock? To see her was to want her. Having a bed in the same room threatened his already weak control. Damn, all he wanted was to hold her, kiss her.

He drew in a deep breath, then knocked on her door. No answer.

"Ariel, I only want to talk to you." He waited for several moments, but still the door remained closed. "Ariel?"

Tendrils of alarm wound around his throat. "Ariel?" He turned the knob and opened the door.

The room was empty. His heart clogged his throat.

"Ariel?" He whirled around and dashed downstairs to search all the rooms. Ariel was nowhere to be found.

Panic drummed in his chest. Where could she be? What

had happened to her? Had the reporters returned? Or someone worse? Horrible scenarios played through his mind, each one worse than the other.

Rand gripped the edge of the kitchen doorframe, bowing his head. His earlier helplessness was nothing compared to this. Where was she?

Twenty

Rand dashed for the telephone. He'd call in his family. If they all helped, he'd find Ariel. As he lifted the receiver, he caught sight of a piece of paper on the kitchen counter. Had that been there during his first mad dash through the room?

His glance went first to the signature at the bottom of the note. Ariel. Her handwriting was flowing and passionate, like Ariel herself.

Rand—

I have gone to stay with Stephanie until the baby is born. I do not wish to ruin your life any longer.

Ariel

Beneath her signature, she'd added another line.

Enjoy your peace and quiet.

Relief enabled Rand to breath again. She'd gone to Stephanie's. All he had to do was drive over there and bring Ariel back. She belonged here with him.

He hesitated. Or did she?

Seeing her only made him want her and added to the pain of knowing he had to let her go. Perhaps she was better off at Stephanie's. She'd be safe there.

Recalling the intrusive reporters, his spirits fell. In fact, Ariel would be much safer there than here. Rand plowed his fingers through his hair. Maybe this was the best course of action for the time being.

But he didn't have to like it.

And he still intended to ensure she was all right.

He dialed his sister's apartment and she answered on the second ring. "Steph? It's me. Is Ariel there?"

"She's here." Stephanie's voice was strangely formal.

He didn't speak for a moment. "Can I talk to her?" He could apologize, at least.

"She doesn't want to talk to you. Good-bye, Rand."

She clicked off before Rand could protest. Damn. He'd wanted to hear Ariel's voice. Was she really that angry with him?

Evidently.

Rand hung up the phone, then kicked the wall. Like that helped. Determined to thrust Ariel from his mind, he straightened. He now had an entire evening to himself—something he hadn't had in weeks. He should enjoy it.

He'd call his friends and see if they could get together at Smiley's. He hadn't had a chance to do that since Ariel's arrival.

But Dean's phone went unanswered and Dwayne and Roger begged off with excuses. Odd, they were usually always ready to hit the bar.

Left on his own, Rand fixed a sandwich and settled in front of the television. But the sandwich tasted like cardboard and the shows did little to hold his interest.

Rand grimaced. What did he used to do before Ariel

burst into his life? Though it was only three weeks ago, he had a difficult time remembering.

Or was it that television paled beside Ariel and her erratic magic? He had to admit, with Ariel around he was never bored.

Now the evening dragged and he found himself going to bed earlier than usual. *You're turning into a slug, Thayer.*

As he laid on the bed, staring at the ceiling, sleep eluded him. The more he sought it, the more it stayed out of reach. In his dreams, he could be with Ariel, but he was even denied that.

By Saturday morning he'd hardly slept at all. Climbing out of the shower, he pulled at the towel so roughly, the rack fell from the wall. "Damn."

Repairing it took some time, but not enough, so Rand measured the cabinets and shower. Maybe he should redo the bathroom.

He shook his head. Now he sounded like one of his sisters. Didn't he get enough of that from them?

Thinking of his family brightened his spirits slightly. It was Saturday. He was guaranteed at least one phone call for some emergency repair and several others to come look something over.

By ten o'clock, he knew something was wrong. No one had called—not one single sister, not even his mother. Had the world ceased to exist while he wasn't looking?

Rand peeked outside. Some neighbors were climbing into their car while children across the street played in the snow. Life continued. So why did he feel like he was in an insulated bubble?

He'd call Vicki. She always had things to be fixed around the house as her husband was less than handy with such things. But she was reluctant to talk to him.

"No, everything's fine, Rand. Don't need you," she responded to his query.

"Well, how about the kids? I'm free tonight." What *was* he saying?

"No, thanks. We have it covered. Got to run. Bye." She ended the phone call almost as abruptly as Stephanie had the previous night.

What was going on? Calls to his other sisters were just as short. The kids were fine. No, he wasn't needed. So long.

In desperation, he called his mother. She provided the first clue for this unusual day. "I can't talk. I'm on my way to a meeting at church."

"I . . . okay."

"What's the matter?" Amusement tinged his mother's voice. "Too much peace and quiet?"

Rand hung up the receiver, realization dawning. Peace and quiet. That was it. Ariel was somehow ensuring he received the peace he'd always wanted.

Well, then, he'd just enjoy it. He'd show them.

He paused in the middle of the kitchen. The question was, how?

Ariel paced the main room in Stephanie's apartment, much to Stephanie and Dean's amusement.

"You're going to wear a path in the rug if you keep that up," Stephanie said from within Dean's arms where they cuddled on the couch.

"I can't help it." Ariel cast them a glance. They looked so happy together. At least this love worked for some people. "I can't stay still."

She continued pacing, holding her hand at the small of her back against the ache that had plagued her all morning. What was Rand doing now? Did he miss her? Was her plan working? Though Rand claimed he wanted nothing more than to be left alone, Ariel couldn't see someone as active as him actually enduring it.

When the phone rang, Ariel's pulse jumped, but Stephanie took her time in answering it. Within a few sentences, Ariel could tell it wasn't Rand on the other end.

"That was Mom," Stephanie announced as she hung up, amusement dancing in her eyes. "She just returned from a church meeting but had to tell me that Rand called her earlier today. For Rand to call Mom just to chat is a first." Stephanie grinned. "I'd say he's bored out of his mind."

"Good." Ariel returned the smile. If nothing else came from this, at least Rand would realize that having what he wanted wasn't as good as he'd thought. Now he had boring peace and quiet. Perfect.

If only she didn't miss him so much.

Of course, being around Stephanie and Dean, who were totally devoted to each other, didn't help. Not that their sniping at each other had stopped completely. It just took on a new undertone filled with subtle meaning, and added glances so potent Ariel could feel them across the room.

Perhaps staying here hadn't been one of her better ideas. Their touches recalled Rand's delicious lovemaking, the feel of his skin against hers, his seductive kisses.

The ache in her back twinged suddenly, stronger than before, and Ariel pressed against it in an effort to dispel the pain. Only this time the ache continued, moving around to her front where it felt as if someone were twisting her insides. She gasped, clasping her belly. What was that? Even the growing pains hadn't hurt like this.

"Ariel?" Stephanie was up off the couch in an instant. "Are you in labor?"

"I don't know." Ariel had never witnessed the actual birth of a child. "It hurts."

Dean snapped to attention now, his gaze going to her belly. "How far apart are the pains?"

"That was the first hard one, but my back has been aching all day." His obvious concern frightened her. Was something wrong?

"Why didn't you say something?" he asked.

"I thought they were because of my huge belly." She'd had aches for the past week, no doubt a result of her off-balance body.

"They can be early labor, too. Let me know if you have another pain."

Ariel nodded and turned toward the kitchen. Did labor

consist of nothing but pain? Why hadn't someone warned her of this before she decided to have a baby? No wonder none of the other Fae had had children. With very little pain in their lives, the Fae had a low tolerance for it.

She'd considered herself brave for enduring the constant aches. Now this latest ripple through her belly attested to something worse. Could she be brave enough for that, too?

After pouring herself a glass of juice, she lifted it to her lips, then dropped it on the counter as another more agonizing pain wrenched her insides. She leaned over, clutching her belly.

By the Stones, that hurt.

Dean rushed to her side and wrapped his arm around her, his expression concerned. "That wasn't even five minutes apart." He steered her toward the bedroom. "You'll hate me for this, but I want to check you."

By the time he finished, the pains had increased in both frequency and intensity and Ariel had decided she would turn *him* into a toad later as well.

"I can't believe it. You're already dilated to seven. We need to get you to the hospital now." Dean pulled open the door and called to Stephanie. "We have to go. Give Rand a quick call, then start the car."

Ariel straightened, barely able to talk as another ripple tore at her. "Is . . . is the baby coming soon?"

"Too soon. Looks like you're one of the lucky ones who has silent labor."

Lucky? Ariel wasn't so sure about that.

Dean led her to the main room, encountering Stephanie as she hung up the phone.

"No answer," she said, her gaze darting from Ariel to Dean. "I'll keep trying him from the car."

Ariel sat in the back, Stephanie beside her while Dean drove. The pains came one after another, harder, faster. Was having a baby worth this? She actually cried out as she was seized by more agony.

Stephanie held her hand. "Breathe slow and deep, Ariel. Concentrate on something else. It'll help."

"Where is Rand?" Ariel wanted him, needed him. He would make the pain go away.

"I don't know." Stephanie squeezed Ariel's hand. "But we'll find him. Don't worry."

Worry? Ariel wasn't worrying.

She was dying.

"This is ridiculous." Rand tossed down his tools. He'd decided to work on the CD cabinet he'd been building, but even working with his hands hadn't eased his restlessness.

He'd never felt so cut off in his life. He'd always taken for granted his family's intrusions in his life, griping about it constantly, but without them he didn't know how to act. His family was a part of him.

And, to be honest, not all the calls had been work related. He'd been invited for many a meal, to share in special moments in his nieces' and nephews' lives. Moments he'd been proud to witness.

Even more than that, he missed Ariel with an intensity that ate like fire at his gut. For all his protests of not wanting a woman in his life, that was exactly what he wanted—one woman. Ariel.

He stalked into the kitchen and grabbed a soda. She'd come into his life, turned it upside down, and introduced him to a chaos he hadn't known existed.

And he loved it.

Almost as much as he loved her.

Rand groaned. He'd been so blind, so stupid, denying what he'd known all along. Ariel had not only stolen his seed and his life, she'd stolen his heart.

Existing without her was painful, foolish, and wrong. He couldn't let her go . . . even if it meant giving up all that he held dear.

Ariel wasn't safe here. He'd seen that with his own eyes. A faery didn't belong in the human world. Therefore, he'd live in the magical realm with her.

Which meant he'd never see his family or friends again. With the time difference, he couldn't come back to visit. Their lives would be over before his child took its first step.

Rand crushed the can, spilling soda over his hand. He tossed it into the sink, rinsed his hand, then turned for the front door.

It didn't matter. He needed Ariel. To go on without her wasn't living. If she couldn't stay in his world, then he'd go to hers. Simple as that.

He pulled on his coat and shot from the house. He'd go to Stephanie's and face Ariel. He'd apologize for being seven kinds of a fool and tell her he loved her. Maybe it would mean something, maybe not. He'd learned enough of her world to realize emotions were subdued.

Perhaps she *couldn't* love him.

He raced out of the driveway. Didn't matter. He loved her enough for both of them. As long as they were together, he'd be happy. Hell, with her in his arms, he'd be ecstatic.

His cell phone jangled when he was halfway to Stephanie's apartment, startling him with its piercing ring. After a day of total quiet, he welcomed it. "Yeah?"

"Rand, where are you?"

He recognized Stephanie's voice, but she sounded breathless. "Nearly to your place. Why?"

"Get over to the hospital now. Ariel's having the baby."

Rand's already frantic heartbeat jumped several notches and he crossed two lanes, incurring several blaring horn blasts, in order to turn at the next corner. "I'm on my way."

Thank God, he didn't encounter any cops along the way, as he only slowed for red lights. He dashed into the Birth Center at the hospital and found Stephanie waiting. She ran toward him and enveloped him in a hug.

"Dean has her in delivery now. If you hurry, you can make it." She passed him on to a nurse and before Rand had time to blink, he was shoved in a birthing room, decorated to resemble a bedroom at home.

Dean and a nurse stood near a bed. On the bed was Ariel, her face pale, her hair damp. Her gaze found his at once and he flinched at seeing the confusion in it.

"About time, pal," Dean muttered.

Rand ignored him, hurrying to Ariel's side. "It'll be all right," he murmured. Hell, what did someone say to a woman giving birth?

"Make it stop hurting." Ariel squeezed his hand so tightly he almost winced.

"It will. Once the baby comes, it will."

"Why didn't you tell me it would be like this?" She threw her head back, stiffening in obvious agony.

"I . . . I . . ." He'd assumed she knew. *Stupid, Thayer.* Hadn't he learned Ariel's knowledge of his world was limited?

Her breathing was too fast. Rand touched her cheek. "Breathe with me. In. Out. Slowly. In. Out." He had to calm her.

"I—" Her words ended in a cry. "I need . . . I feel . . ."

"Time to push, Ariel." Dean gave them a reassuring smile. "That's what you're feeling. With the next contraction, take a deep breath and push."

The head of the bed was elevated and Rand wrapped his arm around Ariel's shoulders to hold her firmly as she followed Dean's instructions. She was so brave, his little faery.

She pushed with such intensity, Rand feared for her safety. Was this normal?

Dean coached her, telling Ariel when to push, then when to stop. It was only a matter of minutes before the baby emerged.

"That's enough." Dean's eyes twinkled as a high-pitched cry filled the room. "Congratulations. You have a beautiful little girl."

The nurse whisked in and, amid a flurry of activity,

dried and wrapped the baby in a blanket and laid her on Ariel's chest. Ariel's expression softened as she touched the baby's face and soft blond hair, and examined the tiny fingers.

"It's a baby," she murmured, her awe obvious.

"She's beautiful." Rand forced the words from his choked throat. "Like her mother."

Ariel met his gaze, her smile warm, her eyes damp. "But she has her father's eyes. See?"

The baby blinked, revealing chocolate brown eyes, which appeared to focus on Rand. His heart swelled with a new love. His daughter.

"Do you have a name picked out?" Dean asked.

Rand glanced at Ariel. They hadn't discussed names. In fact, he hadn't been sure Ariel would even give him a say in the matter. "Do we?" he asked.

She nodded, her gaze returning to the baby. "She's already told us her name."

Rand started, then remembered. He grinned as he took the tiny hand in his. "Her name is Rose. Rose Thayer."

"An appropriate name for a beautiful young lady." Dean paused beside them. "We're done here. If you let the nurse take Rose, we'll get the preliminaries out of the way and get Ariel cleaned up."

"Do I have to let her go?" Ariel asked, her hold possessive around the child.

Rand understood completely. He didn't want to allow this miracle out of his sight for a moment.

"You'll barely be put back together before she'll be with you again." Dean smiled. "Trust me."

And because it was Dean, Rand did. Following instructions, he went to register Ariel, only to return and discover the waiting room filled with his sisters and mother.

They all demanded information, one voice overrunning another, then hugged him, as many as two or three at a time. Rand blinked to keep tears from falling. Damn, he'd missed them. He had never thought it possible, but he'd miss every single one of them.

Dean emerged, back in street clothes, and came to stand beside Stephanie. "Congratulations, Rand." He extended his hand. "Rose is definitely the healthiest, prettiest baby I've ever delivered."

Stephanie gave him a warm smile, a husky note in her voice. "You probably say that to all the parents."

The look Dean sent Stephanie startled Rand. What was going on here? That was definitely a more-than-friends type of exchange. "Have I missed something?" Rand asked.

In answer, Stephanie snuggled against Dean, who hugged her close. Good humor shone from his eyes. "It's a long story. I'll explain later."

Rand studied them. His best friend and his sister. Why hadn't he seen this coming? "Are you happy?" he asked Stephanie.

Her smile lit up the room. "Totally."

"Well, then, that's great." Rand hugged her, holding her tight. With a shock, he realized he would never see her again. God, he'd miss her. He released her finally and clasped Dean's hand again. "Take care of her."

Evidently Dean heard something in Rand's voice, for he sobered. "Is there something you're not telling us?"

Rand hesitated. He wanted to talk to Ariel before he said anything to his family. He echoed Dean's earlier words with a wry smile. "I'll explain later. Can I see Ariel now?"

Dean nodded. "Rose should be with her by the time you get there. I'll give you a few minutes, then everyone is going to want to see this new addition to the family."

Rand nodded and hurried toward the room. Ariel's magic would return now. With it and their baby, she had no reason to remain. He quickened his pace. *Please, don't let her leave until I tell her how I feel.*

Ariel relaxed in the bed, her earlier agony only an unpleasant memory. She had a child, a lovely girl with a sparkle in her eyes and roses in her cheeks. She would be a wonderful pillywiggins.

That thought made Ariel hesitate. Did she really want her daughter to have that kind of life? No longer queen, Ariel couldn't be sure what kind of reception Rose would receive. Would Titania even allow Rose to join the faery court? With Titania's disdain for half-breeds, she might even decide to imprison Rose as she had Robin.

Ariel's chest tightened. She wouldn't allow that to happen. Her magic was almost as powerful as Titania's.

Or was it?

She searched within herself, but found nothing, not even an ember of magic. Shouldn't it have returned by now? The baby was born. She placed her hand against her soft, but flatter belly. "Where's my magic?"

"You foolish, foolish pillywiggins."

She jumped as Oberon, King of the Fae, appeared beside her bed. A handsome faery with dark hair and eyes, he wore his commanding presence as easily as others donned a shirt.

"Your Majesty," she said, bowing her head.

The light in his eyes was kind, though his expression was rueful. "Don't you know what you have done?"

Ariel smiled. "I had a baby. She's wonderful. You have to see her."

Oberon shook his head. "I received your message, but I didn't realize why you'd stayed until I felt the shift in the magic. Haven't you ever wondered why female Fae don't have children?"

She'd learned the answer to that. "Because they don't want to become out of shape and ache and suffer pain."

"No, little Ariel, don't you remember the old legends? When a Fae gives birth to a child conceived by a mortal, she becomes mortal."

What? Mortal? Ariel bolted upright. "What did you say? That's not possible. I'm Fae."

"You *were* Fae." Oberon took her hand in his. "Your magic has gone into the child. She is now fully Fae, but you are mortal with all the limitations that go with that."

"I . . ." Ariel couldn't find words as her initial horror faded away. Mortal. She was mortal.

Like Rand.

Oberon disappeared abruptly as a nurse wheeled in Rose's tiny bed. Ariel bent to touch her sleeping daughter's back. She was so lovely, so perfect.

Oberon reappeared as the nurse left. "There is a way to get your magic back. But you must act quickly, within minutes."

She could get her magic back? Ariel turned to face him. She wasn't entirely sure she wanted to know the answer. "How?"

His gaze flickered to Rose. "You must destroy the child before it is thirty minutes old. Only then will your magic return to you."

Destroy Rose? The thought horrified her. "Never." How could she harm this precious life?

"You're dooming yourself to a pitifully short existence, Ariel. Think about this." Oberon approached the crib. "Would you prefer I do it for you?"

"No." Ariel seized the baby in her arms, startling Rose awake. "Don't touch her. She's worth more than magic, more than eternity." More than anything Ariel could gain as a faery. In fact, mortality might be the best thing that could happen to her.

"Don't leave yet." Rand rushed into the room, his hand outstretched. "Take me with you, Ariel. I love you."

His words released the weight already leaving Ariel's shoulders. He loved her. She met his gaze with a tremulous smile. "I'm not going anywhere." She'd already made up her mind.

She faced Oberon, her chin up. "I'm staying here with Rand and so is Rose." Now that she'd made her decision, she experienced a new sense of calm, of rightness.

Rand glanced at Oberon as if just noticing him. "Who's he?"

"Oberon, King of the Fae."

"Did he come to take you back to the faery realm?" A fierceness entered Rand's voice that made Ariel smile.

"I'm not going back," she murmured.

Rand touched her cheek, studying her face. "Do you know what you're saying?"

Pleasure rushed through her, bringing tears to her eyes. "I love you, Rand. I'm mortal now and I want to stay with you . . . if you'll let me."

"Let you?" Rand bent to kiss her, careful of the child in her arms. "I want you with me always."

This was what Robin had meant when he described love—this giddy, wanting-to-laugh-and-cry-at-the-same-time, effervescent feeling. Ariel nestled against Rand as Oberon released a snort of disgust.

"Mortals and their love," he muttered.

"You ought to try it sometime," Ariel said. What would Titania be like if Oberon actually loved her? If she loved him?

"Not for me." Oberon crossed his arms and studied them. "Life will not be easy as a mortal, Ariel."

"I know." Ariel still had much to learn about the human ways. "But I want to be with Rand."

"What about your daughter? She is fully Fae, you know."

Rand's eyes widened. "Rose has magic?"

"It should remain dormant for now. She will discover her magic when she enters the human period of puberty." The Fae king frowned. "Are you prepared to handle that?"

To Ariel's surprise, Rand laughed. "After three weeks with Ariel, I'm prepared to handle anything." He tightened his hold around her. "I've discovered I like a little chaos in my life."

"You will have that." Oberon grinned, then bowed his head. "Take care, little Ariel. Blessed be."

Without another word, he vanished.

Rand touched Rose's cheek, his finger enormous against it. "So our daughter will be magical, eh?"

"That was where my magic went. Into her."

"And you don't mind?" Rand's gaze probed her face.

"No." Oddly enough, she didn't. Her magic wasn't who she was. While it had been a part of her, she'd discovered she was much more than that. "Not as long as I can be with you."

"Good. I don't intend to let you go." Rand kissed her with such tenderness tears slid down her cheeks. He caught one on his finger. "No more opals."

"Do you mind?" Brief doubts surfaced. What if her magic had been what he liked best about her?

"Well," he drawled, his grin contagious, "I'll miss the green Jell-O flooding my kitchen, but I'll get by." He cupped her cheek in his palm. "I love you, Ariel, magic or not."

"I love you, too." She leaned forward for his kiss, then froze at hearing a multitude of voices approaching.

"Looks like the family is descending." His affection for them lingered in his voice. "What should I tell Mom?"

Ariel glanced from Rose to Rand, her spirit lighter than when she'd been able to fly. "Tell her the wedding is on."

They entered then, all his sisters and mother, exclaiming over the baby and embracing Ariel in a series of warm hugs. Ariel couldn't stop smiling. Her days of loneliness were over.

The little lost faery was found.